Hope yo

Tally V.

THE SILVER MEN

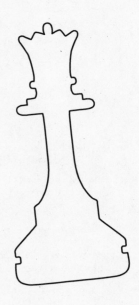

TALLY VIVARAIS

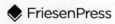 FriesenPress

Suite 300 - 990 Fort St
Victoria, BC, V8V 3K2
Canada

www.friesenpress.com

ISBN
978-1-5255-9701-5 (Hardcover)
978-1-5255-9700-8 (Paperback)
978-1-5255-9702-2 (eBook)

1. YOUNG ADULT FICTION, ACTION & ADVENTURE

Distributed to the trade by The Ingram Book Company

DEDICATION

This book is dedicated to my parents for loving and supporting me throughout this entire endeavour. To my mother and sister for reading it first and helping me make it stronger. To my loving fiancé, Malcolm, for being just as excited as I am to have this out in the world. To every expert and novice who helped me answer the tough question and shove me through writer's block. Finally, to my little brother who won't read this because it isn't a comic book. Sorry, bro.

CHAPTER 1

The sound of banging metal startles me awake. From my bed, I shift my gaze to find Bethany pacing outside our rooms, slapping a wooden spoon against the bottom of a pan to rouse us. When we're awake, she drops it dramatically over her shoulder and it falls with a large *clang* as it hammers the floor.

"Time to get up, sweeties," Bethany says with zero sweetness. "It's a good day to be alive, so long as you don't piss me off."

We're all in various states of "What time is it? Why is this happening? Please make it stop" as Bethany smirks, taking pleasure in our misery.

"Meeting in the courtyard in ten minutes," she says marching up and down the hall. "Be there or be left behind." She circles her arms in an attempt to usher everyone out of their rooms, clapping her hands at them when they don't move fast enough.

I tuck my head under my pillow, trying to visually say, *Absolutely not. Leave me alone.* Bethany hasn't always had the best bedside manner, but she knows how to grab our attention.

When the rumblings of footsteps go quiet, I slowly lift my pillow to gaze across the room. To my disdain, Bethany stands in the doorway, staring at me. My roommates, Cat and Lily, have already scurried off to the meeting.

"Come on, Talia," Bethany says. "You don't want to be the last one out there again, do you?" I groan and flip my head to the topside of the pillow; the cool change of air is welcoming.

"Maybe if we didn't have these meetings at six a.m.," I say toward the ceiling, "I would be out there on time with everyone else."

"Thanks for the advice. Now get up." Her voice is harsh and cold. Cuttingly serious.

I groan loudly to cement my obvious exhaustion, and I climb out of bed. I push my floppy braid back over my shoulder and rub the sleep from my eyes. Bethany glares at me as I pass her.

Not impressed? I think. *Boohoo, me neither.*

Bethany's lucky I love her; she's like a sister to me. A sister in arms with one common goal: Don't die.

Years ago, Bethany and I were being placed together into our squad, a.k.a. the group of strangers we would spend the rest of our lives with. Squad assignments were made based on living relatives, ages, and requests. Each has two elders, a male and a female, kids, very few teenagers, and a couple of random adults. If requests were made, then the military tried their best to keep people together.

Anyway, Bethany was put into our squad by mistake. She'd been requested to join another, but by the time anyone realized the mistake, we'd grown too attached to let her get taken away. So, we put up a huge fight, child hysteria is more like it, until the elders in our group made sure she could stay. Ever since then, despite our disagreements—of which there have been many—she's still one of the only people in the squad I can trust without a doubt.

When Bethany speaks, everyone listens. When she walks into a room, everyone acknowledges her presence. When she has a request, it's done before she finishes her sentence, save for getting me out of bed, of course. It wasn't always like this, though. A few years ago, our last elder died from an unknown sickness, and since Bethany was already an adult at the time, we argued with the military enough for them to agree to let her take over. Although, it did come at the cost of a huge slash to our already low resources. We would've given anything to stay together. So, we adjusted the paperwork to say that she was the squad leader, and no one tried to fight it.

Bethany is far from perfect. She is cruel, calculating, and manipulative. She also has days where she can't get out of bed, days where she would rather be any-where than here. Always looking for a solution, that girl. Unfortunately, I'm sure she'll find one soon.

Then there are days like this when she has these crazy plans that make me want to hit my head against a wall. Days like this when she wakes us up at 6:00 a.m. for a meeting.

I whirl around to face her, my early morning annoyance boiling over. "What is this about, Beth?" I ask. "Because if this is another one of your 'We can rule the world' speeches, can't it wait until after lunch?" Her glare doesn't change; it's too early for her, too. Her long, raven-black hair catches the light of dawn shining through a window. She looks startlingly determined.

"This isn't just some speech, Talia," she says. "This is real life. I've been working with Charles on this for a while, and we are positive that this will work. But I have to convince everyone else of that, so I really need your support on this. Can you do that for me, please?"

I roll my eyes and mumble, "Fine." Bethany smiles and pushes past me. I watch her walk off and contemplate running back to my room to sleep again. But if Bethany needs an extra vote, I'll always be on her side.

As I step outside, the heat hits me like a roaring tidal wave. I'm only wearing a tank top and cotton shorts but sweat immediately begins to gather on my skin. I look back at our squad base, longing for my bed.

The base is a mid-sized, red-brick house with a lot of windows. Vibrant, green vines stretch along the walls to make it look like something out of a fairy tale. I've lived here since the first squad assignment day.

I turn to look at the sign staked in the front of the property that reads "*SQUADRON 83 BASE. NO TRESPASSING.*"

I look around to see that everyone is still in their pyjamas, and most of them are just as sweaty. Bethany cuts through the crowd and steps up onto the sturdy crate that she uses for all house meetings. Why doesn't she just build herself a stage? I have no idea. Everyone knows that she has a flair for the dramatics.

Bethany faces the crowd of thirty-five, and the voices, once buzzing, are now a respectful murmur. She lifts a hand, and the silence is like no one is there at all. Bethany looks determined, as in, scary determined. She takes a deep breath and speaks.

"It's time," Bethany announces. The faces around me change from furrowed brows to shock, depending on how 'in the loop' the people are. Although she pauses, Bethany's words never falter. She's thought hard about this. She's ready. "As some of you know," she continues, "Charles and I have been working on this project for a while, and this time I am absolutely positive. Charles's remote will work, and when it does, we will take over. We will be the rulers of the Silver Men!"

There are several gasps around me, and despite the heat, goosebumps rise on my arms. I watch Bethany, my heart beginning to race.

"Think of all the days when we went hungry," she says. "The times when we were afraid to fall asleep because we weren't sure if the cold would take us in the night. Those days are over. Squad eighty-three will take what we need! Squad eighty-three will never go hungry; we will never be weak again!" She takes a breath, letting the weight of her words sink in. "Who's with me?"

Bethany looks over the crowd, her chest moving fast, trying to catch her excited breath. Everyone stands gawking for a second, then they rumble like an old jet. She's got them.

Bethany finds my gaze. I nod to her, inferring a congratulation. She nods back a thank you.

Largely because of the excitement of the morning meeting, I find it nearly impossible to pay attention to the details. I was never really the battle strategist, but I'm kept around for when people need a reminder of who commands respect around here. When people snap without thinking, I don't hesitate to either become the voice of reason or the swift punch in the gut, whichever seems most required. Nick, another of the close circle, slams his hand on the desk, startling me out of my daze.

"This has waited six years!" he shouts. "It can wait for another day!" A bead of sweat crawls down his dark skin. I consider giving him an elbow in the gut, but he's standing and I'm sitting, so I settle for a toe-stomp instead. He yelps and I smirk.

Just doin' my part. From the corner of my eye, I can see him glaring at me. Nick has been making the same argument for the last twenty minutes: "It's too soon. Let's prepare." But Bethany is always quick to counter with, "What time is better than the present?"

Both solid points, but I know who'll win in the end. Everyone knows who'll win. The heat eats me alive in the cramped room, the War Room, as Bethany calls it. The place is small, with a dusty old table, three cracked wooden chairs, maps covering the walls and making it look much smaller than it already is, and a single white fan eating up way too much electricity. No one dares stand in front of it. Even though the breeze would be amazing, we wouldn't want to steal it from the rest of the room because we may find out that one person in the room is making dinner that night and, surprise surprise, there isn't enough for everyone, and you are last in line. So yeah, we don't stand in front of the fan.

"Well?" Bethany is staring at me, and I quickly realize so are the rest of the people around the table. I feel the heat of embarrassment rise to my cheeks. I lower my gaze to avoid her chilling stare. She sighs and restates, "Are you ready to go now?"

I'm taken aback by the question. *We're leaving now?* I shake off the surprise and tighten my shoulders. I know what my leader needs. "I'm always ready," I say. She gives me an appreciative nod before slamming both her hands down on the table.

"Then what are we waiting for?" she says. "Let's rule the world. Outside, thirty minutes."

Thirty minutes, I think. Thirty minutes and then thirty-five miles. Thirty minutes, thirty-five miles, and a high likelihood of death.

What do I pack?

I shove a spare t-shirt into my old school bag that has a cartoon sprawled across the front. Childish? Whatever. It's been a long time since I've had to go to school. I won't be gone long, one night at most. I consider packing more. I'm not the most decisive person, and I'd hate to wake up tomorrow and realize that my outfit isn't "take over the world" enough. I roll my eyes at my thoughts. *Anything is fine. It's just one day.*

I grab the first pair of shorts I see and shove them into my bag, along with a pair of socks, a small blanket, and a miniature pillow. If I need to sleep on the ground, I'm not doing it without neck support.

I peek over at the photo frame collecting dust on my bedside table. A little brunette with bangs that she tried to cut herself, wearing a pink-and-white striped shirt and sitting happily on a man's lap. He has the same ocean-blue eyes as her, but her hair is undeniably like that of the woman next to him. While the man has dirty blonde hair, the girl and the woman have dark, reddish-brown hair. But the girl has a smile that is a combination of both of them, too genuine to be matched by any one person.

Sometimes I miss them; other times I go a week without the thought of them even crossing my mind. But those smiles belong to before the war ... before the Silver Men.

Before the creatures I'm about to release.

I shake my head to clear it, cursing myself. There is no room for doubt. It's too late now. I swing my pink bag over my shoulder and march out of the room. I have a purpose. I have a mission. I've lost too much to give up.

I make it outside and it seems that almost everyone is present. The few still inside the house are packing food. Those poor souls will have the heavy bags. My stomach and I thank them for their sacrifices.

I spot Bethany's black hair in the crowd, but I know better than to walk up to her. She's in her own world up there, and to step into it would land me on food duty for sure. Thankfully, my best friend James comes to my side and lazily throws an arm around my shoulders. I sigh and push him off me. Normally I wouldn't care, but it is *way* too hot to be so close to a six-foot-three dude. He fakes a whimper before backing away and laughing to himself.

"Morning to you, too," he says as if I'm the problem.

I'm too tired to humour him so I keep my eyes forward, unwavering from the tree-covered horizon.

"*Morning to you too, James,*" he mocks in a girlish voice. "*What a fantastic day for world domination, don't you think?* Why, yes," he says in his own. "I do think so, Talia. Like I always say, world domination is best on a sunny day."

He turns to me, pausing for a laugh, but instead, I jab my elbow at him. He dodges it easily, knowing my tricks after so many years.

James is the only thing I have left from before the war. We met in first grade when he "accidentally" threw an apple at my head. He must have apologized every day for an entire month before we both forgot what he was apologizing for. Soon after we became friends, and in later years, best friends. We still rarely leave each other's side. When our parents died, the only thing we had left was each other. I'll be damned if I ever let that go, and I'll damn him if he tries. When the squad groupings started, we both put each other down as next of kin, guaranteeing us a spot together. And together we have been ever since.

His eyes look relaxed and unburdened. *Let's ruin that.* "Do you think Charles's remote will work?" I ask, practically whispering. James grabs onto my arm, a comforting gesture. I look up to see that his smiling face has a look of uncertainty. When he realizes that I've noticed, he shoots me a smirk to cover his worry.

"I really hope so," he says darkly. "'Cause if not, I'm counting twenty-three dead bodies." He nudges me off balance for a second, but my dancer's feet quickly fall back in step. "Besides," James adds. "Charles is a genius at this sort of stuff. You know that. I have total faith that this will work."

He turns toward the rising sun if only to hide his true emotions, but I know he's just as scared as I am. I step in to hug him, wrapping my arms around his waist even though the weather is too damn hot. But some things are more important than breaking a sweat. James wraps his arm around my shoulder to return the gesture.

The squad begins to walk together, although split into smaller groups. Everyone's mostly quiet, save for a couple of people who characteristically never shut up.

We march for what feels like years until a towering metal fence comes into view. James starts cheering, and everyone erupts with him. *This is what we've been waiting for.*

Does he not realize this means we're only about half a mile away from probable death? Sure, cheer away.

There are hundreds of these gates spread across the country, each one containing a dozen Silver Men alone. It only takes one to kill everyone here and then everyone it runs into for the rest of its robotic life, however long that is. But sure, cheer on.

The first gate is a simple passcode lock. I say "simple" because Charles has it open in a matter of seconds, with some sort of code-cracking device, I presume. He tried to teach me once, but I got lost after he started adding letters into math, and then he started making up words, I'm pretty sure. Besides, I'm more useful in the War Room.

On the other side of the gate, there are hundreds of old storage lockers, some used to hold cherished items that people loathed to give up. Now they contain the most dangerous creations on the planet. I feel a twist in my stomach, and I pull James closer. He leans down to my height, his face right next to mine. I look at him, our gazes are perfectly aligned.

"Where're the guards?" I whisper. James sniffs a laugh and straightens. He looks back down to me and smiles.

"Come on, Tal. Don't be such a coward. There haven't been guards here for years." My panic starts to ease, and I nod. "Do you even pay attention in the War Room anymore or do you only keep an ear out for sass?" he asks, putting his hand on my shoulder.

"Stay back everyone," Charles announces.

So much for not panicking. *Well, at least we'll have a running start. How kind.*

My stomach churns as Charles plugs his black box into the second larger lock station. I watch attentively, refusing to take my eyes off him for even a second. I look for the first sign of trouble, so I'll know when to run. "And in three," he says. My entire body starts shaking with nerves. "Two." I grab James's arm, hopefully not for the last time. "One!"

I close my eyes only to rip them open at the sound of thick steel screeching against more steel. The sound is loud enough to scare away the birds from the trees, as the sky fills with squawking and fluttering wings. Charles presses an ironically big red button on his remote, and the Silver Men take a step forward into the light of day.

And at once, I am breathless.

The Silver Men gleam in the natural sunlight; they sparkle like nothing I've ever seen before. They're smooth, still polished, yet almost too human in shape. "Bipedal liquid metal robots used for speed, efficiency, and a simple method of painful executions," as Charles would say.

It feels like an invisible rope is tie to my hand and it pulls me forward. I break through the crowd, my heart beating faster the closer I get. Close enough to touch them. They shine as if diamonds were embedded right into the flowing metal. I get so close to one that I can see my breath fogging up its chin.

"I've never seen them this close before," I say, in awe of these metal men in front of me. Charles looks over to me and nods.

"Be thankful for that," he says. "One touch from these things and you're as good as dead."

My eyes linger down to the deadly machine's hands. They sparkle as much as the rest of it. I feel myself wanting to step back, wanting to fall back, and run far away from these things. But the other part of me, the "why would I ever do that" part, says to touch it. After all, only their hands can kill me, and Chester has the remote control anyway. For some reason, that's the voice that wins. I lift my exhausted arm to his perfect face, inches away, and a bead of sweat drips from my brow.

"Sorry, Tal. I call dibs on this one!" I jump as James grabs both my shoulders, yanking me back. I elbow him for the scare but turn around with him anyway.

"Who said you were getting one?" Bethany shouts from ten feet away. James stops short, pulling me with him.

"Me," James says. "I want that one. Didn't you hear the dibs?" He gives Bethany a boyish smile, indicating that he thinks he somehow won this argument and that she is now going to leave him alone. But he pulls me back because we both know Bethany isn't going to let him win anything.

Instead of getting into a fight, though, he heads toward the Silver Men. I turn to James, annoyed.

"Would you mind not picking fights with the scariest person we know?" I ask, making him laugh.

"I mean, she's the one that keeps backing down," he says. "So maybe she's afraid of me, maybe *I'm* the alpha dog now!" He punches the air in front of him, moving his body in a wide circle until he's lightly punching my shoulders. He stands tall until a shadow appears behind him, and the sun is suddenly in my eyes.

I hold up my palm to shade it, and as the sunspots fade and the image becomes clearer, my breath catches in my throat. The creature standing behind James is unmistakably one of pure destruction.

My jaw drops, and I gasp, James catches on. He closes his eyes and turns around slowly, bracing himself for what he might see. I grab his elbow, pulling him with me as I take a step back.

"Jesus!" James says, his voice shaking. He backs into me, moving us further away. The Silver Man glides like ice on a heater, sliding towards us.

Over the crowd of our seemingly unaware friends is a burst of cackling laughter. Realization clicks into my head immediately and I curse. "Bethany," I say, and turn toward the laughter. "It's not nice to emotionally scar your squad for life." James postures himself perfectly as if he didn't just lose his heartbeat.

"Bethany." He deepens his voice, and his posturing only makes Bethany cackle louder. A few people surrounding us even look over with a cocked brow before going back to their conversations.

"What?" Bethany asks through tears, gripping Chester's remote in her hands. "I thought you wanted this one. Is he not good enough for you now?"

James steps towards Bethany, towering over her, a very brave gesture considering what just happened. "I'm good. I'll let you keep it."

Bethany straightens her shoulders, still no match for James's height, but fully confident. "Just don't forget," she tells him, poking him in the chest with her finger, "I will always be the alpha dog." She winks at him before she melts back into the crowd.

James turns to me, defeated, then he pushes past me sullenly. I slap his back and follow him, hiding my smirk.

I wake up last, as usual. I feel like my eyes are plastered shut, and I rub them, begging them to stay open. The flap on my tent is ripped open, and I'm attacked with a large brick of sunlight aiming perfectly into my eyes.

"Come on, Talia," Elliot calls. "I need to pack the tent." I roll onto my side to hide at least half my face from the evil sunshine. "Fine, be that way," Elliot says, exhausted.

A patter of footsteps enters my tent, pausing just next to me. "Why do you always have to be so stubborn?" Elliot demands. I wave a hand in dismissal but am greeted by a much worse welcoming. I'm hoisted into Elliot's arms, but I'm too tired to do more than struggle a bit.

"Put me down," I groan. But Eli pulls me out of the tent to where I'm attacked by full brutal, unforgiving sunlight.

"If you insist," he says, and the ground hits harder than the light. In hindsight, I really should've seen this coming. I push myself to sit up.

"Can I at least have my pillow?" I call.

Elliot gathers my belongings, which may or may not have been covering the
entire base of the tent, and drops them on the ground next to me. I show him a
finger in gratitude, and he salutes back before disassembling the tent pole by pole.

As much as I would love to fall back asleep on the dirt out of spite, I have little
trust that my belongings would still be here when I woke up, and/or I would find
myself waking up in a shallow grave. So, I turn over and start shoving my things
into my backpack. I pick out my outfit for the day and change on the spot—it's
nothing they haven't seen before, we're a small household. I shove my pyjamas in
my backpack and heave it over my shoulder.

The walk back to base is just as silent as it was on the way here, save for Charles
and Bethany mumbling plans, tips, and tricks. They whisper too quietly for me to
hear, no matter how hard I try. Instead, I can catch gossip from Sandra and Emma
and overhear someone else complaining about dirt in their boots. Time passes
slowly, and when I'm not trying to eavesdrop, or walking with James, I walk next
to one of the Silver Men that march alongside us.

I can't help but think about how they were never meant to be this dangerous.
They were just supposed to be a way to make the enemy quit, to replace soldiers
so we didn't need to send any more of our population to a fight where we had
next to nothing to gain. A simple method gone tragically wrong. The Silver Men
were locked up quickly once their murderous tendencies were realized, but the
original structures couldn't hold them. The Silver Men were, are, too powerful.
So instead, they broke out and killed hundreds of millions before the government
finally found a way to properly store them.

A twang of guilt pierces my stomach. Are we really this stupid? Can we really
expect a happy ending the second time around, or are we dooming humanity, one
step at a time?

The sun beats down with unmerciful heat. The sweat that is soiling the backs
of most people's shirts makes it almost look like it has been raining. I suppose with
the sudden clouds it could be. It's amazing how the skies that were a perfect blue
only a mile ago are now filling with dark clouds. A cold, quick drop of water lands
on my nose, and with a blink of an eye, it's pouring rain.

I turn to look at Charles just as he scrambles to hide the remote. Instead, he
fumbles it, dropping it into a puddle.

"No!" he yells as he falls to his knees to quickly find it in the dirty pool of water. He fishes for it and then pulls it out like a trophy. He shoves it under his shirt and tries to wipe it dry. He looks up, more concerned than I have ever seen him in my life. He stares at it for a moment, and then he looks up at us with dread-filled eyes. His skin has gone waxy pale.

I know what it means. I scream until my lungs give out. "RUN!"

In a panic, we all scatter. Blood-curdling screams echo from too close behind me. At one point, I turn to look over my shoulder to see a Silver Man grab Emma by the neck, the raindrops on her skin showing blue electricity jumping over her body before she falls limp. The Silver Man drops her corpse, her body hitting the ground like a ragdoll, her eyes fixed forward.

Wide-eyed, I slap my palm over my mouth in shock. The Silver Man turns to me. There's no time to mourn, only time to run. The air burns my throat as I push, knowing it can catch up. But maybe I can hide.

My thoughts are scattered as rain pelts my face. I see an old blue barn up ahead and decide to duck inside to catch my breath, if only for a minute.

The air in the barn is thick and heavy with dust. Around me is nothing but a couple of old rotted hay bales.

Nowhere to hide, must keep running.

The screams have died off, and I'm not sure if it's because everyone has gotten away or if everyone is dead. I have to get out of here.

I rush out of the barn only to be greeted by a Silver Man just outside the door. It stands, stoic and eerily beautiful. Hot rain slicks over my face, mixing with my tears. I stumble back a step, but I can't get away. The Silver Man reaches for me.

Suddenly, my body jolts with the strong shock, electricity that hits my teeth, my bones, my eyes. I think about my parents.

See you soon.

My vision blurs, blackens, and then I feel nothing at all as I hit the ground. Dead.

CHAPTER
2

I feel dazed and confused as I stir in a small bed. *Oh God, what is that?* My head feels like there isn't a single spot that isn't occupied by a rusted nail. I peel my eyes open and blinding light is all I see until everything slowly comes into focus.

I'm in a small room. The bed I'm on is pushed against the far wall. The walls have a short wood panelling covering the lower half and a spoiled-milk-coloured paint covering the top half. I shiver from the cold of the room and pull the blanket closer. I'm so tired. Maybe just five more minutes. I squint, willing the pain to subside so I can fall asleep again.

Wait. A frozen wind rushes down my spine. I shove my eyes open. Where the hell am I? I shoot up into a sitting position and notice a little girl with strawberry-blonde hair and wide green eyes sitting across from me and staring as if I am some sort of creature. I'm not, am I?

Now, wait a minute. What am I? Who am I? My brain is clouded with a big grey ball of smoke that I don't quite understand. I can't see anything or remember anything. I jump up and grab the little girl's arms, holding them tightly to her body to keep her from running off.

"What is going on?" I rush out, finding myself out of breath. "Who are you?" The only response I get is from her wide eyes and furrowed brow as she stares back at me with dark fear. As I hold onto this child, something clicks. *Let go, she's just a child.* I quickly release her shoulders and shove myself to the far reach of the bed and pull my knees up to my chest. Where am I? What's going on? Why can't I remember anything?

The last thought echoes in the darkest reaches of my mind, banging back and forth and smashing like pots and pans. I can't remember. I can't remember. *I can't remember.*

The little girl studies me for another second before turning and running out of the room. My head rattles and I'm worried it might break. The pain spreads the more I move until my entire body feels like glass preparing to shatter. A hot tear of frustration drops down my cheek. I lift my hand to wipe it off. *No scales, no fur, probably human. That's a start.*

I whip my head up at the sound of something trumpeting down the staircase adjacent to my open door. A blonde boy stops short of the last couple of steps as he ends up on the wrong side of my glare. He takes his next steps carefully as if approaching a dangerous animal. He studies my face as he enters the room. I feel the need to push myself further back into the wall, but of course, there's a wall in my way. I roll my eyes and bring myself closer to sit on the edge of the bed, facing him head-on.

He smirks and straightens his back. "Hello, Talia." My brave face turns sour. I look down and try to find the information. Talia. Talia, Talia, Talia. It doesn't register. "Don't even try to deny it." My eyes snap back to him. "We found your name stitched on your backpack." His smirk grows bigger. "Cute," he adds. I jam my nails into the palms of my fists and grit my teeth in frustration. I want to wipe his smug look right off his face.

"Listen here, you impudent little child." I stand up to match his posture. He's a couple inches taller than me. *Guess I'll have to make my words big.* "I don't know what you think you know, but I can assure you that you don't know *anything* about me." How can he know anything if I don't know anything?

He looks behind him at a small wooden chair on the wall, grabs it, and swings it around so he's sitting on it backwards, accepting my challenge and gesturing a palm for me to take a seat as well. "Enlighten me." I want to be stubborn, to refuse and stay standing, but I'm tired, so I sit down, cautiously slow. "Who exactly is Talia?" he says in a way that would make a psychologist clap, and a peal of sick laughter rolls out of me. I laugh for a little too long then pause and see that he never started to laugh along with me.

"Beats me." I scoff.

He cocks his head and studies me again. A grinning curiosity. I look past him to see an old man with a grand white bread walking past the doorway. The boy leans into me, so uncomfortably close that I can smell his minty toothpaste.

"What squad are you from?" The old man turns at the sound of the boy's voice and rushes in immediately, raising a hand to the back of the boy's head.

"Ow!" The boy rubs the back of his head and turns to see who assaulted him, only to immediately cower back into a small bubble. "Hey, Doc, how you doin'?" His voice is a few octaves higher.

"You idiot. I told you to come get me immediately when she woke up." Doc studies me. I just woke up and I'm already so sick of people studying me. "Hello, Talia." I roll my eyes and heave another chuckle.

"Who's Talia?" I retort.

Now it's Doc's turn to be confused. He has a little bit of a potbelly, but more in a Santa Clause way than a beer gut. He looks over to the boy, who shrugs, shakes his head, and turns back to me.

Doc moves close to me and grabs my face and squishes my cheeks. He rotates my head, analyzing me. I feel a sudden white rage inside me, and I grab his wrists and pull them away. I hold them there for a second. The boy stands up to defend Doc. I'm in no mood to fight off both. I throw Doc's hands down to his sides and retreat in the far corner of the bed again. Doc looks like I physically hurt him, but I didn't grab him that hard. *What a big baby.* "Talia," he adds with a softer tone.

"Stop calling me that!" I don't like the empty feeling the name gives me. It's like a hollowing in my chest. Like, rather than a missing puzzle piece, the whole damn puzzle is gone. *Goddammit. I'm an empty puzzle box.*

Doc sighs, visibly relaxing. "Young lady." *Oof, I don't like that.* I hold up a hand to pause him.

"Wait, let's go back to the mystery name." I twirl a finger to illustrate my point. Doc re-straightens his posture and glares. I think I'm bothering him. *Sucks.* "What was it again? Talia?" I fake a shiver. "I guess it'll do for now. But let's consider changing it to …" I make a rainbow with my hand. "*Master.*"

"Who the hell are you?" the boy exclaims with both disbelief and a hint of amusement.

"That's a question we *both* want an answer to. Unfortunately, for now, the answer is Talia." I've successfully made everyone in the room uncomfortable and baffled. Was that my mission? No. Do I enjoy that it happened? Absolutely.

The room goes quiet for a few moments until a black woman at least in her fifties peeks her head around the wall and into the room.

"Am I interrupting something?" she says in equal part sass and apathy. *I like her.* Doc and the boy eye each other, waiting for one of them to say something. She is wearing a purple cardigan with blue jeans and shiny hoop earrings. Her salt-and-pepper hair is trimmed near the scalp, and she pulls off the look nicely. When no one says anything, the woman continues, "Well, my apologies for butting in on the telepath convention. In the meantime, I have some clean clothes for our guest to borrow."

"Oh, that's me!" I jump towards her and she puts her arm around my shoulders as she leads me out of the room.

"And can I get your name, dear?"

"How do you feel about 'Master'?"

She laughs. "Not while I'm around." I smile and let out a laugh for that.

"I guess Talia will have to do."

"Well, Talia, here are some old clothes, and here's Donney's room." She reacts to my confused stare with an explanation. "Donney's room is the only one with a door. He refused to let us burn it when the weather got cold. Said something about needing a retreat, so he doesn't kill us all." *Hahaha, get me out of here.*

I grab the clothes from her and give a quick nod in appreciation. The door is plain and white. The wood looks thin, so I guess I can see how you wouldn't get much heat from burning it anyway. *Kill us all? Who on earth am I bunking with?* I shove the thought aside as I pull open the door to see exactly what I expected—a mattress was lazily thrown in the corner of the room without so much as a box spring to keep it from touching the floor, and a few random clothes scattered around the floor. I do my best to ignore the underwear. I shut the door behind me. I let out a sigh as I lean back and allow myself to slide down the inside of the door to sit on the floor.

My head is pounding. All these people, and well, everything, is making me rather uncomfortable, to say the least. I try to feel my tongue, but it is bone dry. Along with my lips. Scabs dust off as I rub them together. *Don't pick at them, don't* ... I can't help myself. I bite off the first layer of skin. I know I'm bleeding, but I continue to pick at it with my fingers until all the old, dead skin, albeit some new stuff as well, is gone.

Satisfaction aside, I scan the room for anything, something ... a mirror! A small hand-held mirror sits lazily on top of a pile of ... here's hoping ... clean t-shirts. I crawl over to the pile, excusing the stinging pain coming from my skinned knees. I hold the mirror up to see a pair of vividly blue eyes and a million freckles on a slim face. *Meh, nothing special.* I was kind of hoping for a supermodel, or maybe a robot eye, something cool. I study the mirror, reach up, and pull my eyes wide and my cheeks long. *Ah, shoot.* The blood from my lip has flowed down my chin. I use my wrist to wipe it off.

Nothing special. I push myself onto my feet and let the mirror fall back down onto the pile of shirts. I grab the clothes lent to me, skipping out on the underwear. I'd rather go commando than share. A medium-tight sports bra is mildly more acceptable.

The door opens. My heart skips a beat and I immediately grab the second thing I see to cover myself (the first was the underwear, and I'd rather die). This boy is a different one from before, early twenties, sporting brown ruffled hair and a six o'clock shadow. He stands there like it's his first time seeing fireworks. Once he realizes what is happening, his amazement turns into an annoying smirk. He's about to quip. I can feel it in my bones.

"Can you close the door?" I chirp out before he gets the chance to get quippy with me. He pauses, confusion flooding his face as if asking why he would want to do that. I grab a plain pillow off the bed and throw it in his direction and hit the side of the door instead. *Imma blame it on the brain thing.* "Preferably sooner than later."

"A'ight," he says in an annoyingly deep voice. "But to be fair, you're in my room." He has a cocky confidence as he strolls out of the room as if it was his choice. *I guess that was Donney.* What a charmer. I don't waste any time slipping on my loaner shirt. My brain pushes me in front of the door and before I can protest, my hand is on the knob. Twisting, *dammit brain,* pulling, *crap,* and open.

Here we go.

I take a step through and immediately see Donney sitting on the stairs, staring attentively at his hands. I try to walk past him, but he looks up and sees me before I can leave.

"Where do you think you're going?" I steel myself so he can't tell that I am perturbed at his less-than-welcoming presence. This is, after all, the guy who said he needed privacy so he doesn't, and I quote, "kill us all." I try to continue walking past him, but he stands up and blocks my path, quite easily, I might add. Standing right against him I can see that he is much taller than me. My eyes barely meet the tip of his chin, and he's slouching. "I asked you a question."

I point to myself and look around, checking to see if he's talking to me. "Who, me?"

His smirk returns and he checks me out, up and down. Creepy much? "It's good to know what you look like with your clothes on." He shoots me a wink that makes me roll my eyes into the back of my skull. "Usually I have to buy a girl a drink before I get to see that show."

"Have you always been this much of a dick?"

"No, it grew bigger with puberty." He's quick, I'll give him that.

I squish my face into a fake forced smile "Real mature."

"I'm Donney." He stretches out his hand, which he holds there while I stare at it until he understands that I have no intent on taking it. "Just know that if you ever need anything, don't ask me." I feel like I'm locked in a stare-down filled with unbreakable tension and potentially murderous thoughts.

"Are you always this charming?" I throw into the mix; he's not getting the last word.

"Pretty much." He takes a hand and runs it through his hair. "Usually the ladies swoon."

I cackle. "What *ladies*? The sassy old lady or the five-year-old ginger?"

His face turns to stone. Have I offended him? His energy just switched to a dangerously negative one. Am I scared? Yup, that's fear. I take a step back and watch cautiously as he silently pushes off the wall and sits back on the stairs, glaring at me as I walk past. A cool shiver runs through the air as I head back to the room I woke up in, or try to … where was it again?

I stumble through the halls until I see the first boy's head looking out of a room. "Talia! What took so long? Couldn't figure out how to put a shirt on right side in?" I look down to see I had indeed put my shirt on inside out. Dammit. I was in such a hurry to get out of that room, I hadn't noticed. My face flushes with heat. I take a deep breath and look up.

"Hey, I don't even remember my name, let alone how to put on a shirt. What's your excuse?" He looks down quickly. *Idiot. Point: me.*

"Real funny." I push past him to get into the room. It feels warmer than before. I guess clothes can do that for you. Doc sits on the wooden chair with what looks to be an advanced first-aid kit sprawled out on the bedside table beside him.

"Talia, please, take a seat." I stare at him, waiting for a *just kidding* or something. This is freaking creepy. Among the Band-Aids and alcohol swabs sit several empty vials and various needles.

"Nope." I turn to leave the room, but the blonde boy stands in my way. Pfft. He might be bigger than me but that doesn't mean he's stronger. I try to push past him, but he stops me with ease. What if I charged at him, would that work? The space behind me is limited, so I can't get much of a running start, but it's better than staying in here with happy Mr. Stabby.

"Don't even think about it." The boy glares at me. My posture straightens and my eyes widen. This isn't *really* a telepath convention, right? How hard did I hit my head? "Talia, for God's sake, would you just sit down?"

"Okay, I'm agreeing to be called this for the time being, but do you have to use it in every goddamn sentence?"

"Just sit *down*. It's only a couple of vials to figure out what's wrong with you. Believe it or not, we're just as curious as you are, maybe even more so." The boy closes the distance between us until I fall onto the bed. *Humph, cheap.*

"Just in case you didn't get the memo, this is a me problem. In no way is this your problem or even your business, so yeah, thanks for the clothes, but I'm going to be getting on my way."

Doc's soft voice etches up from beside me. "Listen, girl." I glare, but he shrugs and continues. "We want to help you. This isn't ideal for anyone, but in case you don't remember what the world is like out there, it's no place for a girl with no memory. Now, we can help fix you, or at the very least help get you back on your feet enough to leave and survive once you do, or you can leave now, and we won't stop you."

"Doc," the boy snaps back.

"No, Montey. She's free to leave. We aren't kidnappers." Doc looks me sweetly in the eyes. "We are just people that want to help." Doc holds a hand out to me, and I know what he wants, he wants my blood. What he will do with it I have no idea, but at this point, what do I have to lose? I reluctantly place my arm in his hand. He gives me a gentle nod. The alcohol is cold, but it wipes away a notable amount of dirt. "You might want to look away." He preps a small needle and places it over a dark purple vein.

"Nuh-uh, I'm watching." How do I know that he's not going to switch the needle out for something else while I'm not looking? Okay, I'm starting to think I'm a little paranoid by nature. I look into Doc's soft brown eyes and note that he looks as if he's pitying me, or maybe that's just my lack of trust in general. The needle pinches as it breaks through my skin. He fastens it on with a small piece of tape and grabs the first vial.

He fills about six. Six vials of my blood sit on the table. I feel lightheaded and my tongue is sticking to the roof of my mouth.

"Montey," I spit out. He looks taken aback by the sound of his name. "Can you be a dear and get me some water?" He looks at Doc, who looks at him right back. *Freaking telepaths, I tell you.* Without another word, Montey leaves the room to just Doc and me.

"Between you and me, and I really mean that, what do you remember?" Doc straightens his vials and puts everything back into his dirty brown leather bag.

"I just don't, I guess." I know nothing about myself. Do I like hockey or soccer, chocolate or vanilla, cake or pie? Thankfully, I still know what pie is. "I remember the difference between cake and pie if that helps." I think I've just seen the impossible. I think I just made Doc *laugh*?

"I'm glad to see that brain damage hasn't compromised your sense of humour, as far as I'm aware, at least." He straightens his back and looks me deep in the eyes, like he's staring into my soul or something. "Tell me, though, what do you know of the Silver Men?"

The words send chills down my spine They are the creations that destroyed the world, the liquid-metal robots created by the military to get the Wastelanders, the people who live in the barrens on the outside of the country's borders, to stop attempting to invade what is rightfully ours. We got what we wanted in the end—an entire nation leaving us alone. We just never wanted this. "I know them." *Why do I know this?* Unfair.

"Interesting," Doc says as he studies me more. "What of them do you remember exactly, and have you ever run into one?" A fool's question; no one runs into a Silver Man and lives. Not anymore.

"They're monsters. No one survives their touch."

"Do you remember how they started?"

"War machines. Death to all those who dare come in their way." I don't know how I know this. It's like a door of information has a slight crack in my memory and I can feel it there, but it shines no light of my own—my personal memories are just dark.

"You were young when they were created; by the time you could have an opinion, they were at their worst."

"Nothing meant for death and destruction is ever good."

"But that's just it, that wasn't their purpose. They were peacekeepers. At least, they were supposed to be. Bulletproof so they could rage on in a battlefield without dying, electric hands to stun the enemy but never to kill, no faster than they needed to be, all of this so we didn't have to waste human lives on a war with no upside. Then came the download. A new update meant to speed up the process a bit."

"Only they turned into death machines instead? Yeah, I don't really care. They're still death machines now." I lean back, tired of storytime. I know how this one ends. Everyone gets locked up "for their safety"— "safety in numbers." What a load of bullshit.

Doc studies me again. "So, you remember all that, but not your first name?"

"Well, thank God it was written on a backpack, right?" I want to go home, wherever that is.

CHAPTER
3

Doc left me about an hour ago to stew in my thoughts, hoping something might come to me. Instead, I'm just bored. I've considered taking a nap so I don't have to be awake, and who knows, maybe I'll dream of something useful, but this bed is hilariously uncomfortable—like they took a towel and loosely sewed it to some springs. The glass of water Montey brought me a while ago is empty on the table, and I'm thirsty again, but I refuse to leave this room. I feel like there's one too many people in this house who wouldn't mind me disappearing really quick. How many people are in this house, anyway? More than one, that's for sure. At least five. I do not have the numbers in this game. Maybe they'll be nice, but from what I've seen so far, only about two-fifths won't kill me given the chance. I won't turn my back on the little ginger either; no underestimating happening here. No siree.

The door to my room opens a crack, then nothing. *It's okay,* I think. *I don't think hearts need to beat, anyway.* "Hello?" I say like a person in a horror movie that's about to get killed. When no one answers, I look around the room for any sort of weapon, but there is literally nothing. *Maybe it was the wind?* Yeah, a wind that could turn a doorknob, yeah, one of those doorknob-turning winds, very common things. Of course, I realize that I'm in a basement. *There goes that theory.* I take a deep breath to steady myself, and I push myself off the "bed" and balance myself on my feet. My vision gets spotty. I shake it off as I step toward the door. The floor creaks underneath me and a hand pushes through the crack in the door. I step back, catching myself. The hand holds a small white napkin and briskly waves it up and down. The door opens more and Montey walks through. My fist quickly gets acquainted with his arm.

"Ow, dude, what the hell?" He rubs his arm. "What was that for?"

I roll my eyes and move back to the bed. "You know very well what that was for. You scared the shit out of me." I sit down, only to see him giggling. "What? What's funny?"

"You know exactly what's funny," he says in a voice mocking my own. "I scared the shit out of you."

"Dick. What do you want?" He drops his arms and stares at me, like, *done playing now? Fine.*

"I just thought you might be bored, that's all. I figured I'd keep you company." He shrugs.

"And what exactly did you have in mind? Swapping stories of our childhood, telling our favourite jokes? In case you haven't realized by now, that conversation is going to be a little one-sided."

"Oh, I hadn't thought of that." He fakes obvious disappointment. "Oh wait! I had." He backs up and reaches out of the door and pulls in a box of chess. He gestures to it like a woman on an old-fashioned game show. "Care for a round?"

He sits down in front of me and moves the table between us. He quickly sets up the board and places the pieces appropriately, pausing every few seconds to make sure everything is correct. When the board and pieces are finally set up, he looks over to me. His eyes are a crazy shade of blue, and his hair is blonde and curly, not super curly, but in a nice, wavy way. I smile at him, and he grins backs.

"Why are you staring at me?" he asks quizzically.

"No reason," I spit out quickly and turn my attention back to the board.

"Okay, well, white goes first," he says. I study the board in front of me, mostly to avoid eye contact. I could be studying my next move; he wouldn't know the difference. "That means you. You go first."

"Right, right, I knew that." I reach down and move one of the pieces with the round head in the front row diagonally. A roll of laughter falls out of Montey. "What? What did I do now?"

He wipes away tears of obnoxious laughter. "You've never played chess before, have you?"

I pause and scowl at him. "HEAD. INJURY."

Montey rolls backwards and keeps laughing like he'll die if he stops. Right now, kinda hoping that's the case. He rolls back and wipes tears from his eyes. "Okay, lesson one," he points to the round head pieces, "these are pawns. They can only move forward and can only kill upwards diagonally."

"That's stupid. Won't they run into each other? What do they do then?"

"Well, then they're stuck, unless they kill someone, or someone kills them."

"This doesn't sound like a very friendly game."

Montey looks me deep in the eyes. "I never said it was." A chill runs down my spine.

"All right, tell me how to win then."

CHAPTER

4

We play for another hour or so, a couple rounds, one after the other. I haven't won a single match. I'm starting to think he's cheating. Although, I suppose it's easy to make up rules when the person you're playing against has no idea what you're saying. Like, how am I supposed to know "advanced moves" like when he gets to steal one of my pieces every time I sneeze? The move is called "sneeze fire." Randomly moving the tower thing, sorry, *rook*, with the king every time I'm about to win, that's definitely something he made up. *Castling? Such bullshit.* Not that I call him out for it. Apparently, flipping the board in anger is just as good as a surrender. I'm not a big fan of that.

The game is not one of my favourites, but I do appreciate the idea of it. Trying to get ahead of your opponent without letting your guard down? Definitely something I would want to note down somewhere. Actually, come to think of it, it is my favourite, by default of having literally nothing to compare it to.

I think I've been playing on autopilot this round. The board comes back into focus and I study the potential moves. *Son of a gun.* I move my knight two up and three to the right and I look up to see Montey panicked and gawking at the board.

"… Checkmate?" I say as he slowly looks up to meet my eyes. A half nod is all it takes for me to jump off my spot on the bed and squeal, "YES!" Egyptian dance, the Charlie Brown, and even a little bit of the cha-cha-slide. Suck it. Suck it, Montey.

"I can't … How?" He stands up to match my height and I instantly freeze. He seems angry, distraught, and confused all at once. "I've been playing this game my entire life and you learned how to play it TWO HOURS AGO." Heat builds in the room as he yells.

"So, no rematch?" He turns around to face me, a deft calm as if nothing happened. For a second, you can hear a pin drop.

"Oh, you're getting a rematch." He grins and sits down to reset the board.

As he's setting up the board, a holler comes from upstairs. Dinner's ready. Montey nods for me to join him. "Yeah, no, I'm good. Just, uh, consider bringing me leftovers?"

"Nope, you either come up now and meet the people that are housing you in your 'current condition' or you starve down here."

I tap my chin as if I'm actually thinking about it. Let's face it, the choice is obvious. "I'll starve." I get back in bed and pull up the blanket. "Shut the lights off on your way out."

"You're a real piece of work, Talia. You know that, right?" I turn on my pillow to face him, and my hair rolls into my face, making my point slightly moot.

"Artwork," I correct before rolling back.

The lights flicker off, and my fatigue, like a rock in the front of my mind, adds weight onto the lids of my eyes.

I wake up too soon. The singular light bulb hanging from a frighteningly loose wire in the ceiling flickers on and off. *Ghost house? First telepaths, now ghosts? What have I gotten myself into?* I lull my head to the side to see Montey flickering the light with a plate of food in his other hand.

"Okay, you caught me." He stops flickering the lights. "I never actually intended for you to starve, although with the death glare I'm getting from you right now, I'm thinking I might be better to kill you slowly than not at all." I am glaring, aren't I? I loosen my stare and shove the entirety of my weight off the bed and roll purposely on the floor. The mattress isn't high from the ground so it's not like it *hurt*. A much easier way to get up if you ask me.

"Can I eat it, or are you going to force me into cannibalism?" I eye the food as drool pools in my mouth. Vibrant greens, golden carrots, and a chicken leg.

"If you go with cannibalism, can you eat Donney first? He might be gamier than me." He lifts his unused bicep. "But I'm sure the salt in his blood would be great for flavour."

I stare at the food more, my mouth watering so much that I'm probably going to die of dehydration before I die of starvation. Montey gives in and hands me the plate. Defeated, I take it and drop myself back on the bed. My hair has officially fallen out of its braids. I pull the elastics off the bottom and tug them onto my wrists. I pull the strands out and let them flop down. My hair is actually pretty long. I want to cut it. Yeah, on second thought, I don't think they'll let me near scissors.

"So, tell me, aside from the fact that I'm a stranger, why has no one else bothered to come down here?" I gesture to the door. "I'm sure there isn't just the five of you here."

Montey is sitting in front of me, legs crossed, leaning back on his hands. He is emanating a calm that I am really grateful for, especially since every time I go to look for memory or even try to relate a thought to a previous one, my brain fires back at me like a fly running into a bug zapper. Another thing! Why the hell can I remember what a bug zapper is when I can't even remember my favourite colour?

"Dunno." Montey interrupts my thoughts with his reply. "Maybe they think you need space? They're all really nice for the most part, so I wouldn't think they're avoiding you to be malicious." He lolls his head back and closes his eyes.

"If you're tired, you can leave. Don't let me keep you here."

"I'm seventeen and am constantly working in gardens or walking to a chicken coop, I'm always tired. That doesn't mean I'm ready to give up your amazing company yet." He looks at me with that sly smile of his, extending the idea that the last sentence was complete bullshit, to say the least.

"Oh, thank God," I say wittily in reply. "I was so worried that I would be left alone without a semi-decent chess player protecting me." I give him a sly smile of my own and he humphs.

"Screw you, I'm a good chess player."

"Whatever helps you sleep at night."

Donney comes into vision as he walks past my room. He looks in and our gazes meet for a second. I think he scowls? Okay, I mean, our first encounter wasn't the greatest, but it also wasn't the worst. Who pissed in his Cheerios? He keeps walking without a word.

Montey turns to follow my gaze, only turning back when he doesn't see anything. "I wouldn't worry about him. He's a bit of a hothead, but you're not a threat."

"How would you know?" I stare into him with a determined thought to scare him. He should be afraid of me; I'm afraid of me. Montey opens his mouth to reply but I speak again before he can get a word out. "I need some air, any chance I can go outside?"

"I honestly don't think that is a good idea." He jumps up to stop me in my path. He's a little too close to me. I can smell his cologne, or I suppose in today's world, his natural scent? Weird. Whatever. He smells like a memory, which is annoying, to say the least, considering I DON'T HAVE ANY. I face my pale feet, careful not to allow him to attempt to read my expression, which I'm sure would read exactly what I'm thinking.

"I'd like to go outside, now." He pauses, reluctant, but he steps aside and allows me to pass.

"Don't think you're getting a free pass." I step out into the hallway and look left to see more doors, and right, where I came from, which has Donney's room, a bathroom, and the stairs. I walk that way. "I'm coming with you."

"Believe me, I didn't actually think that you were going to trust me for ten minutes." I keep going, scanning the hallways, making only careful moves, sure not to open any doors, despite how much my curiosity wants me to. I find the stairs and climb. One foot in front of the other. Taking the steps is harder than I thought it was going to be. Air is heavy on my chest. I pause at the top to gain my bearings. Montey, only a half-step behind me, puts his hand on my arm. He whispers into my ear, "Are you sure about this?" *Say no now, say no forever.*

"I'm sure." I catch my breath one step at a time as I move towards the door. Gravity is definitely at least ten times stronger than normal; I swear the ground is calling my name: *nap on me, Master, only for a minute, don't I just look so soft?* My vision spots then fades in and out. I close my eyes and take a deep breath. I widen my eyes, and everything is clear again. Okay, no worries, only a minor setback. Onwards and upwards. I look to Montey and give him a determined nod. He shrugs and holds a hand out for me towards the door. He jumps ahead and pulls it open for me.

"I got you."

"Thank you," I say with a small curtsey.

"Maybe don't bow too much, you might fall over." I punch him in the arm as I walk into a vestibule. It smells like mildew and old cigarettes, as if they're soaked into the walls. The grey carpet on the floor is matted up and so dry that it almost crunches between my toes. I regret this already.

"Here, wear these." Montey hands me some worn-out brown slippers that will definitely be like wearing absolutely nothing. Might as well. I grab them from him and pull them on. They're warm, like someone had just taken them off.

I look outside and it's bright, bright light coming from the sun, its rays digging into my face and making me really hate the sun. Like, who does this guy think he is? Shining all over the place. I discover that I hate the sun. *Zap.* Got it, a memory. I've always hated the sun? Did the sun kill my dog? I wouldn't be shocked. I lift my hand up as a small shield and Montey holds a finger to me, telling me to hold on. He looks around and grabs a baseball cap hanging on a coat hanger in the corner of the ugly, peeling, green-painted room. He dusts off the sun-stained, once-red-now-pink hat and tightens it around my head.

"There, perfect."

I give him a quick nod. "Where are we going?"

"I was going to ask the same thing." Doc's round figure stands in the door connecting this section to the rest of the house.

"Oh, uh, I, uh …" says Montey. "Hey Doc, how are you? Did you have an extra helping of vegetables? You don't look a day over thirty-nine."

Doc rolls his eyes at Montey's obvious attempt at flattery, though Doc seems to be more annoyed than flattered. "Can I speak with you in private?"

I chime in, "I don't think that's a good idea." They both stare at me as if this is the first time I've ever spoken. "I want to go for a walk, and I, frankly, do not care where. I just need a break from that room. I'm not a captive." I pause, staring at them. "Am I?"

"No, of course not." Doc is the first to reply. "I just was thinking of your health."

"I made it this far, didn't I?" Montey shoots me a side-eye as if to say, *no you didn't*. I give him one right back, hoping Doc doesn't catch on.

"Montey, where are you taking her?" he asks with more force this time.

"Doc, don't worry, it's just a small walk. We'll be back in an hour at most. Fresh air is good for the health."

An old woman with greying ginger hair steps around Doc. "Hey, if you two are going for a walk, I think you can make it to the coop and back before it gets dark." The suggestion gains the freckled woman a glare from Doc.

"Good idea, Sara." Montey gives a too-wide smile to Doc. "Can you grab us the baskets?" Sara nods and scurries off. Doc never removes his wrinkled eyes from Montey while he does everything in his power to avoid the lethal gaze. Sara comes back not a second too soon with cloth-covered wicker baskets.

"Here you go." She hands them off to me with a quick smile and leaves as quickly as she came.

"Fine. Go," Doc says, clearly wishing we'd change our minds. I'm leaving this house, if only to prove that it's not my prison. I grab the bronzed knob on the thick white door and shove the door open as if my life was dependant on it. I run out and face that son of a sun, consider showing it a pretty bird, but the hat makes it bearable. I look back to the door I came from, expecting to see Montey, but instead, I see Doc holding Montey's arm, scolding him for something. They both look at me at the same time. Creepy much? I look away as fast as I can, but I know they're still watching.

"Hurry back," Doc says. Not a question.

Montey hands me a basket and walks ahead in silence. I follow him, careful not to say something I shouldn't.

CHAPTER
5

"How long have we been out here?" I say, trudging forward.

"Literally thirty minutes," he replies with a small hint of amusement in his tone. "It's still a good forty-five-minute walk there, and then we have to get back before dark."

"Or else what?" I challenge him.

"Not a good question to ask in this economy."

"What's that supposed to mean?" I scrunch my eyebrows, confused.

"It means that we are given enough to live well until everything gets back up and running. You don't piss anyone off or you don't get even half of your fair share. It helps that we have such handy people in our garden, but that doesn't mean they won't happily make your shares into compost."

"They'll starve you for coming home late?" I ask. He scrunches his face, clearly displeased with my tone, or question, or maybe he just smells something funny.

"No. They won't starve me. It's you that they'll starve. They have no reason to feed you. But they lose government support if I die."

"You do realize how ridiculous that is, right?" I almost trip on a rock but catch myself. Montey says nothing and just shrugs. I mean, what do I expect? They know nothing about me, and I know nothing about them. Maybe they want to eat me and that's why they're keeping me. *Chances of them being cannibals are low, however...* How does the government, or lack thereof, have anything to do with this? Do I ask any of this out loud? No, of course not. I'm pretty sure I won't get any actual answers, anyway.

More silence, more walking. My calves are on fire.

"There." Montey points to a speck in the distance that I have to squint to see past the sun.

"That?" *No way have we walked this far for* that. "That's what we walked over an hour for?" It's a hovel with a red roof that looks like it just needs one gust of wind to collapse.

"C'mon, Talia. It's what's on the inside that matters." He playfully punches me in the arm and holds a hand to his heart. I grab where he hit and try to scowl through a smile, and he runs ahead. I do a slightly quicker walk, but I don't run. I don't think I physically *can* run. *Running bad.* Montey looks back to find me about a hundred metres behind him.

He throws up his arms, like *dude, you're still back there?* His arms flop down next to him and he tilts his head and his blond curls fall with movement. I finally reach him and keep walking past him.

"How do you have so much energy?" I ask the boy now trailing behind me.

"I do this *way* too often." He appears at my side, keeping perfect pace with my now- determined march. The hovel approaches quickly, and I start hearing them.

So.

Many.

Chickens.

The stench is almost agonizing. I look to Montey, who is very "been there, done that." I harbour a glare and keep moving. The heat settles on me as soon as I stop moving, but I allow Montey to unhinge the gate and enter first. The fence rests around the hovel about twenty feet around, enough room for the fowl to run freely. Montey enters the rather large coop. It looked pretty small from afar, but now that I'm in it, it looks like you could easily sleep fifteen people in here if you got rid of all the chickens. Being out of the sun is a relief too. I'm definitely going back with a burn.

"What are you waiting for?" Montey asks while relocating a chicken and grabbing two brown eggs from the nest and gently placing them into his basket.

"Right." I turn so I'm standing eye to eye with the creature. I swear it stares into my soul, and I stare right back. I lift my arms to pick it up, but she jumps out of the nest, abandoning her eggs. *What a good mother.* I tsk and grab the three eggs she was holding hostage. I turn around to show Montey the eggs. He's already watching me, hands on hips, as a disappointed mother would when her son comes home with mud from head to toe.

"What?" I say, throwing up my free arm. "I collected three! Last I saw, you only had two." Montey shakes his head and keeps picking up the hens, one after the other.

"We'll each grab a dozen. Okay?"

"Will that be enough? How many people live with you?"

"It'll be enough; besides, we have a deal with the squad that owns the coop. They only let us take a certain amount and we give them frozen vegetables in the winter. Win, win."

"Is that why we had to walk so far?"

"Yeah, but we make them walk for the vegetables too, so, we're even." Montey huffs out a laugh.

"Don't think I didn't notice you avoiding the question for a second time." I pick up a fluffy chicken, move it to the nest next to it, and collect more eggs.

"What question was that again?"

I roll my eyes and haltingly reply, "How. Many. People. Do. You. Live. With?"

"Oh, that question! I don't think you've asked that before, have you? When was the last time you asked?"

"Don't think that I don't know what you're doing," I say as I wag a finger at him.

Montey humphs. "Why is it that your head injury only acts up when you need it to?"

"Montey!" I startle a couple of hens, and I turn to face him. "Would you answer me, for the love of all that is good?"

"It's not even a secret. I just have fun toying with you, and it's fun to torture you with the fact that I know something you don't."

"I have amnesia!" I mime choking him. "You know EVERYTHING I don't!"

"Debateable, but whatever. There's twenty people in our squad." He turns back to the chickens "Squad number one-thirty-eight, since you didn't ask."

"How many squads are there, anyway?" He quirks his eyebrow, a look that holds confusion, amusement, and amazement all at the same time

"You have a really odd selective memory. You get that right?"

I look up and mock thinking really hard. "Yes," I decide.

"I don't know, actually." He pauses. "I would assume thousands, if not tens of thousands. The world was all but destroyed, but there are more survivors than we can see around us. Plus, the country is pretty big. I swear the only bright side is that the Wastelanders didn't win."

Right, the Wastelanders. The people that live below the border in the Deadlands. The ones that started the war. The reasons that we have one-hundredth of the population than we had before. The reason that we live in these stupid squads. *Freaking Wastelanders.*

A red heat fills my head. I try to shake it off, but it wells from my stomach to my ears, heating up a fire in my soul that I didn't know was there. An inexplicable feeling of anger that makes me angrier than the whole idea in general. I hate all of this.

"I'm done. Are you done?" I spit out. Montey pauses and looks at me, concerned. He gives me a faint nod. "Good, let's leave." I don't look back as I push through the fence and head back off in the direction we came.

We walk for forty minutes until Montey stops under a tree.

"What are you doing?" I want to get back and out of the stupid heat.

Montey lays down and uses a protruding root as a pillow. "Resting."

"Uh, didn't we have to get back before sundown?" *Come on! Move it!*

"You've made good pace. We're fifteen minutes ahead of schedule. We can rest."

I could strangle this boy. "We can rest when we get back," I force through gritted teeth. He pops open an eye and looks at me up and down. "Why are you in a hurry?"

"I'm not, I just ..."

"Talia. Sit. Down." Now I *really* don't want to sit. I look out at the vast number of green trees that surround us and the string of small old houses that were torn down for parts or firewood long ago. The sun glints off a cracked window and catches me in the eye. I turn my eyes to the ground to hide from it. I look to Montey, who is staring at me intently. I slowly kneel and sit across from him.

"Thank you," he says in a bit more of a "now, was that so hard?" kind of way. The grass is cool and slightly damp from the shade. I kick off the slippers. I scan my feet to find several new blisters. They sting when I touch them. I wince at a bad one. *I'm so glad I got shoes for this hike.* I swing my legs out straight so I can lean back. The air feels smooth rolling into me. I look up to the sky to see the cotton-candy clouds, a delectable mixture of baby blue and powder pink. One looks particularly like a dog. I shine a hint of a smile and look over to Montey, who is already watching me. He has such a boyish grin. I go to say something, but he speaks before me. "What's making you smile?"

Reluctant, I take another calming breath. "Clouds." I look back up to the dog cloud, which has been blown away by the wind and now looks more like a unicorn. Montey scoots over off the root and out of the direct shade to lay down next to me.

He points to the unicorn cloud. "That one looks like a dinosaur."

"No way! It's obviously a unicorn!"

He tilts his head and squints his eyes. "I guess. What about that one?" He points to another cloud. I move over so our shoulders are touching so I can more accurately see which one he's looking at.

"Oh, bunny. Definitely a bunny."

He lets out a wholesome laugh. "Yeah, I see that too." He is grinning from ear to ear. His eyes match the green in the grass. He is really beautiful. He turns quickly to meet my eyes; my heart skips a beat and I force my eyes away.

"We should go," I say, maybe too quickly, and sit, slip on my slippers, and stand. I adjust my hat and look down. He gives me a half-smile but nods and stands up with me. I grab my basket and start moving out.

He keeps up beside me until the house is in sight. The sun is still up, but barely. He jumps in front of me. "Talia, there's something I have to tell you." His eyebrows lay flat, making his face read cuttingly serious.

"What is it?"

"You can't tell anybody I told you, and I really don't think I should be telling you, but I also think you really should know. It's just that—"

"Montey," I cut him off, "tell me."

He closes his eyes and looks to the skies. He exhales and faces me. "It's time someone told you where we found you …"

CHAPTER

6

I don't think I can catch my breath. Answers, finally some answers. If I could force the words out of his throat faster, I would. I would do *anything*.

"We found you outside a barn. Your clothes were soaked through, your hair was covered with sweat." I find myself devouring every word. "You were about a three-hour walk west of our base. We were going to collect beef not too far from where we found you. Your heartbeat was weak but at least there was one. As for the others ..."

"Others?" My eyes snap to his. He nods, and I turn to walk in the other direction. I can't handle this, I have to process this. He grabs my arm.

"Yes, Talia. There were others."

I don't think I can breathe. "Well, where are they? They can tell me who I am! Why didn't anyone tell me this sooner?"

"Because, Talia." He grabs both of my shoulders, forcing me to look him in the eyes. "You were the only one with a heartbeat."

His words sink in slowly, and suddenly I know I *can't* breathe. I try to shake his grip, but he holds my shoulders so tight that I know it's going to leave a mark. It only makes me want to break free more. I shove my arms against his chest, and he only pulls me in closer until he can completely wrap his arms around me.

"Shh. It's okay. It's going to be okay."

I think I'm crying. "How is any of this okay?" I say through ugly hiccups.

"It will be." Why am I crying? I don't know these people. The thought is enough to turn me stone cold. I stop crying, and I stop fighting Montey's grip. He loosens, and I pull away slowly.

"How many?"

"How many what?" Montey adjusts my hat and fixes my wet hair so it's all tucked behind my ears.

"How many bodies?" He grabs my cheeks softly and studies my eyes, and his eyes wander to my lips. "Please, tell me."

He hesitates. "Thirteen." My eyes go wide. Montey thumbs away what's left of my tears. "Thirteen bodies."

"Can I see them?" My request takes Montey aback. He pauses.

"No." His response takes me further aback.

I yank myself away. "Why not?"

He turns away and continues to head towards the house. "Because you aren't supposed to know!" he yells back in a cold frustration, but he doesn't stop moving. "God, I shouldn't have told you."

"Then why did you?" I shout, having not moved from where he left me. He stops in his tracks and turns to face me. He determinedly marches towards me, probably to keep the conversation at a lower volume.

"Because," he says through gritted teeth, "you deserved to know what you came from. Because you are the only person left alive, the only witness, the only one who might have any idea how all of those people, all of those people under thirty years of age, died of what seems to be electroshock." I look for the memory, only to be greeted by another sinister zap. *I know, or at least, I should know.* I am more determined than ever to get my memory back. What else should I know?

A thought occurs to me, slower than it should have. "Is that why people have been ignoring me? Is that why I haven't seen anyone?" Montey doesn't say anything but he nods. "They're terrified of me. They all know that I'm suspect number one in the largest mass murder since those goddamn creations killed the entire remainder of the world!"

"No, honestly, they don't all know." His words force me to look at him again. What is up with this boy?

"The whole truth, Montey. *Now.*" The intensity of my stare is enough to burn through diamonds.

"I've told you all I know." He starts to walk away.

I huff. "Okay."

"Okay?" He turns back to face me. "I finally tell you that we found THIRTEEN dead bodies near where we found you barely alive, and all you have to say is 'okay?' You know what? Fine. Maybe you're a sociopath and you don't actually care about all of those people who were, by the way, no older than twenty-five years old at most. All children. All dead. You don't think that you survived for a reason? You don't think that maybe you should be a little more concerned–"

"Shut up," I say in the quietest voice possible. "Shut up, shut up, SHUT UP!" I stand as tall as I can to look him dead in the eyes. "You don't get to tell me what I'm feeling. You barely know me! I barely know me! I am terrified that they could have been my family, my friends, and now they're all dead and I have no idea who they are. I say *okay* because I have nothing else to say to you." I spit at him like I can't get rid of the poison in my mouth. "I can't start talking about this because then I won't be able to stop. Who knows, I might not have even known those people.

"They might have been complete strangers. I might have gone out for a stroll, fainted, and never have actually met them. I don't know if I loved them, hated them, or had no idea who they were, and the thought of that scares the shit out of me. So, you, last of all, *you*. You don't get to say jack shit to me about what I should be feeling or what I should say because inside I'm screaming louder than anyone can hear, and all I'm feeling is fear and you can never underst–" I am silenced, and for a good few seconds I can't understand what's going on until I realize that Montey's lips are pressed against mine. He's passionate and cautious, every thrust a different feeling, and I am *not* a fan of this. I pull off of him in the nicest way possible and avoid spitting, sure not to insult him.

"You know all that we know. Really, but the only people that know are me, Doc, Donney, and I'm sure Donney's told Clary by now." That throws me. I recoil from his grip to stand on my own.

"Why would our neighbourhood psychopath tell an eight-year-old what happened?"

Montey's shoulders release; he seems thankful for the temporary change in topic. "First of all, Clary is eleven. Second of all, she's Donney's little sister." Ah shit. I see why he doesn't like me after that comment.

"Okay, first of all, they look literally nothing alike." Clary has strawberry blonde hair and potentially a million freckles. Donney has tanned, flawless skin and dark-brown hair.

"Yeah, it's a long story. The only reason I know is that I once guilted Bea into telling me. Long story short, Donney was tossed around to over a dozen foster families before the war, then, once the extinction event hit, he and his foster sister elected to not join a squad. Rather, they became looters and robbed abandoned houses for supplies until one day they came across Clary. She was only about three at the time, and her parents were nowhere to be found."

"Holy crap. That's terrible." I can hardly bear to picture a child on her last leg, starving, with no one to help.

"Yeah, and here's the worst part. Donney's foster sister didn't want to take Clary with them. She thought it would be too hard to sneak around with a baby.

She voted to drop the baby off near a government facility and hoped she would be found. Donney, on the other hand, insisted they take Clary with them. His sister wouldn't back down, so she left them in the middle of the night. No one has even heard from her since."

"Huh. So, Tinman does have a heart." I raise my eyebrow, attempting to lighten the mood.

"You'd never know it, though. He keeps it well hidden under his metal core."

"Still a dick," I sing as Montey laughs.

"Yeah."

I laugh with him. We laugh and laugh until we don't. "Is that all I need to know?" I ask, ready to go back now.

"No, one more thing. The only reason why you haven't seen anyone is because Doc told everyone to stay away."

My head lolls in exasperation. "Why?" I breathe out the word. I don't know if anything can surprise me anymore.

"He just wants to make sure everyone is safe. He's not the villain here."

"No, apparently I am." I push past him, but he catches my arm.

"That's not what I meant, and you know it."

I'm about to reply when I turn back to the house to see a small figure that appears to be facing us. *Doc.* "We have to go, and please," he looks me deep in the eyes, "don't say anything." I can feel the desperation flowing from him.

"I won't."

CHAPTER 7

"There you are!" Sara says as soon as we step in the door. Doc never takes his eyes off us.

"Wow, Sara, you've never been this glad to see me before," Montey says proudly.

"Not you, sweetie, the eggs." Montey rolls his eyes and hands over the basket. She also grabs mine. "I'm baking a cake." She smiles and places the eggs on the cracked marble counter.

"Wow, I don't remember the last time I had cake!" Montey licks his lips.

"Me neither," I add. Everyone in the room pauses and then bursts into laughter. I'm too tired for this. I smile at them and excuse myself. "I need to rest." I kick off the "shoes," place the pink hat back on the rack, and move to the stairs, leaving the same way I came.

I see Clary sitting off to the side of the stairs. She looks at me and looks away as if she were told to not even look at me.

"Hi," I start, "I'm Talia."

"I know who you are." The words quickly leave her, as if she were never supposed to say them.

"I know who you are too, Clary." She actually looks at me this time. Surprised and wide-eyed. She smiles sweetly.

"Do you like chutes and ladders?"

I guess the look on my face answers *yes* on my mouth's behalf. "Come." She ushers me along. "I'll show you."

She twists around a couple corners until we enter a room with several other children in it. Most of them are tangled up with their hands and feet on various colours of a play mat with someone shouting instructions like, "Left hand green."

A little blonde girl, younger than Clary, shouts, "Right foot green!" She flicks a plastic arrow for the next instructions.

"Talia and I are playing chutes and ladders if anyone wants to join!" Immediately, a little brown-haired boy in the corner of the room shoots his hand up. He places his book down. The boy can't be more than twelve, but the book he's reading looks hilariously big. He comes to sit next to us. He picks up the green piece, claiming it as his own.

"Okay, I'm red," Clary says, grabbing the red piece and holding it up to her hair. "For obvious reasons. Talia, you can be blue." She places all the pieces on the starting square.

Clary spends the next fifteen minutes or so teaching me how to play and then we have a couple of practice rounds. I think I like chess better. At least winning takes more effort than losing. At this rate, it seems like both take the same amount of dice rolling.

The one kid, the quiet one, still hasn't said a word. I obviously don't pressure him, but I'd be lying if I said a few questions hadn't occurred to me. His name, for starters ... Clary just keeps calling him Green, as in "Green's turn" or "You found *another* ladder, Green? I think you're cheating." Although I don't see how one could even consider cheating at this game. Unless he secretly has telepathic powers and is controlling the dice. I stare at him inconspicuously. Brown hair, brown eyes, probably not harbouring some secret superpower. We play a few rounds. I win none of them but I'm willing to chalk it up to luck since that's all this game is anyway. *I'm not salty.* You're *salty.*

"Your turn." Clary breaks me out of my mind space and hands me the dice. I smile at her. I roll them onto an unoccupied part of the board, careful not to hit any of our pieces ... again. "A ladder! Nice roll, Talia!" The little girl's smile makes me smile, so pure and innocent and ...

"What the hell?" Donney stands in the white-framed doorway.

I should probably apologize for what I said. "Hey, I just wanted to–" He holds up a hand to stop me. *Rude.*

"Clary. Your room, *now,*" Donney says, not taking his eyes off her. Without another word, Clary gets up and leaves. I watch her back as she exits the room. Donney's attention is now focused on me. *If looks could kill ...* He holds up a finger and opens his mouth, ready to say something, but instead, he shuts his mouth and follows Clary out of the room. I look to Green.

"What's his problem?" I say, quietly enough so only the kid can hear me. Green shrugs, stands, and starts putting the board away. Once finished, he saunters off and puts his nose back in his book.

I'm starting to think Donney doesn't like me. *I'll live.* I consider watching the others playing the flick-limb-on-coloured-circle game, but I think I need to sleep.

I head back off to the room, and just inside is Montey with his nose in a book. I tilt my head to try to see what book he's reading so attentively. *The Art of War.*

Comforting.

"What are you doing in here?" he asks, noticing me.

"I should ask you the same thing. I thought I was coming here for peace and quiet from a house that would rather see me dead."

"Funny, I thought I was doing the same thing ..." He places his book closed on his lap. "Minus the dead part." The book looks worn, like, read-a-million-times worn.

Comforting.

He catches me staring. "Want to look?" He smirks.

"Huh? Oh, no. I'm good. I honestly just want to sleep." I move over to my bed.

"Okay, sweet dreams." He picks up his book and keeps reading as if I never walked in.

I cough, clearly trying to grab his attention. "So, not to be rude, but do you actually plan on going to bed anytime soon? Because I have a head injury and I do actually need my rest. But hey, if you wanna stay, then knock yourself out." I lay down.

"I think I'll stay."

I lift my head off the pillow. "I didn't think I'd have to say this, but Montey, get out." I hold up my hands as if to say *what are you doing?* I sweep them like sweeping him out of the room.

"Hey, I said I was coming here for quiet; I don't think you *sleeping* will interfere with that." His nose never leaves the book. I stare at him, slightly slack-jawed, thinking of anything I can say to get him to get out, short of calling "*fire!*" But that seems a little excessive. Then again, he's yet to move. *Drastic times?*

Maybe it's best to just leave him be. What's he going to do that no one else is going to do? Him, I trust. The rest of this house? Not so much. Not that they have actually done anything *bad.* But I wouldn't put it past them. Plus, I think Donney still might try to kill me in my sleep. Fine, sleep, don't care about Montey. At least he's being quiet. I flip my pillow so it's cold side up and practically fall onto it. The back of my head is still sweaty from my walk, and it's not exactly cool in this room. Can I blame the excessive body heat?

Talia, sleep.

Right, sleep. I force my eyes closed.

"And don't snore this time," Montey says.

I snap my eyes open. "I don't snore."

He keeps his thumb in his book but lets the book down enough to make eye contact with me. "Yes, you do, and it's not adorable, either, more like a walrus with a sinus infection." He pulls his top lip in with his canines sticking out, mocking a walrus. I throw my pillow at him. I hit his face dead-centre. He looks like he's trying to be stunned, gawk-eyed, but a small smirk falls through. He throws the pillow back and misses me.

"Wait, who's the one with the head injury again?" He feigns anger before standing up and moves towards the bed to grab the pillow and starts hitting me with it. I'm defenceless! I hold my hands up, trying to grab the pillow with every swing, but they all land. I reach out, grab the pillow, rip it out of his hands, and start swinging back.

"Hey! Knock it off!" He laughs.

"No way! You didn't stop, why should I?" Another hit landed.

His hair is completely dishevelled. He grabs hold of the pillow, a blatant tug of war, a stand-still. We both let up and let go. My cheeks hurt from smiling ear to ear.

God, I hope I don't look nearly as ridiculous as he does. He looks completely crooked, his hair appears practically on backwards, though I'm sure mine is no better. Montey reaches over to tuck my hair behind my ear. His hand is warm, and I have to physically restrain myself from leaning into him. His hand never leaves my face, but his eyes find mine; they are such an impossible colour of green. Not a single speck of any other colour, if you excuse the black as night pupil that is slowly shrinking the delectable green.

I don't like this! We're too close. This is uncomfortable. *He keeps you safe.*

An inch apart, no less, no more, sigh. My heart beats in my ears, everything else is astonishingly silent. His hand pulls away, and before I can open my eyes, a soft whap strikes me in the side of the head.

"'Appear weak when you are strong.' Art of War." I'm frozen in shock.

"Montey, what the hell?" I stare at him through the hair covering my face, mouth gaped open. Although, not lying, I'm glad that's over. Still, I feel … wrong? Like, what just happened?

"Bet you didn't see that coming," he says through a gigantic grin covering his face ear to ear. I don't think I can even force a smile on. He sets the pillow down behind me. His smile fades slightly. "I'll leave you so you can rest now."

He picks up his book and chair on the way out. He places his chair just outside the doorway, but just barely sitting in the hallway. A minor semblance of privacy, but I'm still frozen in place. I don't think I can sleep now even if I want to.

"I'm—" I start when Montey shushes me. I shrug and get up to leave.

"Wait. Where are you going?"

"I am going to pee. As I was trying to tell you before you shushed me." I grin at his embarrassed face.

"Right. Okay, have fun." He hides his face back in his book. I shake my head as I leave but I can't shake the grin off my face. As I head down the hallway, I overhear Clary and Donney talking inside Donney's room with the door shut.

"… not that bad, right?" says Clary

"No, but it is a little odd, don't you think?" replies Donney

"Maybe, but if you want me to stay away then I will."

"No. Odd is not something to be feared, but to be run towards, searched, and solved. She's probably not a bad person; we just need to give her time to adjust."

"Okay, if you say so … wanna play again?"

"No thanks, kiddo, I think you got me beat."

"Okay, I'll clean up then," Clary says as she rushes out the door and sees me standing. She pauses, staring right at the door. I am now dumbfounded. Donney must see her staring because he follows her out and sees me. He starts to glare and then laughs.

He says, "You're turning a little red, dear." I turn away in a huff and go straight into the washroom. I stare at myself in the mirror for a good minute.

I am a bit flushed, aren't I? *Dammit.*

You're turning a little red, dear, I mock in my head for a bit. I turn on the sink and splash water on my face. I stare at myself again, waiting for the redness to subside, then I start to head back to my room, only to see Donney blocking my way.

"Now isn't that better? As positively pale as you were the day we found you."

I scoff. "Screw off, Donney."

"Me screw off? You were the one eavesdropping on a private conversation." I can't think of anything to say. Once again, I find myself without words. I wonder if I was always like this. Donney remains unmoved in front of me. My temperature rises as I stare him down; however, he never lets the grin on his face slip, even for a second.

"Are you going to let me through?"

"Well, I wanna know how much of that *private* conversation you heard."

"Look." I look him dead in the eyes. "I wasn't there for any more than a minute. I'll let you think over all the incriminating stuff you might have been talking about in that minute while you get out of my way." I try to push past him but he's stronger than an ox.

Donney leans in a little too close for comfort, which seems to be something he enjoys doing, and whispers in my ear. "Look, maybe you accidentally overheard a sentence or two of that private conversation, but I think that it is definitely enough to get your brain moving. So, while you think about all the things we could've been talking about, just know that it doesn't concern you, and I hope I don't have to bring it up to anyone that our new little troublemaker has a listening problem. I think you're better off to forget everything you heard, *okay*?"

There's a threat to his words, one I am not very fond of. I'm about to tell him where he can shove it when Montey comes around the corner to see Donney blocking my path.

"Donney, what the hell? Let the girl go." Montey rushes towards us.

"What are *you* going to do about it?" Donney says without taking his eyes off me.

"Back off, Donney. I don't want to have to deal with your bullshit today."

"It's funny how you think you have a choice." At that, Donney lets go of me, turns, and shoves Montey into the wall and lifts him up by his shirt. "Listen, your little girlfriend and I were just having a conversation about ears, that's all. So, why don't you screw off back to your rabbit hole and we can all forget any of this ever happened?" With that, Montey grits his teeth and nods and Donney places him back on the ground. Montey turns and heads for the room as Donney turns and faces me. "You can go too." He tilts his head, gesturing to emphasize his point.

"Oh, can I? How kind of you. Honourable, really." I glare at him as I pass him and follow Montey down the hall. I find him in my room red as a beet. His fists and his teeth are clenched. *What do I do?* I'm about to place my hand on his shoulder but he turns around to face me and goes off.

"Who the hell does he think he is!?" He's asking me, but I know he doesn't want an answer. I tilt my head under his, forcing him to meet my gaze. "Did you know that he does this thing where he teaches all the kids to call me Lucifer? He tries to convince everyone that I'm the villain! That I'm the one who they should be afraid of. He makes me so mad; I swear I could … I could …"

"Hey," I say so he focuses back on me. "You're looking a little red, dear." I giggle as Montey stares at me, his gaze lightening up more and more every second.

"That's not funny." He tries to keep a straight face but just can't do it. He starts to laugh. *Good.* He should be laughing. He deserves to smile.

"It's okay, okay? Don't let him get to you, he'll get what's coming to him." I kiss his forehead. He smiles and leaves for the night.

Okay, that was too eventful and now I actually am exhausted.

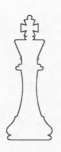

CHAPTER
8

I think I got maybe five hours of sleep, no dreams, just randomly waking up in a pool of, presumably, my own sweat. *I am the epitome of grace and beauty.* The house was eerily quiet last night. Almost haunting.

I stumble out of the hall and into the bathroom only to see a long lineup of kids. Donney comes along and walks right to the front of it, kicking the kiddos out and claiming it as his own for a good ten minutes. When he finally leaves, you can tell the kids almost cheer but are definitely holding back. Donney walks past and winks at me. I give him a look of disgust as he walks away.

When I finally get to the front of the line, Clary jumps beside me and hands me her pink hairbrush. I look at her with confusion until she feels the need to say, "Oh yeah, I forgot. It's to brush your hair."

"I remember that much, silly. I was just wondering why you wanted me to use your hairbrush."

"To brush your hair," Clary says slowly and, honestly, quite condescendingly. I look and her and nod and start brushing my hair. "Good job!" she says a little too loudly, just as Montey walks by and looks in.

"Did you get all dolled up for me? How thoughtful."

"Yes! Let me just put on my lipstick quick." I hold up my middle finger and wipe it over my lips.

"Nice," Montey says with a chuckle.

The smell of cooking food lingers downstairs. I look to Clary, who invites me to go first. I lightly jog to the stairs and run up. I poke my head out of the stairway. I see Sara from yesterday standing over the glass-top stove and hear the sound of eggs popping in the grease. At the white-painted wooden table, there are a couple of kids I saw last night. There's Green, yes, I am sure that is not his real name, and next to him is a blonde girl, maybe fourteen.

Clary runs up behind me and takes the seat on the other side of Green, her strawberry hair glowing from the sun shining in the window. Bea's the first to see me, and she smiles but doesn't say anything. Bea, bless her soul, the woman that saved me from being naked, and frankly, the first friendly face I saw here. A couple of other older people, okay, maybe more middle-aged, all stand at the island chatting with Sara. Sara turns around to place an egg on a plate and sees me.

"Talia! Good morning! It's nice to see you not locked in your little tower of a bedroom." Her smile is bright and innocent.

I reply in kind, "Good morning, Sara, I see you're making good use of the eggs."

She holds a finger to her mouth. "Shh. I still have enough for the *thing* I mentioned, but I also have extra, so here!" She hands me a plate with an egg in the corner and a spoonful of garlic mashed potatoes.

"This smells," I take a deep breath, soaking it in, "amazing." I think I might be drooling. I sit down at the table at the spot across from Clary. She smiles at me, and a plate is placed in front of her next. I swear she inhales it.

A hand presses down on my shoulder. The owner of the hand speaks. "Good morning, Talia." *Donney.* "I almost forgot you existed. I'm almost disappointed to see you."

"Good to see you're in a good mood this morning, Donney," Montey says, glaring at him. Donney gives up his hold on my shoulder to throw his hands up in surrender, backing away with an ear-to-ear grin across his face.

"Now, you two knock it off. Today is going to be a good day," says Bea, switching her glances from Montey and Donney. Donney grabs a plate off the counter, winks to Clary, and heads downstairs.

"Does your room really need more crumbs?" I yell after him.

"Good point!" he yells back from the bottom of the stairs. "I'll eat in your room!"

"Don't you dare!" I say with a mouthful of food. He doesn't reply. *Great.*

The group of adults at the counter all rolls their eyes. "Where are my manners?" Sara asks. "This is my sister, Mary." A woman with red hair, less greyed than her sister's, waves. I nod in greeting. "This is George." George has a jawline that could cut glass, and impossibly dark skin. He nods at me, I nod back. "And this is Bea, short for Beatrice." Bea hits her.

"You know better than to call me that," Bea says, more joking than anything, and everyone chuckles.

"We've met." I turn my eyes to meet hers. "Morning, *master*." Everyone else looks around in confusion but Bea just smiles.

"Morning." She gives me a wink and they turn back to each other. I guess I was interrupting something?

I eavesdrop on the conversation; it's something about a drone they found? Drones are how the government sends us things like medication and canned foods. One being found on the ground is very concerning. This means it was most likely sent crashing deliberately, as it's extremely rare for them to fail. Who would crash a drone that could be bringing life-saving medication to someone in need? *Selfish bastards*.

"How is it?" Sara chimes in over her shoulder. She turns her head and smiles at me while I have a mouth full of potatoes. I give her a thumbs up and a stuffed-cheeks smile. She shakes her head and turns away. "So, Talia, Doc told us about your … incident." I sit straight, as if someone dumped ice down my back, completely frozen. I stand up, finished with my plate, cautious with each step.

"Oh yeah?" I place the plate on the counter and wash it with the soap and water that fill the sink.

"Yeah, pretty scary, huh?" She and the other three adults are watching me now. I don't think I can move an inch. There are only four of them, but I feel like there are a million eyes on me. I need to be careful about my next words. I open my mouth, but Bea saves me.

"Losing all of your memories is unimaginable, especially in today's world. Memories of good times along with the hope of life getting better than it is now is what a lot of us live for." The other girls nod in agreement and I'm careful not to let the breath I've been holding out all at once.

Honestly, now that we're talking about what I think we're talking about, I no longer want to talk. "Yeah, it sucks. Like, could you imagine having everything you loved ripped away, and then not knowing what was ripped away?" My words come out like a rude joke, but I won't apologize. "Now imagine that you can feel it with every step you take. Could you imagine not being able to have any happy memories to hold onto, imagine them burning in a fire, sent up into ash with no chance of ever putting the pieces together? Now imagine all of that is just creating an empty hole in your chest. Missing everything that was. That's how I see every day." Everyone is staring at me now. I don't think they know how to respond, and I don't think I want them to respond.

CHAPTER
9

The next few days go by without anything eventful happening. Montey checks in, we play chess, and I let him win. *Appear weak when you are strong.* I don't leave my room much; he brings me down my food. Doc has checked on me a couple of times.

Apparently, my blood tests were "inconclusive." Whatever that means. So, he shines a bright light in my eyes, squeezes my arm, says something along the lines of "we'll know more soon" or "fingers crossed we know more soon." I don't know how crossing our fingers is going to help.

I'm freakin' broken. I feel like a mess of a human being. No one, other than the two aforementioned, has come to see me, which is good. I don't want to see them.

All I really do is think about the things Montey has told me on our walk. Everything is sinking in. I probably had a squad. *Had* being the operative word. Thirteen people died, minimum. Who knows if there were many more? Why did I survive? What is so special about me? Also, I wonder if this is the only lie that's been told to me. Maybe they're lying about that too. God, I could just scream.

"Hey." My head snaps to the doorway. Donney. I almost forgot he existed.

"What do you want?" I snarl.

"I deserved that." He doesn't move. "I'm not apologizing either, so don't hold your breath."

"Oh, thank you, I was worried I was never going to breathe again. What do you *want*?" His face doesn't change from a neutral expression.

"Never mind." He rolls his eyes. "This is stupid." He turns to leave. *Wait!*

"Nu-uh. No, you're not coming here just to leave." I get off the bed to stand opposing him. "If you want to say something, cough it up." He turns back and gives me a dirty smirk. I study him for a moment. His skin is a paled tan, no freckles, no imperfections, nothing.

"Or else what?" He leans into his words; his smile hides a dare. A dare—*that* I was not prepared for. "That's what I thought."

I sigh, defeated. At least he's to the point.

"Screw it. Clary wants to play more board games with you."

I freeze, taken aback by the invitation. "Why me?" I have to force the words out.

"Because she sucks at board games, but she seems to be able to beat you. It helps her confidence knowing she's better than someone." That knowledge makes him chuckle. "Annnd, she's worried about you. You haven't left this room and you're starting to smell."

I elect to ignore that last part. "She doesn't need to be worried. I'm fine."

He rolls his eyes. "I don't care. She just wants to play board games." He almost looks like he's begging for a second.

"Does she know?"

Donney's face fades into something darker. "Do you?" Stone seriousness.

"If I said no, how would this conversation end?" I squint; a challenge.

"I ain't a fortune teller, but I can tell you, in my best judgement, it won't be good … for you." A fierce opponent.

I take a breath. I don't think telling him no would be a good option. "Then yes. I do. But unfortunately, I don't know what you all want me to know. I still have no memories, and I wish to God I was making that up." I don't think I took a single breath between words. I catch my breath once the sentence is finished. He does nothing but stare at me, expression perfectly neutral. A perfect poker player.

"Yeah, she knows. She doesn't really care. And frankly, neither do I." My eyebrows crease together. I'm sure I look as confused as I feel. "Don't get touched or anything, I still hate the fact that you're here and I wish I never dragged your sorry ass back here, but, well, shit, you're here, and Clary wants to play … will you go play with the damn girl?" He moves out of the way of the door frame, gesturing down the hall. I'm sure he's not leading me to my death. *Why, oh why, would I put that thought in my own damn head?* I pause for a second as I enter the hall. I could just run back …

Donney sees my hesitation and shoves me down the hall. I stumble but catch myself. "Would you just go? She's eleven, not evil."

"Does that go double for you?" I snarl, halfway down the hall.

"Yes? I'm going to go with yes."

"So, twenty-two and evil?" He scoffs and follows close behind me like a jailer leading a convict on the green mile. He leads me to the room, watches me sit down with Clary, and leaves without another word.

Clary smiles at me. Clearly, she's been waiting because she already has a new board game set up. "Hi, Talia. Let's play a game." Well, worst-case scenario, I can always just play board games for the rest of my life. *Dreadful.*

At least I've taken a shower now. Clary isn't actually too subtle with her hints, including but not limited to her inviting me to play a game called "shower." It's where I take a shower. That's it, I just … shower. Frankly, it's more fun than a good portion of the old games she makes me play. But even that beats sitting alone in my room. She keeps trying to get me to do other things too, like changing my clothes, or leaving to get fresh air.

I've started having dinner with them, upstairs, in the bastard of sunlight. Montey sits on one side of me and Clary sits on the other. No one asks questions anymore. Maybe they had them answered. A little unfair, dontcha think? They get answers when I don't? *Not even a speck of light in the shadow covering my mind.*

But I don't think it really matters. I'm okay here, I really am. I know I've only been here for a week, but I guess when this is all, you know … you get used to it pretty quickly.

I don't think Donney is much warmer to me now, though. Then again, I don't really see him being "warm" to anyone, Clary excluded. He seems like he tolerates everyone. Montey, however, is helping whenever he can: he helps with dinner, solving crossword puzzles—

practically any time there's an issue, he's the one they call. An all-around good person.

"Pass the salt, please." Mary, Sara's sister, adds to the idle chit-chat that covers the table, including discussing what movie to watch and what Emma, a thirteen-year-old Picasso, should draw next. Nothing important. I avoid participating, but Montey drags me in more often than I'd like. I usually just cut my contributions short and pass it off to someone else. I'm even in on a couple of inside jokes. Unfortunately, this does nothing for the lifetime of a chasm lost in myself. *Boohoo.*

Montey drags me into another conversation. "It was crazy! Right, Talia?"

"Not as crazy as Doc's story about the time he fought a shark in Hawaii!" See? I'm really getting good at not talking about anything.

"Tell us the story again, Doc!" Emma says, excited and eager.

"Well, okay." Doc starts to ramble on about a story I've heard twice already since I've been here. The world before the war seems crazy, like it never actually happened.

Montey leans over so his hair is against my forehead. "Hey, let's go for a walk." I nod as we excuse ourselves to put our plates away. I ignore the shoes and just grab the hat before stepping outside into the colours of the setting sun.

"None of this feels real," I say as Montey shuts the door behind him.

"I can assure you it is. It's all real, and I think it's all better now that you're here." He pauses, grabbing my hand. "Do you think you," he looks down at our hands, "might want to stay here?" My mind goes blank. *Do I really have a choice?* But I think I know what he's really asking while avoiding saying it—he means with me. I admit this little thing between us is going fast; I just don't think I can afford to lose one of my few supporters here. I don't want to make a scene and lose him. *Lose Montey, lose everyone.*

"I ... don't know. Some part of me wants to go and see if I have anyone else out there. Wouldn't you?" His face calms; complete understanding.

"I lost people too, Talia." He tightens his grip, and his palms are sweaty. "We all have. The Silver Men took everything from a lot of people. And I get it, why you're asking why you were saved. Honestly, everyone left on the planet has asked themselves that same question—

you aren't special, you just don't remember what you lost." His words circle my mind, cutting slashes in every wall, but I get why he said it. *I'm not alone.*

"The only difference, Montey, is that you know what you had is gone, as in, never coming back. I could have a family out there and I don't even know where they are." Montey's green eyes sparkle with the setting sun, and he looks down, swallowing my words. His eyes find mine, suddenly wide with something I can't quite place, and in a panicked motion, he pulls me in and kisses me. It is rushed and far too short to be sweet. He smiles at me, his little goofy smile, and runs, dragging me with him.

"Where are we going?" I laugh, trying to keep up. He ignores me and hops over a big rock. I follow in suit. He pulls me around to the back of the base where there is a wooden storm cellar door practically lying on the ground. He lets go of my hand to rip it open. The door reveals a small staircase. Montey flashes me a toothy grin before jumping down.

"Come on!" he calls. I scan the surrounding area, but there is nothing prevalent. *This does* not *look like a good idea.* The walls are dark and damp and frankly uninviting, but I follow him down anyway.

The cellar has no light excluding what bleeds in from the open door, and I think we don't have long until the sun goes down completely and we lose all light.

There's a tool bench on the wall and a cement floor; the chill runs from my feet to the nape of my neck. Montey pulls out a metal briefcase and places it on the bench. I stand next to him as he pulls something out of the case.

A radio.

My breath catches in my throat. *Holy shit.*

"We don't have long."

"Long to do what?" I just stare at the radio, with all the dials and wires.

"To contact your old squad. Find out if they're alive."

"How do you expect me to do that? There are thousands of potential channels and that's only if someone is listening. Besides, how do we know if my squad even has a radio?"

"All squads have a radio; it's how the government communicates with us for necessary supplies." I stare in awe as I take the communicator in my hand.

"What do I say?"

"I don't know but be quick and concise, just try random frequencies."

"That's not helpful." My heart is palpitating annoyingly fast.

"Actually, better idea: to get more channels in, just give them a hint as to where we are, and this way we don't have to wait for a reply."

Okay, I have it. "My name is Talia, one-thirty-eight, I'm alive. Are you?"

Montey does a slow clap. "How profound." I hit him in the stomach. It just felt right. "Oof."

I ignore him and switch the channel to another random one, "My name is Talia, one-thirty-eight, I'm alive. Are you?"

I spin the dial, not bothering to wait for an answer, trying to cover as much ground as possible. I do this on maybe a hundred frequencies until the sun goes down and I can no longer see anything in the darkness. I see Montey's faint outline, and he's swinging his legs from where he's sitting on the workbench.

"If you want," he says, "we can come back tomorrow and do the same."

"Don't you think we'll be caught?" I grab his hands, and they're warm.

"It'll be our little secret; no one else has to know." He places a hand on my face and kisses me again. His lips are soft and squishy. I don't really mind this time. It's not great, but it's just celebratory.

"We should get back before someone wonders where we are." I grab his hands and pull him out up the stairs and into the moonlight. You know, the not-evil sky thing.

We enter the main level of the house. Sara and Mary are chatting about who-knows-what, Bea is knitting at the table, and I catch a glimpse of Doc as he heads downstairs. I run off after him.

"Hey, Doc." He turns at the sound of my voice. "I was wondering if there were any more tests we could run, you know?"

He presses his lips in a line. "Honestly, I don't think we can. I fear the only person that can truly tell what happened to you is a neurologist, and those aren't exactly easy to come by nowadays. Especially since we haven't told anyone you are here."

A pang of disappointment seeps into my chest, my head falls heavy, but I understand. I drag myself to my bedroom, and my steps feel drudging, but I make it. I'm sure it's no later than nine but I think I need to rest.

Tomorrow is another day.

CHAPTER
10

My eyes flash open to the reverb of a scream, and the ceiling light spins in my vision. I force myself to sit up. *What was that?* My heart starts to panic. What am I supposed to do? I move to the far side of the bed. I pull my knees close to my chest. *Good idea, they definitely can't get us now.* I shake my thoughts out. I scan the room and jump out of bed, and the spots fade from my vision. Montey is already in the doorway.

"Are you okay?" he spits out. I pause, staring at him. *What the hell is happening?* "Talia, are you okay?" Donney pushes up from behind him.

"We don't have time for this." Montey glares at him.

"Hurry. Follow me," he whispers quickly. He's holding a gleaming silver axe in his hand. The adrenaline is kicking in. I land on my feet and shoot a confused look at Donney.

"Montey, what the hell is going on?" I reply while running behind him.

"A Silver Man got his way into the house somehow and that's when I came to get you." He keeps running. This house is big, and we twist and turn, corner after corner. Down the hall I see a few people scurrying into an unfamiliar room. Donney gestures me into the room.

A scream curdles from the front of the house. *That tiny room is starting to look lovely.* I get in the room and I don't see anyone, which is weird since I'm sure I saw at least ten people come in here. Something cold grabs my wrist, and my heart falls in my chest before I turn around to see Green pulling me into a small hole in the wall, literally a square hole in the wall no more than three feet tall and two feet wide. I scurry inside. The walls are lined with mattresses, and there are shelves holding probably a month's worth of canned food if it were split between all of us.

Montey jumps in the hole and Donney follows suit behind him. I notice that the wall I had entered from is actually metal on this side, and it looks thick too. The boys frantically pick up a metal piece slightly larger than the hole and quickly bolt it shut. The machine is screeching loudly; it knows we're here now. Just before the hole is covered completely, I see it—a Silver Man standing on the other side. I stumble backwards and fall. The last bolt straightens and holds the metal tight to the wall. *Boom!* A bang slams against the metal cover.

The Silver Man is trying to enter.

Boomboom. Everyone in the room backs away from the wall. Donney looks to Doc as I follow his gaze. Doc just shakes his head, like he already knows the answer to the question Donney hasn't asked. *Boomboomboom.* The banging is desperate, then ... nothing.

Everything is silent. I swear you can hear people's eyes blinking. I scan the room for all the children, and I think I see all of them, so my heart rests a little. *Then what was the scream?* No one says anything. No one moves; we're all petrified. *It's here, it's really here.* I can hear my heartbeat, its volume rising the longer the silence lingers.

Finally, there's a cut through the silence as a voice on the other side of the wall creaks up. "I'm alive, are you?" I freeze. *Zap.* My eyes snap to find Montey's and he stares at me, completely terrified. My legs go wobbly and the room is spinning out of control. I don't think I'm breathing. My chest knots and twists. *I think I'm going to throw up, oh please don't throw up.*

The voice says nothing else, but we hear footsteps clacking away down the hallway, as well as the pneumatic hiss of the Silver Man's steps getting quieter as they move away.

I'm alive, are you? My words on the broadcast. There are two possible answers: they are my squad, and I come from a squad of murderers. Alternatively, they could've just heard me and figured *what a better time for a little light-hearted murder?* Either way, I'm not a big fan of how this will end.

"Twenty." Doc's words snap my head to attention. The words sink into me as they sink into everyone.

Twenty.

Twenty people.

Someone's missing.

People's heads are twisting, scanning in rapid succession, hoping to solve the mystery.

Sara notices first, alerting everyone with a bone-chilling scream. "MARY!" She sinks to her knees, George holding onto her arm to keep her balance. Her cries seem to be contagious, as soon as almost everyone in the room is either crying or looking like they're about to.

Montey comes over to take the place by my side. Sara takes a large, suffering breath in and shoves to her feet, casting a dirty look my way.

"You," she says through gritted teeth.

"Me? What did I do?" She doesn't know, no one— *correction: almost no one*—knows.

"You had that look on your face when they spoke."

"You mean fear? Yeah, I'm pretty sure we're all scared, Sara," Montey interjects.

"Dammit, Montey. I know what I saw."

Doc places a hand on her shoulder. "Sara, I think you should take a seat and calm down. No one expects you to be okay with this, but now is not the time to be casting blame."

She moves away, repulsed, her features contorted in disgust. "You can't tell me I'm crazy!"

"Sara, I'm not—"

"I'm not crazy! I know what I saw." She steps towards me. "And this is *your* fault!" Before anyone can say anything else, her fist connects with my jaw. My head jerks with the impact, the taste of metal in my mouth is almost immediate. I wipe my lips with the back of my hand. The blood is darker than I thought it would be. I fight the urge to spit it out, so I don't rile her up further. Someone has already restrained her by the time I straighten my back.

Donney holds her arms behind her back. Clary is blocking the kids in the corner, and it looks like she's trying to shield them; not that she would be an immovable object, but she has a good heart.

Now, back to the matter at hand. I walk up to go nose to nose with Sara. A couple of the other middle-aged women try to get in my way but back down with a glare.

"I can assure you I did not bring them here. I had nothing to do with this." My voice coming off as poison that I am willing to spit. "I would never condone the senseless murder of a woman that so many loved. If you think I would do something so foolish then maybe you *are* crazy." I walk backwards through the silence; a couple of the kids are whimpering.

"I think that's enough for tonight," Doc says. "Sleep it off. We have all the time in the world to grieve but not if we die down here." He nods to Donney, who lets Sara go. She doesn't push or fight.

Does she believe me? Or is she afraid of me?

Everyone faces the walls and rips the mattresses down; they cover the floor in a matter of seconds. I stare at the metal wall. Is it still out there? Will it wait? Guess that's a tomorrow problem.

Unless we die in our sleep.

Yeah, unless that.

The night rolls on for days, or what seems like it. I can't sleep, and frankly, after today's affairs, I don't think I'll ever sleep again. The scream, replaying over and over in my head, curdles my blood.

I wonder what the original purpose of this room was. There's enough food down here to feed everyone comfortably for a while. Albeit it is disgusting canned food that is most definitely not suitable for prolonged human consumption. The ceiling is oddly flawless, with not a chipped paint speck in sight, excusing the wooden hatch. The hatch looks like it was originally an old door that someone strapped to the ceiling, with hinges on one side and three sliding locks on the other. Slightly rusted but otherwise seemingly untouched. I wonder what's on the other side.

I don't think it's a good idea to try to open it either.

Yeah, but what's on the other side?

No.

None of my business.

I sit up. My legs are crossed, taking up the entire space from the body on my left to the body on my right.

On my left lies a too-still George. His chest is moving, so he's not dead.

Too soon.

On my right is Donney. He's a bit more fidgety, but he's yet to turn to face me.

I wonder what's on the other side of that door. I brush off the thought. The room is running out of things for me to look at.

Screw it. I pull myself up towards the ceiling door. I rub my fingers over the wood.

"Shit," I exclaim, in no more than a hushed whisper. Donney fidgets a bit but nothing damning, but c'mon, I got a stupid splinter. The wood sticks out of my index finger. I suck on it to pull it out. Damn door.

I can't take a hint, can I? There's a cool breeze coming from the other side of the door. The locks are cold when I touch them. I grab onto the first lock and try to turn it, but the rust fights me.

Take the hint, Talia. I fight back. The lock eventually gives enough for me to slide it loose.

One down, two to go.

I have to reach for the second lock. It's a little further away from me; my hands run colder the longer I hold them up.

Just a little further.

Gotcha! My hand reaches the lock, and the rust is weaker on this one. It slides with ease.

Looking down at the last one is like looking down a mile-long street when you can see your destination in the distance. It's there, now if only I could reach it.

I take a tiptoe step forward, and then another, and then …

I fall with a smack. My vision goes blurry until it resets to the light of the room. I'm being held down, my hands above my head and a weight on my chest.

"What the *fuck* do you think you're doing?" Donney's face finally appears through the darkness. My face falls. *Great.*

"Oh, hey, nothing much." I shrug nonchalantly through his grip.

"You're an idiot, you know that?"

"Aww, Donney, you sweet-talker, I'm blushing." Our conversation is a low hum in a room full of people, but no one even stirs. His hair falls loosely down his face, falling prey to gravity. He lolls his head to the side and rolls off me, leaving me room to sit up.

"Thank you," I say, not meaning it a lick.

"Seriously, why do you try to get yourself in trouble?" He studies my face, and my lips are pressed in a thin line, expressing that I honestly have no idea. He nods and lays down.

"Hey, Donney?"

"No," he says quickly, not giving me a chance.

Not today, buddy. "Donney?"

"What?" he replies tiredly.

"I'm the reason it's here."

"No, you're not. Don't say shit like that. Nothing could bring those psychopaths here, and frankly, I don't wanna hear another word about it." His voice is stern and filled with meaning. I nod and lie down, being sure not to disturb anyone else.

And that damn ceiling door can wait.

Morning rolls around soon enough … I think, I can't *see* morning, but Doc stands up and turns on the light. The bags under my eyes weigh more than I do right now. I push myself to stand up. I take that back. An elephant doesn't weigh more than I do right now. I pull my arms out, reaching in a glorious stretch, and follow the squad over to the food shelves. They move like cows being herded. I guess when you don't know what to do, you do what the monkeys do. I get in line and quickly snag a can of peaches. I move to the far end of the room and sit down before realizing that this can doesn't have a pull-tab and requires a can opener. *Damn, guess I'll starve.*

My shoulders loosen of exhaustion and a shadow blocks the light from my lap. I look up to see Green holding a can opener, arm outstretched as an offering. I take it and nod a quick thanks and he walks away.

I scarf down the peaches like I've never eaten before. No one speaks to each other. The only sound is the sticky, slopping sound of people eating anything from canned beans to Italian wedding soup. I cringe. The sound of people eating is not enjoyable.

Doc stands in the middle of the room and claps once, and everyone's attention turns to him. "Okay, I hate that it's come to this, but we'll now be leaving the base." No one looks shocked; it's like he's stating the obvious. "We're going to be heading to Squad Thirty-Five base. They were disassembled after their elders passed, so their place will be empty. If you get lost, just keep heading west until you reach the clearing. You'll see it eventually." Everyone nods somberly. "There are supply bags on our way out and it'll be dark in the room, so make sure you find one." His eyes find mine, but I turn away instantly. "Everyone," he says, insinuating that I, too, have to grab a bag. I look back up and Doc gives Donney a look that is very "you know what to do."

Donney walks to the middle of the room, right under the ceiling door. "Stay back." His voice is a mixture of sleep-deprived and determined. Before now, I didn't think there could ever be such a combination. Everyone follows his instructions, pushing up against the wall. He looks over to me, rolls his eyes, and undoes the third sliding lock. When he lets go of the door it falls and immediately a heavy iron ladder falls into the room. *Oh, that would've hurt.* Donney looks at me again, and I sheepishly turn away. *I get it, okay?*

Doc twirls his hand, motioning for everyone to climb. One by one they climb. I shouldn't go. This isn't my family. I'm only causing them pain. Everyone has climbed up the ladder with the exception of Doc, who is now glaring at me, careful not to make a sound. He's not leaving until I do.

Got it, self-pity can wait. I push myself to my feet and head over to the ladder. The rungs are freezing cold. Doc reassures me with a thin-lipped smile and a hand on my shoulder. I reply with a smile of my own and take the ladder one step at a time until I can step off into a pitch-black room.

Once my eyes adjust, I grab one of the supply bags tucked off in a corner and throw it over my shoulder. Donney is leading the charge, his axe in hand, near the small light bleeding in from presumably the bottom of a door. He holds up his hand. 5 … 4 … 3 … 2 …

Light pours into the room, taking every shadow with it and everyone pushes out. The rush of light blurs in my eyes and then everyone is gone. No one stays behind for me this time. The world hushes and then mutes around me. Air in, air out. The sun immediately invades my space as I leave the room. I'm in the vestibule, and I look back to see wallpaper torn from the wall. *No wonder I didn't notice the door before.*

A scream bursts from outside and I fight the urge to run out again. I think it found us. Soon enough, everyone will be caught. Should I run? Should I–

The light comes from the door shadows, and I turn around. I want to see it. And there it is, the Silver Man standing in front of me. It raises a hand and holds it up to my shoulder. I can't explain why, but I mirror it, holding up a hand and placing it even with its own.

It advances, only a step, and as its cold hand touches mine, I close my eyes and wait for the zap. A cold rush of energy bursts through my chest and rolls out through my hand. It feels … electric. The rush is emptying but not painful.

What is happening?

A rattling comes from the machine. It convulses, sparks spitting out of cracks you wouldn't otherwise notice. It crackles, and a large bang of screeching metal smacks it down and it falls to its knees. I look up to see Montey and Donney standing directly behind the machine. Looking back at the Silver Man, I can see the metal axe sticking out of its head. Donney steps on it to gain leverage as he rips the axe out of his hand.

"What are you waiting for? Move!" I jump over the busted machine and burst through the door behind the boys. Montey reaches back and grabs my hand, the weight of him pulling me along. The ground moves below my feet in a blur, every step pounds through my legs, but I keep moving, I can't stop, not while he's holding my hand, and he definitely won't allow me to let go. I try, but he just squeezes harder. The air is moving from my lungs, which are not willing to cooperate. Once we reach the forest, I have to watch the ground more. *Jump, twist, duck, jump, jump, duck.* I'm following Montey's movements rather than making any actual calls for myself, but I know I have to keep moving.

I don't know how long we run for. I didn't even think running this long would be possible. *Jump, duck, jump, jump, dodge.* We reach the first small clearing, and we see others of the squad waiting by a tree, drinking water from a round canteen, passing it around like it's the most delicious thing in the world.

The three of us walk up and they immediately pass it to Montey, who takes a sip and passes it to Donney. I think my mouth would be watering if I had any excess to give. But there's only a limited amount, and they're not very likely to share with the strange murderer. One of the middle-aged men, whose name I cannot remember, holds out a hand to have the bottle handed back. Donney looks almost perturbed and ignores the man. Donney twists to pass the canteen to me.

"I'm okay," I say while dying of thirst.

"Don't play the martyr, Talia, drink," Donney says without taking his eyes off the man. I give a clipped nod to whoever may be looking and grab the canteen. I take a sip, but I won't allow myself to take more, no matter how much I want to down the entire thing.

"We should be in the clear now," the man says when I pass him back the canteen, "but the base is still a couple of klicks west. So, we should keep moving." Everyone nods in agreement and start walking. I look back to where we came from. The trees look dense and unending. Out from the trees pops a little girl. I don't recognize her, but she's far away. I lift a hand to wave.

"Talia? What are you doing?" Donney calls back.

"The little girl! She's waving." Donney rushes to my side and looks to where I am looking at the girl.

"There's no one there ... Talia?"

"I feel dizzy ..." The world starts to stir and spin, and then it starts to shake. I fall to the ground. It tightens my back, and I jerk left and right, unable to stop myself from this terrible calcium taste filling my mouth. The world goes silent as I'm forcefully rotated to my side.

The world fades in and out, in and out, in and out ...

CHAPTER
11

The forest floor goes on forever. I think I'm flying. I try counting the pebbles, but I forget what I'm doing every few seconds and restart. The dirt is so pretty.

I'm standing in a crowd filled with blank and blurred faces. The bug zapping in my head is ticking every second. My vision not willing to focus, and I only see a girl with black hair stand on some stupid soapbox. I can hear her voice, but it's all coming across as gibberish. *Zap.* I try to focus but it only makes the pain in my head grow. The crowd bursts out cheering. I can't explain why, but I cheer too! Yeah, girl! You do that thing! *Whatever thing that is …* My cheering turns the heads to me; blurred, unrecognizable faces turn, and the crowd drops silent. A face pushes through the crowd. This one isn't blurry. This one is perfectly clear. Blonde hair, hazel eyes, slim features. When he finally reaches me, his stressed face relaxed. *Zap.*

"Hey, Tal," the boy says, a sly smile so sharp it could cut glass.

"Hi." *James.* The words fall into my head like finishing a sentence it's finished a thousand times.

"You know, it's been a while since you've been here. We all miss you."

"I … I sent you a message."

He pulls me into a tight hug, which turns into him playfully messing up my hair. "I got it, and we're coming for you."

"Who's we? Who is everyone?"

"The pieces will start to come together now. Give it time and it'll all be clear. But for now, you have to go back."

"Go back? Go back where?" He smiles at me and then everything, James included, starts backing up a mile a minute, like an elastic pulling far past its breaking point.

My eyes jerk open only to immediately close again. The pain sears through my vision, making the light become fluorescent. It feels like I've been hit in the head with a brick.

Or rather ... an apple.

My dream floods my head and a small part of the grey fog lifts.

Holy crap. James. I search my memories for anything else, but it's accompanied by its usual bug zap, all of it. I can't remember anything. Except for James, who is crystal clear.

I reach up to rub the sleep out of my eyes. Once I finally manage to pry them open, I see Montey sitting at the foot of ... whatever they have me on.

"Where are we?"

"Holy crap, Talia. I totally thought you were a goner this time. No more death scares, you're past your quota." Montey rushes to jump over the bed to hug me, but it feels ... wrong. Desperate. My arms are held down and he just squeezes harder.

"Montey ... you're hurting me." He lets go only to hold my arms with his hands instead like he's afraid I'm going to run. His hair is dishevelled, and he has dark bags under his eyes narrating his exhaustion.

"Sorry, I ... I just I couldn't. You had a seizure." Right. The shaking, the forest floor, the craptastic taste. *Seizure makes sense.*

"I'm okay now, okay?" His eyes are wide and looking right at me, but he's looking, not seeing. "Montey."

He shakes out of his trance, and his forest-green eyes are bloodshot as he finally meets mine. "Right, right." He lets go and pushes away. "Sorry."

"Hey, I'm okay, okay?"

"Okay." He looks at me up and down, as if waiting for something. "You know you can trust me with anything, right? I mean, I can obviously keep a secret. 'I'm alive, are you?'"

I throw him a cooling stare. "Don't say that so loud! Someone might hear you!"

"I'm just saying, you can trust me." He smiles sweetly, prompting me to answer.

"You're an idiot if you don't think I do."

His shoulders relax and he smiles, but it feels forced. "I'm going to get us food. I think you should stay here."

"I'm not hungry." *I'm starving.*

"I'm sure," he says sarcastically. "I'll be right back." He hesitates then pushes up and makes his way out of the room.

The room around me is everything but ideal. The floor is cement, and the walls are ... also cement. *Am I in a prison or something?* That being said, it is cooling, which, this time of year, isn't exactly a bad thing. Although I am the only thing in here, excluding the gigantic blanket that I guess I kicked off while in my hallucination, dream, memory thing. *Whatever.*

I can't help but have my mind wander back to James. I try to pick apart the memories to gain anything else, but it seems like almost anything that isn't him is blurry. But I remember him. His personality, his spotty attempt at bravery, his laugh. *Lest we forget his tendency for murder.*

Now, that's the part that doesn't make any sense. James isn't a murderer. I've known him for nearly my entire life; he wouldn't. He couldn't.

He did.

I'm startled by the sound of creaking floorboards coming from outside the room. "Come in?" Another creak, but no one enters. "Would you just get in here already? I'm not exactly one to talk to myself ..." *out loud* "... so don't expect to overhear a damned confession or something. You could just ask." Clary peeks her head around the corner. I immediately feel a bit of shame crossing my face.

"They don't have any board games here." She holds up a beat-up deck of cards. "But I can teach you how to play a few games ... if you'd like."

My lips press in a thin line. "I don't know if that's a good idea ... I don't want you getting in trouble."

"Donney's okay with it, I already asked."

"What about everyone else?"

Clary looks genuinely confused at the question. "What about them?" *She makes a valid point.*

I shrug. "What games do you know?"

She smiles wide and starts passing out the cards. "I'll teach you."

CHAPTER
12

"There you are!" Donney says, finding me and Clary laughing about the fact that she *TOTALLY* cheated. Which she says she didn't, but I know she ... doesn't matter. "I've been looking everywhere for you."

I turn to look at her. "I thought you said he was okay with you being here."

"I was guessing ... but he doesn't seem *too* mad, so I guess my guess wasn't too off."

Donney gives Clary a stern motherly look. He sighs. "I don't have a problem with it, and I wouldn't have if you just would've told me where you were. You really think I wouldn't want to know your every whereabouts today of all days?"

Clary looks genuinely ashamed, her head bows, and her eyes close. "Sorry ..."

"Don't worry about it, kiddo, just go and get dinner okay?"

"You got it, boss!" She does a mock salute before running out of the room. Donney laughs and shakes his head.

"Hey, sorry, I should've che–"

He holds up a hand to hush me. "She knows how to take care of herself." His tone is instantly cold. His hand is on the doorknob when it opens from the outside, and he bounces back, startled. I have to stifle a giggle. Doc pushes in.

"Hey, glad you're both here." His voice is old and tired. Crackling from time.

Donney's eyes narrow suspiciously "Why?"

"Donney, as you know, after the events of this morning, Talia should probably lay low."

"I did nothing!" *I did everything, but nothing they can prove.* My arguing seems pointless, and Doc continues.

"I know that, and I think that they do too but for now, I'd rather you stay here." He holds out a hand, illustrating his words.

"What does that have to do with me?" Donney's suspicion doesn't waver.

"Ah, yes, thank you for reminding me. Donney, you'll be her babysitter."

"Nope! No, not a chance." Donney is already trying to run out of the room.

"Yeah, Doc, I hate to agree with Donney, but I don't need a babysitter."

"Then call it a bodyguard. I just need to make sure that everyone is safe."

Donney pauses with his hand on the doorknob. I don't think he wants to disobey a direct order from his squad leader, but he also wants zero part of this babysitting gig.

"… from me?"

"Yes."

Ouch.

"And that you're safe from everyone else."

"Yeah, not happening, old man. I'm not volunteering for this. Make Montey do it! At least he can tolerate her!" Donney smiles viciously at me.

"Then consider this me voluntelling you to do it. Besides, Montey is needed in making a new garden so we can at least have some food for when winter hits." Doc tries to place a hand on Donney's shoulder, but he ducks, making Doc angrier.

Donney snarls, "Can't anyone but me do this?"

Doc replies by pointing at Donney in a mildly threatening way while backing out of the room like some cartoon villain. Donney lets his head fall in defeat.

"Oh, c'mon, Don, I'm a hoot."

His eyes are sharp as he glares at me. "Call me that again and I might just help them kill you," he says, watching the door shut behind Doc.

I blink butterfly eyes at him. "Promise?"

"For crying out loud, are you actually trying to die?" he says, exasperated.

I shrug. "I'm good either way. Let's say I have a self-destructive personality with a contingency plan."

He looks at me in disbelief. He nods, and without saying another word he disappears out of the room.

There goes that idea. I guess I could … rest more? I'm tired of resting. As ironic as that sounds. My eyes flash to Donney as he re-enters the room holding a big soft chair. I chuckle as he tries to fit it through the door, twisting it in odd ways until finally it cooperates and squishes though. Donney throws a fist up in a mini celebration that he seems to be having for himself and flops down in the chair.

I throw my arms up like, *dude, what?* He seems to understand perfectly as he gestures to the lack of seating area in the room.

"Clary didn't have a problem with the floor," I say matter-of-factly.

"Clary doesn't tend to see things that need improvement. Everything is good enough."

"Words to live by?" I lift my shoulders.

Donney flops down in the big armchair. "Not if it can be improved upon easily."

"Uhm, I watched you try to smush that oversized armchair through the door. I don't think that that can be called 'easily'."

"Do you see a single bead of sweat on my forehead?"

I lean in close and remark, "I can't tell, come closer ..."

Donney squints his eyes suspiciously. "No."

"Wise move." I lean back on the bed. I am outrageously bored. "Donney?"

"No," he says stagnantly.

I lift my head to look at him. "Is that your favourite word?"

"No."

"I'm sold. I'll play along, what is?"

He looks over to me and a small smirk grows, and I already know I'm going to hate his answer. "Beg." He winks. I mimic vomiting. He rolls his eyes, but the smirk doesn't fade.

"Has anyone ever told you that you are deeply disturbing?"

He taps a finger on his chin. "No, I guess that makes you my first." He winks again. *Alright, no way out of it, I'm vomiting.* "Just do me a favour, be a good baby and be quiet."

"Hey! We agreed this wasn't babysitting!"

"Now, dear, I know your memory ain't up to par, but I clearly didn't agree to shit. Now, shh."

I scowl at him. "Come on, Donney. I'm bored out of my mind. Let's play a game. I now know three different card games." I hold up three bony fingers.

"Okay! Let's play a game!" he says, smiling uncharacteristically wide. I narrow my eyes, preparing. "How's about the *quiet game*."

There it is. I huff and fall back on the bed. "What am I supposed to do now?"

"I could, honestly, not care less." He leans over and shuts off the light, forcing me to either get up, which I do not feel like doing or sit in the darkness for the indefinite future. The latter sucks ... but I *really* don't want to get up.

About an hour later I finally get up to turn on the light. This place is prison-like enough without the dark, damp feel of one. Donney flashes his eyes open to see me standing at the light switch.

"Hey, what the hell?" He gets up and reaches over me to turn the lights off again, to which I respond by flicking them back on. He stands over me in a threatening stance, trying to get me to back down. I don't think so. Once he sees I'm not backing down, he huffs and plops back into his chair.

"Hey, if you're so apathetic to the genuine reasons to hate me, then why do you?"

He closes his eyes, trying to pretend that the lights are still off. "No. We are not having some stupid heart to heart."

I move away from the door and around so I'm standing in front of him. "You aren't curious to know why I think you hate me?"

"No, because I don't hate you. I strongly dislike you. Therefore, your point is moot."

"I think," I say, and Donney groans. "I think that I remind you of her."

He leans forward—a challenge or a sudden interest? "Who's her?"

"Your foster sister. The one who abandoned you."

CHAPTER
13

He snarls in disgust towards me before looking over my shoulder to the wall, practically burning a hole in it. "How do you know about her?"

"A little birdy told me. That doesn't matter. I just wanted to tell you that I'm not her. So, if you could stop hating me for some stupid memory of yours that I have no control over, that'd be great."

He says through gritted teeth, "I know you're not her. She left, she left me when I was twelve years old. I haven't heard from her in eight years. She's not coming back, and you are nothing like her." I can feel his heat welling up in the room. His face is red with anger. "I swear, if you ever bring her up again, you'll have me as an enemy, and in case it wasn't obvious, I'm one of the only people you have right now."

"Got it. History is off-limits. I'd offer you a piece of my past as an apology, but, oh, right! I don't have one! Treasure what you have, you idiot. At least you have something." I huff back over to my bed and plop down. Lucky idiot, who cares if you have a past? Most people do. One thing I know is that it's not fair to treat people like shit in the present because you were treated like shit in the past. It's called personal growth buddy. *Look it up.*

"I'd like to go back to the quiet game now."

"Works for me." I slam my back on the tiny cot, and the coolness of the pillow is welcoming. Donney closes his eyes again, intending on sleeping his way to winning the game. *I think I've struck a nerve.*

We sit there in silence for an uncomfortable amount of time, and it almost passes off as normal. I hate the quiet game.

My stomach grumbles an ungodly noise. "I'm hungry."

He doesn't move from his chair "Yeah, no shit, it's seven. You haven't eaten all day."

"Can I go get something?" I ask.

Donney's head raises from a loose sleeping position. His eyebrows furrow, questioning my question. "No? Why would you think I would let you do that?"

I lift my hands. "Can *you* go get me food?"

"I thought we've already clarified that I have to babysit you."

"Then let's go together!" I gesture to the door. Come on, boy. What are you waiting for? This is stupid. If he knows I'm hungry, how hard is it to just get me some damn food!?

He pauses before lolling his head down again. "No."

I roll my eyes and my head follows. "Then how do you expect me to eat?"

"Well, you see, I've realized that if you starve, you'll be quieter faster."

God, what a dick. "Donney, go get me food or let me go. Either way, I'll be fine."

He looks up to the ceiling. "Why do you test me like this?" He looks back over to me, his blue eyes scowling. "Let's go."

"Together?" I push myself to stand up, and all my muscles pull in protest. *Don't let him see. You'll never get out of here if he does.* I straighten my back. I have pulled three different muscles already.

"I'm not letting you out of my sight. Let's go." I follow him too close. I wonder if it's literally a prison out there. Given the look of my room, I wouldn't be surprised. The door opens and I almost fall out over Donney. He shoots me an annoyed look, but he bites his lip and continues through the door.

This place is surprisingly lacking in prison features. *Why am I disappointed?* Donney continues down the hall. He doesn't seem to move confidently.

I narrow my eyes. "You don't know where you're going, do you?"

He stands up straight in front of me. "We are going to the kitchen," he whispers.

"Yeah, no, I got that bit. Where is that again?" He's most definitely lost.

"I know exactly where it is, I'm just giving you a tour." He opens every door on our way. *Bullshit, he's lost.*

He reaches for another doorknob.

"Before you open that door, tell me, what's in the room?"

He opens his mouth to speak, closes it, opens it, holds up his hand, drops it. "Screw it, you're starving." He gestures for me to turn back around.

"Wait." I turn around to go in the other direction. "Can I try something?"

"No. Why would you think I would say yes to that?" He motions his hands faster, rushing me along. I completely ignore him and walk around him. I know very well he could stop me if he tried, but he's not trying, so I'm gonna keep going. I move three doors down to a threshold before hearing the voices inside.

"How long did you think you could keep this from us, Doc?" I know I've heard the raspy voice before, but I'd be damned if I remembered her name.

"Honestly, I never thought it was any of your business," Doc replies, and a not-so-civil unrest stirs in the apparent crowd.

"How is this not our business? She killed Mary and Sara."

Are they talking about me? Is Sara dead now too? Did she die in the attack? Why did no one tell me? What are they talking about?

"So much wrong with that. She did not kill anyone. Unless she managed to turn into a Silver Man while we weren't looking and then turned back. Second of all, how is this information relevant?"

"She was found surrounded by over a *dozen* dead bodies."

Yeah, that'd be me.

Donney places a hand on my shoulder, reminding me of where I am. I open my mouth to say something, but he holds a finger to his lips, quieting me. "I think the kitchen is this way," he says, loud enough for the people in the room to come to a quick hush. I smile at him. He pushes me through the threshold. I stumble to keep myself on my feet, which my body attempts to fight.

Around the room I can see several people standing around Doc; they seem to be surrounding him. I can only remember a few of their names. George is standing tall, skin a gleaming purple. Bea is sitting in the corner of the room, nose in a book, clearly disinterested in the conversation. A few of the people I have seen before, but their names are lost on me.

"Ah, hello, Talia, Donney." We both give Doc a nod. "Talia, you remember Karen?"

Oh right, Karen, the woman who would sit at a dinner table filled with conversation and say nothing. *I guess she's grown pretty chatty since then.* "Of course. Hello, Karen." I nod, she snarls. Great. At least I can note that she is not one of my biggest fans.

"I'm assuming you two are hungry," Doc says, addressing me and Donney.

I look up to Donney and smile sarcastically. "Starving." He rolls his eyes before moving around me to the fridge. He opens it and the room immediately smells spoiled.

"It's not the food," Doc says after judging my reaction. "It's the fridge. It's been off for a while now. The food is still good, though. Eat up." Donney grabs bread and puts on room-temperature butter, cold chicken, and half a tomato. He cuts it in half, hands half to me, and shuffles me out of the room.

"What the hell is this?"

"Sustenance," he says loudly, still shoving me down the hall until we reach the room and he shoves me inside and slams the door behind us. "Damn. You really do love listening to conversations that you have no part of." He shoves a finger in my face.

I push it aside. "Technically, I was a part of both of those conversations … technically."

He shakes his head to himself. "Eat."

"Oh, this is food?" I point to the lazy breaded monstrosity.

"Okay, then give it to me. I'll eat it." He reaches for the sandwich, and I quickly shove it in my mouth, only to grimace. It's chewy and there are just … so many wrong textures. He tries to suppress a smile, but it cracks through. "Good?"

"Did you add toenails when I wasn't looking?"

"Close! Fingernails." I start to spit it out. "Wait! I'm joking, don't waste it." I continue to chew, hating literally every part of it. Then again, what do I expect for food that was manufactured minimum of six years ago? *Brought to you by your friendly neighbourhood government.*

It's so awfully dry yet soggy. "I'm making lunch next time."

He shrugs "Or … I'd like to revisit the quiet option."

"I literally hate you," I reply tartly.

"Oh, thank god. I was worried I would have another girl falling over me. This saves time."

"This is literally the end of the world. The only reason anyone is 'falling over you' is because reproduction is now imperative to the continuation of the human race and you're one of the only options."

"Did you just say you want to mate with me?"

"When did those words *ever* leave my mouth!?"

He leans in too close for comfort, and I shove in another inedible bite. "It's subtext, my dear." He winks and pauses for a second before straightening his back again. I stretch aversion over my lips, which only makes him laugh. *I'm so glad I get to be a part of this conversation.*

The door smacks open and Montey stands tall in the doorway. "What the hell are you doing in here?" Montey says to Donney.

"Babysitting," he says

"Bodyguarding," I correct, to which he rolls his eyes.

"Not my choice, *trust* me." He places a hand to his chest, imitating sincerity.

"I don't think I could trust you as far as I could throw you," Montey retorts.

"Now, that's unfair. You can't throw at all. I feel like you should be able to trust me at least equal to the same amount as a grape. Then again, I'm only marginally less likely to choke you." Donney winks to Montey.

"Donney, get out," Montey says sharply.

"No can do. Boss Man told me not to let her leave my sight." He places himself next to me and throws his arm over my shoulder. *Zap.* I shake him off and he looks hurt, but not as much as Montey looks angry.

"Consider this my shift. You can come back when I have to go back to the garden tomorrow."

Donney bats his eyes. "Promise?"

"I promise," Montey says in a baby voice. He goes to pinch Donney's cheek, but he smacks his hand away and gives him a warning glare. I chuckle, which is appreciated by not one, but two glares. *Worth it.*

"Just go, Donney."

Donney salutes sarcastically. He reaches the door and turns around to me and winks so Montey can't see, like we have some big secret between us. It only makes me feel dirty. I pull the corner blanket up into my arms and hold it around me. *Yeah, see you tomorrow, Donney.*

CHAPTER
14

"Uhm, hi," Montey prods.

"Hey." I nod to him.

He takes a step towards me, his stance open and honest. "Did you eat?"

I laugh. "Define eat …"

He narrows his eyes. "Did you ingest sustenance?"

"Then, yeah. Sustenance, sweet sustenance." I squeeze the blanket tighter to my chest. Montey laughs. Such a sugary-sweet laugh.

"Well, I should tell you. It's pretty bad out there. Everyone seems to want to feed you to the fishes," Montey whispers.

"That's reassuring," I say sarcastically while swinging my feet off the bed.

He smiles sadly. "Talia, I'm not going to lie to you. They pretty much all blame you for what happened and, in all honesty, can you blame them?" I recoil in shock. I *never* expected to hear those words out of Montey's mouth.

"What did you just say to me?" I jump up onto my feet to face him.

"That came out wrong." He holds up his hands in defence. "I didn't mean it to say that you are to blame, I just mean you can see why they would want to blame you. I mean, it was most likely your old squad that came after us." I must look like I'm in tears because Montey just melts.

"Hey, hey, hey. No, no. Don't be sad. I'm sure that they're all just scared. They have a right to be scared." I look up to meet his gaze. "*We* have a right to be scared," he corrects himself. "Those people, whoever they are, I have a feeling they aren't just going to give up. For now, please, let's all just lay low."

I nod and sit back down. Montey sits down next to me. The tears slowly well in my eyes until everything is blurry and I can't blink without them falling in droves.

I try to speak but my words come out as hiccups and nonsense. "I ... I ... *hic* ... I can't. This is all my fault. *Hic.*"

Montey immediately turns to hug me. He hugs me tightly and warmly, like he's afraid I'll break if he lets go, and honestly, I might. His arms wrapped around me feel like a home that I've never had. I'm scared of what's going to happen next, and he is the one thing right now that I know is real. This all bothers me a little too much.

Who was I before all of this, and why would I let my squad get a hold of the Silver Men? All these thoughts just make me cry more as Montey grips me tighter.

When I finally calm down, he pulls himself away but keeps a firm hand on my shoulder. "Donney wasn't a complete dick?" He smiles, trying to lighten the mood.

"Oh, no. He was a complete dick, as per usual, but he didn't try to kill me so I'm going to have to say that I'm okay."

Montey shrugs a *what canya do?*

"Hey," I continue, he's so close, I can smell him, and he smells so ... welcoming. Like oak and pine trees. He smiles at me, and when I don't smile back it dims until it disappears.

"What's wrong?" His hand lifts and traces my cheekbone.

"Did I kill Sara too?"

He closes his eyes and takes a deep breath before opening his eyes again. "You didn't kill anyone."

"You know that is not exactly true."

"The radio was my idea, so if you killed them, then so did I. But we didn't; the psychopathic monster controlling it did." *James.*

"Montey." His lips press in a thin line.

"Yes?"

"Is Sara dead?"

Silence fills the room as he slowly nods. "She didn't want to leave. I'm sorry, but it wasn't your fault." I'm frozen in place. I don't care what Montey says, she's dead because of me. I wanted to find my squad, and I guess I did. I look for their faces in the grey cloud again but nothing. *Zap.* I force my eyes up to his. He looks so calm. It's not fair. My lip curls and I turn my body, so he doesn't have to see.

"I'm going to sleep ... I'll see you in the morning."

"Talia, it wasn't your fault, okay?" I don't think I could open my mouth without crying so I don't. He slips off the bed and places himself in the chair Donney brought in, clearly intending to stay the night. I don't think I can fight him.

CHAPTER
15

My eyes pry open in what seems like minutes later, but Montey is passed out cold in the armchair. I suppose now is as good a time as any to give myself a self-guided tour of this place. I push myself off the bed and tiptoe towards the door. Opening it sends a hot breeze into the room. *Close it. It's not worth it.*

When have I ever listened to that idea? I push the door the rest of the way open and Clary pops up in my way. I mouth *"move"* to her, but she stands still, crossed arms, face determined.

"Go back," she mouths back and points to the bed behind me.

"No." I walk around her. She shakes her head disapprovingly and runs off in the other direction. That was really weird.

Whatever.

I walk around looking in doors, and I manage to find a tiny bathroom that looks like its last renovation was in 1952, two bedrooms, one of which is empty and one that has three children sharing a king-sized bed. I'm careful not to make any noise that could wake them.

I keep walking until I find a door that opens to a basement. I'm about to close it when I hear a voice.

"Listen, Karen, if I told you that, would you have allowed this poor girl who, need I remind you, remembers nothing, to stay with us? She remembers nothing at all, she's just scared like all of you are right now. She needed a place to stay and I gave her one. Now, I don't expect you all to move on and pretend nothing happened. I would just like for you all to look at some other possibilities. Okay?" Doc says to the group, speaking only in mumbles.

I feel a tap on my shoulder. I whip around to see Donney just shaking his head at me. I narrow my eyes, trying to study him. *What does he want now?* He grabs me by the arms and pulls me into one of the empty rooms I passed earlier and closes the door.

"What did I tell you about eavesdropping?" he says without turning around to face me. "You're as curious as a cat."

"First of all, I wasn't listening. I was just walking by and happened to pause at the sound of voices. Second of all, what's this about curious cats?" Donney rolls his eyes as he turns to look at me.

"It's going to get you killed." He looks me dead in the eyes, and the look on his face is cuttingly serious. I almost feel intimidated by him, but I can't help but remember what happened earlier.

"And you have a problem with that because?" I take a step closer to show that I am not stepping down.

"Are you kidding me?" His eyes narrow. "Do you have a death wish or something? Because let me tell you, keep doing things like that, and it'll come soon enough."

"Maybe it should," I say under my breath, so he barely hears me.

"What?"

"Did you send Clary to spy on me?" The realization floods over me like a tsunami. He just stares at me with an empty expression. "You did, didn't you? Why? What do you have to gain from me not dying?"

"The satisfaction of knowing I can do it myself when I'm good and ready," he shoots back like a bullet tearing through my skin. I stumble back a step as he steps a little too close for comfort. "You don't get it, do you, dear? You don't get that you're worth more alive than dead. Those people that killed your friends out in that field and tried to kill you are still after you, therefore after us. I have worked too damn hard to keep this place from falling apart to have Karen or someone kill you and dump your body in a ditch for your old squad to find and then come after us again. So, I thought a little additional guard wouldn't be that bad of an idea. Sue me."

"You didn't think so last time you were assigned guard duty." I snuff back.

"In case you didn't notice, it wasn't me guarding you. It was Clary. So, ha."

I study him, trying to figure out if he's lying or not, and if so, about which part? *Got it.* I push up against his body so closely that it is really uncomfortable.

I tilt my head to up meet his eyes. "I get it now." I take a few steps back, giving myself enough space to stand without being in his immediate reach.

"This sounds like a fun game. Is this where I start to guess what exactly you '*get*'? Or are you just going to ruin my fun and tell me?"

"You sent Clary to spy on me."

"Oh my god. How did you guess?" asks Donney sarcastically, with a fake surprised look on his face as he leans against the white wall behind him. "I already told you that, remember?"

"No, no. You sent her to spy on me, but not only that, you had her go get you if I tried to leave the room. You didn't have her wake up Montey or go get Doc. You had her find you."

His smile fades, and I know I'm onto something. "So?"

"So, what is your end game? Is Montey supposed to be this evil mastermind and you're the jackass who turns out to be the hero in the end? 'Cause I'm not buying it. Montey is a good guy."

"Sure. And the devil was once an angel."

"Montey is not the devil. Montey is—"

"A good guy, yeah, I can hear you. Don't forget, I've known him for a hell of a lot longer than you have."

"Are we done here?" I stick up my chin at him, an attempted display of strength.

My display clearly fails. "Are you ready to cooperate and stay in your room until permitted otherwise?"

I roll my eyes. "I'm not a child, Donney. I can take care of myself."

"Uhm, yes you are. Amnesia sends you back to child status automatically." I roll my eyes again. Once more and I worry my eyes won't roll back.

"Whatever. I was starting to get tired anyway." Donney puffs out his chest, proud of himself. It sickens me.

CHAPTER
16

For the past several hours I have just been sitting on the cot waiting for Montey to wake up. Finally, he starts to stir. He blinks hard twice, as if trying to blink himself back into reality. He looks over to me and jumps up, only to slump back into his chair.

"Good morning, sleepyhead." He stretches his long arms above his head, lifting his shirt just a little, exposing his strong muscle lines. I shake my head out of my gaze and avoid eye contact. "Or should I say good evening, because supper is in like ten minutes?" Montey shoves himself off the chair and stalks over in my direction. I push myself to meet his gaze, which is now only a few inches from my face. He tucks his chin up and presses his lips in a neat circle on my forehead.

"Good morning, Talia, I trust that you got some sleep." I giggle and push down a few inches as an invitation for him to sit next to me. He swings down hard enough for the cot to bounce me. I chuckle as I playfully punch his arm.

"I got enough." An obvious lie, judging by the large circles I can feel surrounding my eyes. "But has anyone told you recently that you are the *best* bodyguard *ever*?" Montey rolls his eyes and shoves the heel of his hand to his face in attempt to rub the sleep out of his eyes. His hands fall down his face and lazily slump beside him as he throws himself back on the bed once again, making me bounce. He pulls on the back of my shirt, and I fall next to him, our backs resting against the mattress and our feet dangling off the side.

"I'm sure you wouldn't be dumb enough to leave." *Gee, thanks.* "And no one wants to step a foot near you." However true this may be, it still stings a little. I sit up without a word and Montey flings up next to me. "No one came in, right? No one tried to hurt you?" He looks concerned. His big eyes pierce through mine, waiting for an answer.

I roll my eyes. "No, Montey, of course not. I'm fine, don't wor—"

Donney's leg hurdles through the door. "Ring-a-ding, who's hungry?" The smile etched across his face is uncharacteristic, and he's holding a tray with three plates on it. I can't see what's on them until he places it down on the table. There are three identical meals of broccoli, three small potatoes, and some sort of meat. I wonder where they got it from. Like, who's backpack had a pig or a chicken hidden inside?

"Oh, no. I don't think so!" Montey raises his voice at Donney as he pushes up off the bed and tries to measure up to Donney's height, an impossible feat seeing as how Donney is a solid six inches taller than him.

"What the hell, Montey?" I follow him off the bed and place myself in front of him, untactfully placing myself between two hungry coyotes.

"What is wrong, Montey? Is it the potatoes?" Donney plays dumb with a concerned, almost motherly look on his face, but I can tell he's hiding a smirk under his false visage.

"What the hell is wrong with you, Donney? Get the hell out of here!" Montey tries to step towards him but I am thankfully blocking their path to each other.

"I just thought I'd bring my friends some supper—I just thought since she was supposed to stay in here and you were making sure that she didn't leave …" Donney turns and winks to me and my face annoyingly brightens. "I thought I'd bring you some grub. So, don't be so hostile. I'm just here to enjoy a nice meal with my two favourite chums." I roll my eyes again. This is starting to make my head hurt. I grab a plate and sit back down without a word and start to eat. Montey looks at me with pleading eyes, begging me to help him, but I don't see a problem with Donney eating with us. He's just doing it to get a rise out of Montey, and Montey is making it way too easy.

"Thank you." Donney gestures to me, grabs his plate, and sits down on the bed next to me. "I'm glad someone isn't looking a gift horse in the mouth."

I stop my fork right before it enters my mouth and place it back on the plate. "Let's get one thing straight. You are possibly the farthest thing from a gift, but I am hungry, and I am going to eat whether you're in here or not." I pick up the fork and take a bite of the very salty broccoli, it's delicious. I close my eyes to enjoy the peace of pretending the boys aren't here for a minute. I open one eye to see Donney staring at me, faking a look of hurt and wiping away a non-existent tear. I drop my shoulders and stare solemnly at Montey. "Just eat, please." He exhales in defeat, grabs one of the plates, sinks back into his chair, and grumbly takes a bite.

We eat in silence. Montey and Donney exchange scowls when they think I'm not looking. I'm always looking. Montey is the first to finish eating. He places his plate back on the tray, stands up, and stretches.

"Thanks for the grubs, chubs." Montey snickers and Donney stands up, lifting off his shirt to Montey to show that, without a doubt, he is not chubby.

"Anytime, slime." I cringe at his words as Donney looks over to me. "Almost finished?"

"What, don't I get a clever nickname?" I glare at him and he twists his lips up into a smile.

"Oh, I can think of a few things to call you." I snarl at that, and he winks.

"Watch yourself." Montey steps forwards towards Donney in a threatening stance.

Donney throws his free hand up in defence. "Cool yourself, Clyde. I was just asking Bonnie if she was almost finished with her meal so I can get out of your hair." I look down at my plate to see a stray potato I have just been pushing around for the last five minutes and a couple of bones from the meat. I look up at Donney, and without losing his gaze, I hand him my plate.

"Get out," I say bluntly. When I stand up, I stand opposing him. I look up to him and he looks down to me. This time I added more ferocity to my words. "*Get out, Donney. Now.*" I push him off, and he collects the plates and slowly backs out of the room and tosses me a wink right before Montey slams the door in his face.

"Good riddance!" Montey shouts to the other side of the door.

"Takes a big man to say that to my back," Donney yells back from the other side of the door. I count his footsteps as he saunters away.

Montey smiles to himself as if he just won, although I'm not sure what he won, or what the prize is. He looks over to me and his face falls. "Hey." He grabs my cheeks, making me look at him. "Are you okay?"

"Of course I'm okay. +Why do you ask?" He looks blurrier and blurrier by the second.

"Talia." His thumb heavily wipes my cheek. "You're crying." I put my hand to my face to realize that it is, in fact, wet.

Of course, I'm crying, I say to myself. *Why am I crying?* I look up to Montey with tears running down my face.

"Talia, why did Donney wink at you? Did he do something to you while I was sleeping?" I can tell even the thought is torturing him. I blink in disbelief. "That son of a bi–"

"God, no! Nothing happened, it was just him, okay?" I suddenly find it hard to speak; words are getting stuck in my throat. Montey moves behind me, placing his body so his legs are wrapped around me and his chest is on my back. He tightens his arms around me, and I squirm in his grip, uncomfortable, but stuck. I guess it is kind of nice.

I can feel myself breathing normally again. He moves back an inch and moves my brown hair over to one side and presses his lips against my neck. My eyebrows crease and I recoil from his touch. He stops, turns my head so he can look me in the eyes, and pulls me so close that our lips are stitched together. We turn around and he lays me down, so my head is laid on the pillow, but our lips never part. His body is just barely hovering over mine. I feel his hand slip up my tattered shirt, stopping on my waist. The coldness of his hands makes me jump. *Don't ruin this, Tal.*

Montey pulls away from me, his face centimetres away from mine.

"Hi." I hold his gaze.

"I love you," he whispers. I am stunned by the amount of silence that fills the room next. I don't know what to say.

I have nothing to say.

"It's okay, Talia. I know you must be confused." Montey rolls over and lies down next to me on the bed as we both face the ceiling. "You really don't have to say anything. I just wanted you to know."

We lay there in silence next to each other, his fingers intertwined with mine. We stay that way for a while until the silence breaks. "Can I ask you a question?" The words flow from him while his eyes never waver from the ceiling.

"Of course you can. What is it?" There is a long pause, and I turn to look at him, but his gaze is fixed.

"I saw what you did."

"That is a statement, and I have no idea what you're talking about." He finally turns to look at me, his eyes bleeding into mine. "I saw what you did to the Silver Man."

CHAPTER
17

"Montey ..." I breathe out the word. Not that I can hear it with my heart beating in my ears.

"Don't try to explain it away, either. I know what I saw. You did it. How did you do it? I love you; I can protect you, but only if you tell me." His grip on my arm gets tighter. He digs his nails in, the constriction more and more binding every second.

"Montey. Let go of me."

"Just tell me how you did it!" He shakes me vigorously, and warmth drips down the back of my arms.

I don't know. I want to scream that from the top of my lungs. *He knows.* I want to run, but I know I won't get far. I want to bury myself in a hole and just live there in a nice, quiet hole in the ground. That sounds nice. I could have pictures of my favourite worms hanging on the walls, a nice dirt couch, I could steal carrots from nearby gardens. This could be fun. Montey's words break my fantasy.

"Come on, Talia. Bear with me, this could help all of us. What did you touch it with? You want us safe, don't you?"

I avoid his question. "Who all knows?" he sighs, almost defeated, definitely disappointed.

I don't care. "No one." I let out a sigh of relief. "At least, not that I know of. Donney was behind me, so I don't think he saw anything, and if he did, we would've heard about it by now." Oh God, what if that's why he wanted to keep a close eye on me? My mind is running a thousand words per minute of possibilities. I just sit silently, careful not to say anything that could make it worse.

"Talia, you trust me, right?"

I take a deep breath and look him in the eyes. *No.* "Yes." Why didn't he tell me that he knew earlier?

"So, tell me. What did you touch him with? Was it a magnet? Talia, if this can help us shut them down for good then you have to tell us! We have to protect our family. You want to help me protect them, right?" I try to swallow all of what he's saying, but I keep choking on the words before they even have a chance of coming out.

"Montey." I shake my head, violently trying to shake out my fears.

"JUST TELL ME WHAT YOU DID!"

"I DON'T KNOW!" the scream makes my throat hurt instantly. He lets go of my arms and backs away like I'm a disease. Burning hot tears wash down my face.

"You have the power to stop everything. You could've saved Mary. You could've saved everyone!" He stands tall next to me, pointing down like one would at a disobedient dog. "And you *chose* to do nothing?"

I didn't choose anything! I want to yell back, but I don't think there's anything that can change his mind now. I can't look at him, not with the disgust that now lives in his eyes.

"LOOK AT ME!"

I avoid his stare as much as I can, but his sharp eyes pierce and threaten as he comes closer. My heart hums at the threat.

"What the hell? You have to tell me! We have to know how to defeat those ... those *things*."

I try to fight, but the tears return. Montey has realized what he's done, but he doesn't seem apologetic in the least. His voice softens yet still holds an air of sternness. "Talia, please."

I shove myself further into a corner and grab my arms where he did, and I can feel holes from where his nails dug into my skin. They're slick and wet from blood.

Don't tell him anything. My entire body screams. I protest as long as I can but when he tries to take a step towards me again, I can feel the words fall out like a shield that will make him stay back.

"Montey, I didn't touch him with anything but my bare hand."

He pauses, contemplating the idea, then his face becomes sterner, more ferocious, more ... terrifying. "Talia, for Christ's sake! This is serious, tell me what you did! Don't play games, not when we're so close! Why are you *lying?*" he spits.

He inches closer to me, and I try to move back further but the wall is stopping me. I look him in the eyes. I see anger and contempt. Mine must seem terrified. "I am telling the truth." I look him straight in the eye, my voice is surprisingly calm, my eyes unwavering.

Now he looks scared.

"I was going to die anyway. I wanted to know what he felt like. I wanted to know if he was cold because of the metal, or hot because of the mechanics going off inside of him, gears spinning a million times an hour." My eyes seem to fall to the ground in memory of the shining, liquid-metal man standing before me. The glint of his armour shining from the morning sun. Come to think of it, I'm more scared now than I was then.

No. I'm not scared. Not anymore.

"Talia, that is insane." He stands, pacing. "This is insane"

I press my explanation further. "No one was coming to save me; I was alone in a new house with strangers who already wanted me dead. I was alone, and I was dying either way." Tears that were rolling down my cheeks are now starved and drying.

Montey spins on his heels, brushing his hands through his hair and fisting it halfway through, like a voice fighting to pull it out.

I don't know why I keep talking, but I feel I need to tell this. "I touched it and then it started to shake. I felt the buzz of electricity holding every nerve in my body, begging to be set on fire, but all it did was energize me, ready me with electrical energy, stronger than anything you could ever imagine." A small smile curses my lips at the memory.

I finally meet his eyes, and he looks terrified. "*What are you?*"

I sit in the quiet for a minute as Montey just paces endlessly in front of me. Not willing to open myself up to another attack, I stay quiet.

"You know what you are?" he says under his breath. I look up at him. "Do you want to know what you are?" I swallow my tongue and shake my head. "You're a *monster.*"

Donney rushes into the room. "What the fuck is going on?" His eyes are burning a hole in the back of Montey's head.

"She's a *monster,*" he spits at me.

"Get out," Donney says simply.

"Happily." Montey hits shoulders with Donney on his way out.

Monster? Am I a monster now?

"Talia, you're bleeding."

James came for me. James killed Mary and Sara, I killed them.

I touched the Silver Man and I killed it.

I'm the monster of monsters.

I'm a monster.

"Talia." My chest constricts as I look up to see Donney is still here.

"Leave," I force out. I need to be alone. Donney pauses at my request, staring at me. "I said *leave.*" He nods and does as he's told, following Montey out the door.

I pull my feet up to my chest, wrapping my arms around myself. I can feel the warm wet from the blood that drips from the fresh cuts left by Montey's hand.

I don't know what to do anymore. None of this feels real. James is a murderer, I'm a murderer, *is anybody* not *a murderer?*

Donney comes back into the room with a small box with a red cross on it.

"I asked you to leave," I say, looking at my knees, though they're blurry through my tears.

"I did, then I came back. You just had a seizure; you're not bleeding out too." He holds out a hand, gauze in the other. "Give me your damn arm." His sudden sharpness shocks me into submission. I place my arm in his hand, and he twists it and places the gauze down to grab a spray bottle. He sprays my wound, and I hiss.

"Ouch, dude, that hurt!" He moves his eyes up as if saying *really? This hurt?* He places the bottle down and quickly wraps my arm with the gauze. He then holds out his hand for the other arm. I comply easily this time. He sprays the bottle again; I wince less knowing that it's coming. He wraps that arm and stands to leave.

At this point, I don't even know how to think. I feel so cold and shaky, like I sat out in the winter for a full day. Bumps pop up all along my arms, and thankfully the cold numbs the pain a little bit.

Clary opens the door to see Donney readying to leave.

He points out the door. "Clary, go. Now's not the time, okay?"

She bats her eyes. "Please can I stay?"

He studies her for a minute and looks over to me before escaping into the hallway and closing the door behind them. I pull the blanket closer to my chest, fisting it as if someone wanted to steal it. I use my arm to wipe off the remainder of my tears. *I'm such a coward. I couldn't even keep one secret that will probably get me killed.*

Montey … he…

Just thinking about what he said makes me boil with anger. I imagine the sudden darkness in his eyes in comparison to the beautiful green eyes that lay with me in the grass; they have now turned into a sour lime, bitter to the last bite. The bad taste in my mouth from his kiss still haunts me. My hand shakes, a different feeling than before. This feels normal, like panic.

Oh, panic.

I suck in air, trying to get it into my lungs, but my chest feels like an elephant is covering it. I think I'm suffocating. *After everything, I'm dying now.* God, if this is death, let it come quickly. I feel like my heart is beating out of my chest, palpitating like a hummingbird.

The door opens and I'm soaked through with my tears, shaking and sweating like crazy. *I must be crazy.* Donney frantically looks me up and down before rushing over to me. He sits down in front of me. He looks nervous now, too. His hands bop rapidly, unsure of where to go before resting on my shoulders.

"Talia, it's okay. You're going to be okay. Just, uh, breathe! Come on, no dying until I kill you, okay?" He awkwardly tries to pat my shoulder.

Words ... hard ... can't breathe.

"Come on, Talia, uh, with me. In, out," he mimics deep breathes, "in ... out." I copy him. *In, out.* "That's good! Keep going!"

I breathe, following his direction. I quickly start to feel sober, like a tide has washed over me.

"I am *not* qualified to do this," Donney mumbles.

One last breath. My vision starts to flow back. Everything looks less condensed than before, freer. "Shut up, this ..." *in...out* "... isn't about you."

He pulls away and smirks. "It's always about you, isn't it?"

"Don't you ... " *in...out* " ... forget it."

"Are you okay now?" He looks away from me, towards the wall. Like donning a mask, he slips back into his normal, apathetic self.

Nope. "Yeah, I'm fine."

"Okay, after this, not to make matters worse, but you did just lose one of the five people who didn't want to kill you."

"Oh no, that actually makes everything so much better." I punch him in the arm, and his head snaps over to me as if I were an annoying mosquito, which is probably what I feel like.

"Do you want to rest or ... and I can't believe I'm asking this ..." His face looks tired as if he already hates what he's going to ask. "Do you want to play a game of cards?"

I narrow my eyes. "Are you going to go get Clary, or are you offering to play a game with me?"

"I'll play."

A trap.

"I don't want to leave you alone with her right now. I think she'd be pretty useless if you do that thing again."

"Oh yeah, because you were a great help. What would I ever do without you?"

"If records show anything, probably die."

"Hey! I haven't died yet! Right?"

"I'm chalking that up to dumb luck."

I think about it for a second before scrunching my face and nodding. "That's fair."

We sit in silence. Which, clearly, leaves us both feeling rather awkward.

Donney slaps his legs "So ... cards?"

CHAPTER
18

I've been alone in this room for a while. Donney comes by to ensure I don't starve, but he sucks at that. Frankly, I'd rather starve than eat another one of his "sandwiches." He brought me new clothes again, and I tried telling him that I was okay with my old rags, and no matter how many times they tell me they're "new," I am not wearing any underwear they give me.

Donney sleeps in here too now. He's taken over the chair the past few nights. He's also tried to insist I make him a badge that reads "World's Best Bodyguard." After a comment of that being a really dark joke considering a large portion of the world is now, you know, *mimics throat-cutting noise,* gone.

And yes, I mimicked a throat-cutting noise in my head because it's my head and I can do what I want.

Anywho…

The first night of him staying in the room with me was odd. Like, he just *wasn't leaving.* Like, without an explanation. I fought exhaustion to stay awake until I realized that he wasn't planning on leaving anytime soon. Then it was kinda nice, except for every time it wasn't. He was still an asshole and made a minimum of five comments about either my appearance, smell, or general attitude every hour.

He says Montey wouldn't come in here. I don't know what he seemed so sure, but I trust him.

Clary visits me and we play cards. That might be the only good part of this prison sentence.

Oh! And I've learned something new about myself! I cannot do a push-up to save my life. Not really exciting news, but I don't have much else to be excited about. Scared? Yes. Excited? Not so much.

I'm scared that my old squad might be coming for me and might kill even more people. No matter how much these people want me dead, the feeling is *not* mutual. I'd rather keep as many people alive as possible.

Come to think of it, I don't think I'm afraid of much else. I mean, I've even befriended the spider in the corner of the room. His name is Ralph Jr. His father left him when he was a child. Mother told him he went to join the war, but Ralphy knows that it's all a lie. He was planning on standing up to his mother last night, and I haven't seen him since. I'm starting to worry.

Oh, another thing I remembered. I'm afraid of the Silver Men and what the hell I did to that thing. I'm not even sure I want to know. There seems to be a little too much weirdness in my life for me to keep thinking that I'm normal.

Frankly, I'm still not sure where to go from here. Do I stay here in a house where people hate me? Do I leave? If I do, where would I go? Back to my old squad? Become a looter? Run away to the Wasteland? *Actually, scratch that last one, I'd rather die.*

Either way, I have no idea what I'm doing, yet again. What I do know, as of this exact minute, is that I am hungry and Donney has yet to come to see me today. I'm thinking I'll just go get something myself. It's the middle of the day, so I'm sure everyone is helping with the garden or building repairs or something.

Screw it, it's now or never. I walk my way towards the door and push it open. A wall of heat instantly smacks me in the face. *I'm starting to miss the prison cell.*

Talia, focus. We are on a mission.

Right.

Which way was the kitchen, again?

Right, it's right. I follow my gut down the corridor since I am in no way clear as to which way to go. I notice chatter coming from the basement door again. I look around to make sure I'm not being watched again before placing my ear to the cool wood and listening to whatever I can.

"There's no way she's staying with us. No more, Doc, I'm putting my foot down."

Karen. I'm growing sick and tired of that woman.

"Listen, this girl is just that, a *girl*. She wants what we all want. To be safe and loved." Doc's booming voice commands respect.

"You guys don't know what I know. She should not and cannot be trusted. She's a danger to everyone here the longer she stays." My heart falls in my chest at the sound of Montey's familiar voice. I know I shouldn't be surprised at this point after all that's happened, but I guess I still am …

"Montey, you know I agree with you ever since you told us about how it was her broadcast that killed Mary and Sara. We trust you with this. But you gotta tell us what she did to make you want to see our side," Karen presses.

There's a pause in the conversation. No one says anything, like someone is waiting to take the lead.

"I say we kick her out tonight. At midnight. She'll have no way of protecting herself. And it's not like she will remember how she got here, considering she was unconscious for a good half of it. So long as we make sure she doesn't wake up while we're—uh … *transporting* her. Then she won't know how to find us again and she'll be someone else's problem." Karen is getting on my last nerve.

"We are not making any decisions tonight," announces Doc, with obvious authority that shuts everyone up swiftly.

"How long do you want us to wait?"

"Not tonight, *Montey*," Doc says harshly. I lean in closer and … the door bursts open and I go tumbling down the stairs. I smack my head on each step, until I lie on the bottom step, in too much pain to sit up. My head is throbbing with *immense* pain. My vision is blurry as I try to sit up. Doc is in front of me, trying to pick me up, but I pull my hand away and snarl at the offer.

I look up, trying to gather all the faces I'm seeing but they are all blurs.

All except Montey. I see his face too clearly. He almost looked frightened for a second, but once our eyes meet, I see that he's smiling. He's smiling at me in pain.

I give up. I slam back onto the floor, mesmerized by the stars in my eyes. I hear stomping, which only makes my head feel worse. Someone is stomping down the stairs. Donney falls beside me, eyes frantically searching my body to see if I'm okay.

"What the hell is wrong with all of you? Why is no one helping her?" he yells to everyone and no one in particular. "You're all something else, you know that? She just fell down a flight of *fucking stairs* and all you guys can do is stare at her?" He kneels in front of me. "You're all pathetic."

"Donney." Montey steps forward. "Let her be. She's a monster." The word rings in my head.

Monster.

Monster.

Monster.

I am a monster.

"From where I'm standing, Lucifer … " Donney helps me up. I put all my weight on him, so much so that I'm sure he'll drop me, but he stays strong. "You're the monster."

CHAPTER
19

Donney helps me up the stairs slowly; I struggle to move. Each step I take feels as though I'm stomping on shards of broken glass. I feel like my head is caving in, like someone has taken a hammer to it. It pounds as if it's the only pain I've ever known.

No, wait. I know a worse pain. My mind flashes back to a few days ago, Montey's lips on my neck, his hands around my waist. But when he pulls away, his face keeps shifting to the boy I saw downstairs, his twisted snarl of a smile that could make a statue terrified.

He loved to see my pain.

"Keep going. Almost there." Donney is practically carrying me. My arm over his shoulder must make it hard for him to move up the stairs himself because he takes his time. I can feel him twitch, trying his hardest not to let go. Whether for his sake or mine, I appreciate it. We finally reach the top of the stairs and walking gets easier. Not easy. Just easier.

I am moving slower than I ever imagined possible. I look up to see Clary standing there in shock. Her mouth is gaped open. My vision suddenly colours oddly. I put my free hand to my face and pull it away to see a fresh streak of scarlet blood, and I rub it between my fingers, watching wearily as the crimson streaks over my hand. I notice a drop as it falls to the ground. *I'm bleeding a lot.*

"Hey, Clary!" Donney yells "Go get the first-aid kit, quick!" Clary shakes her head out of the shock, nods to me, and runs off. I focus on the bounce of her short hair as she rushes around a corner.

Donney is practically dragging me now. My face is warm, and I wonder how I must look right now—probably half beaten, despite the fact that I did this to myself.

Good job, Talia, what do you want to do next? Throw yourself off the roof?

We finally reach my room in what feels like hours. Donney slowly lowers me to the bed. Clary follows in quickly after us and my gaze rapidly shifts to the floor. I can't find the strength to look anywhere but down. I'm so tired. If I could just close my eyes …

"Hey!" Donney lifts my chin and forces my eyes to his. "No falling asleep, okay? You could have a concussion. In fact, you most likely have a concussion. No sleep."

Yes, sleep. Please sleep.

Annoyed, I comply. I force my eyes to follow his hand's every movement. He takes a cotton ball and pours something on it, the liquid glistening as it falls onto the cloud-like surface of the cotton balls. He shakes off the extra and the drops fly through the air. He slowly reaches up, using one hand to lift my chin, feeding him the light that the one bulb above gives him, and he wipes my forehead. It stings. I try to flinch away, but he holds me firm.

"Sorry, I should've told you that it would hurt a bit. I'm just cleaning it out to make sure it doesn't get infected." I nod and bite my lip to hold back from crying. Donney places a Band-Aid on my forehead and gives it a gentle tap.

"Ow. What the hell?" My awareness snaps back like an elastic.

"I told you to stop eavesdropping. Just look at where your curiosity got you." He smirks and sits down next to me. "Are you okay?"

"Do I look okay?" I turn to look at him. His blue eyes are glistening with concern, but he smiles for my sake.

"You never look okay."

I punch him in the arm, although in my current state, I don't think that punch would've hurt a fly. I'm starting to think I should give up trying to punch him.

"Well then, there is your answer." Donney runs his hands through his hair and pushes his back to the far wall. I mirror him. I'm sure he's only staying to make sure I don't fall asleep or randomly die from choking on my tongue. Anything like that seems possible today. He stares at me and I stare back at him.

Then it dawns on me. He wasn't in the basement, he wasn't there, he doesn't know. "Don't you want to know why Montey …" Donney sticks a finger in the air to pause me. I comply.

"Lucifer," Donney corrects. I stifle another painful laugh.

"Why Lucifer?"

He looks at me like it should be obvious. "Lucifer was God's favourite until he caused a lot of shit to happen, practically dooming humanity. Now he's just the evillest creature in existence."

"Oh, he's giving you a run for your money, is he?"

He rolls his eyes. "You were saying?"

Right. "Don't you want to know why *Lucifer* called me a monster?" I finish, and Donney takes a deep breath, letting his hands fall between his legs.

"Clary, can you give us a minute?" Clary sits unnoticed in the corner of the room, watching every interaction like a ping-pong match. She quietly nods and heads out of the room, closing the door behind her. He turns back to look at me. "I frankly don't bother listening when the devil speaks."

"But don't you want to know?" I can feel the steam of fear rushing to my face. The voice in my head echoes. *He'll regret helping you. Hell, he might even bring you back to push you down the stairs himself.*

"You aren't a monster, Talia. That's all I need to know, and I don't care about anything else." I snap my eyes up to meet his. How does he not care? *He'd care if he knew.*

Shut up, voice. "You deserve to know."

"I don't want to know," he says with a finalizing smirk as he shrugs.

My eyes flash concern. "Donney." *He should take this seriously. I'm giving him an out, permission to vote against me, an easy maneuver.*

"I really don't care." He pauses and meets my gaze. "Just get some rest, okay?"

"I just woke up! Can't we at least have breakfast?" Coincidentally, my stomach growls, cementing my point.

Donney shakes his head but rounds it out to a nod. "Sure."

CHAPTER
20

Donney walks in front of me as we move to the kitchen. I guess he's acclimatized to being my bodyguard by now.

Does he not know people can attack from behind too?

We move slowly but steadily through the hallways. I wouldn't say I was walking straight; I'm a little too dizzy for that. I make a beeline behind him, careful not to step on his heels. I count the staggering as a success when we finally enter the archway of the kitchen. I look over at all the white-marble countertops and the boxes of cereal taking over the far corner.

Donney pauses at the door, allowing me to move ahead of him. I look at the cereal options. There are boxes of all sorts of colours, with animal mascots plastered on the front. They all look so deliciously, sugary sweet. However, if I am to survive today, I can't take anyone's favourite.

I move them all aside and grab the lonely bag behind them—the bag of cereal has been removed from its box and is now just hiding and staling as people grab the more preferred. I chuckle to myself. I don't think I've ever related to cereal before. I grab the bag and hold it close to my chest with both my arms wrapped around it in a life-threatening hug. I try to take it out into the hallway, but once Donney sees what I grabbed he looks at me, concerned for my sanity.

"Raisin Crumbs?" He pauses and tries to grab the bag, but my fantastic cereal grip holds firm.

"I had to take something that no one would miss. That no one would come looking for." I pause, staring at him, waiting for a response. He only purses his lips together and gestures for me to lead him into the hallway. I step into the corridor and Donney falls in step behind me. Full bodyguard mode, I guess.

My bumblebee legs manage to stagger me back to the room. I could've sworn I heard Donney chuckling, but every time I look back, he is as straight-faced as always.

The door seems heavier than usual, but it's probably just my debilitating headache that's making everything seem like I have the muscles of a premature baby. I shove through and throw myself onto the bed, face first, practically eating the mattress. It is cool and soft thanks to the old comforter balled up in the centre. *If only I could close my eyes ...*

"No sleeping." Donney hits my back with a pillow.

"You're still here?" I try to lift my head to look at him, but I swear the thing weighs like, a hundred pounds. I agree to allow it to fall back down.

My stomach growls again, giving me the strength to somehow flip myself onto my back. *You know what? I'll starve. That'll be easier than getting up.* The weight distribution on the bed changes, so even though my eyes are closed, I can tell Donney is sitting right next to me.

Something hits my face. I open one eye to see Donney fisting a bunch of cereal. He drops another piece, and it hits my closed eye. Too tired to fight, I open my mouth. He takes the opportunity to drop the rest of the handful in my mouth. The dryness is Wasteland level. I almost let a tear fall—*no, wait, I'll need all the moisture I can get.*

I force myself to swallow half of it. I can get a sense of what it tastes like—

my first mistake. It is stale and bland. *Much like Donney's normal food, which you'd think I would be used to by now.*

Donney grimaces. He lets out a dry laugh as I choke down the crusty food, every bit scratching my throat on the way. "Not horrible." I try to smile but Donney just laughs harder.

"That looks delicious."

I crinkle my nose and stick out my tongue. I feel the undeniable urge to scratch the taste off my tongue. "Wow. That was bad! Why don't you try some?"

He raises an eyebrow. "Tempting."

"Yeah, I suppose you could eat whatever you want." I elbow him in the gut.

"Yeah, well, beggars can't be choosers." He laughs and stares at the door.

"You would know." I laugh until I've realized what I said. *Shit. That didn't come out right.* His smile dies slowly, the lines around his eyes falling with them.

"Yeah, I know." The words trail off as if he is lost in a memory.

"I'm sorry, I didn't mean ..."

Donney waves a hand, cutting me off. "Don't worry about it. It's whatever." He looks around, eyeing for any distraction that may change the subject, and his eyes widen. "Hey, look, why don't we play a game of sorts."

"Please, no. I think I have played every card game in the book a million times."

"Well, what would you rather do? 'Cause we kinda have limited resources, and as much as I would love to steal, I mean *borrow,* something from anybody else ... you said it yourself, we probably shouldn't take anything that someone might go looking for."

"Well, thankfully, I have learned how to play a time-honoured game, and I know exactly where to find what we need."

Donney lifts a chin, rising to my challenge. "What were you thinking?"

"Well, Donney ... how do you feel about chess?" I propose.

"Are you okay to be playing chess?" He asks, studying me.

"We'll consider my probable concussion a handicap in your favour. Wanna play?"

Donney holds out the chessboard. "I had to break into Montey's room, highly locked, by the way, to get this."

"What did I say about not drawing attention to me?"

Donney's shoulders slump "C'mon. Appreciate the effort I went through to get this. Besides, all of his attention has been on you since you arrived. I do not think me borrowing his little game would make him want to come in here."

I shrug. "Yeah, okay. Set it up."

We play a few rounds, I win, unsurprisingly every time. "Are you even trying?" I tease.

"I was never one for strategy. My strategy for most things is to shoot first, ask questions later." He reaches to make a move, but decides against it, tucking his hand back under the other.

"That does not surprise me *in the least.*"

"Fine, what's your strategy?" He lifts his eyes to meet mine.

"If I told you that, it wouldn't be a very good one now, would it be?"

"Pretend I figured it all out. Let's pretend I was smart and had you all figured out. Every move that went on in your head and every step it could take. Pretend I know you inside out. Tell me what your strategy is and then change it."

"That was a metaphor wasn't it?" I whine.

He moves his knight on the board, taking my pawn. "Did you get the picture?" I huff. "Yes." *Change my strategy.* I don't have one!

Step one: Make a strategy

Step two: Assume they already know it.
Step three: New strategy
Step four: ???

I acknowledge that this is no help. "But I don't have a strategy."

Donney tilts his head and gives me a disappointed stare. "Yes, you do. You've been playing the defence, scratch that, you haven't even been playing. You're letting the people around you set the rules and tell you what piece you get to play."

I throw up my arms, exasperated. "Okay, wise guy, what's your suggestion?"

He leans over the chessboard, inviting me to inch closer. Armed with my suspicion, I oblige. "You do the thing that no one thinks you're willing to do because they aren't willing to do it themselves." He picks up the board and launches it against the wall, pieces and all.

I stare at him in shock.

"You burn the whole damn board."

"Uh—I ... Dude! What the hell?"

"And you thought I wasn't good at strategy." He tilts up his chin, grinning.

I'm starting to think I need to read that damned book.

CHAPTER
21

Honestly, I don't know how much longer he expects me to be okay being cooped up in here, although considering the alternative, I think I'll be okay. I lay on my back watching my chest rise and fall while I swallow myself into a daydream.

I am sitting outside. Clary and Green are running in circles, Clary chasing him with a stick they found on the ground until Green finds one of his own and they start sword fighting. Clary wins, clearly having done this before.

This is peaceful. The wind blows through my hair, so I tuck it behind my ears. My life-long best friend James comes and sits next to me. He smiles and jokes about the apple and how bad of a cook he is. I try to ask him about our family, but the words just blink out of existence as if I never asked in the first place.

I find a swing hanging from an old maple tree and run over to it without even thinking. James follows closely behind me, pushing me on the swing, threatening to wrap me around the branch if I don't give him a turn soon. So, I do. I move off, and his laughter is like sunshine as he swings around to sit and pushes himself higher and higher until it attracts the attention of the kiddos who now want a turn too.

James obliges and pushes Clary on the swing. Her bright pigtails flow with the movement of the swing, ignoring the wind around her. Green raises his hand for the next turn, and the second Clary sees his hand up, she launches herself off the swing and falls to the ground rolling. I'd ask if she's okay, but she's already laughing. James grabs the swing and stops it so Green can get on. He pushes him just as high and then he jumps off too. I kinda wanna jump off now too.

I hold onto the swing and climb on. James laughs at my determined stance. I bite my lip and push myself higher and higher. I jump, and it feels like I'm flying until—a pillow hits me in the face.

I jump up out of bed and look for the culprit, who is not hard to find. He's the one standing at the door flicking the lights on and off. I groan loudly and use the pillow to bury my face to hide from the light. The only way I know that he's still flicking it is the obnoxious clicking noise.

"Why?" I mumble through the pillow. The clicking stops suddenly, and I rip the pillow off my face to see Donney's face, way too close to mine, with a beaming smile making me jump. "What the hell, dude?"

He gets up and straightens his back, holding out a hand to help me up, which I take for some reason.

"What's gotten you in such a mood?" I take my hand back and place it at my side.

"I just know how badly you wanna get out of here, so … *drumroll, please*. We're going outside!" He smiles brightly, and my eyes widen at the excitement of finally getting out of this place.

"Donney … are you sure this is a good idea?" *Dammit, thoughts, you don't get a say.*

He turns around to leave the room without so much as another word. He grabs my wrist and pulls me along. "Who cares? Let's go." Right, who cares? I'm dragged through the hallway and then into a bright-white foyer turned muddy by gardener's boots.

"Here." Donney hands me a pair of actual running shoes. My eyes glow with excitement as I slip them over my bare feet. Actual shoes, damn. I feel like a princess. "Ready?"

I'm vibrating with anticipation. I can't even manage any words, so I nod quickly.

"Let's go." He opens the door and the sun rolls in. *Today and today only, I will put aside my hatred of the sun for appreciation since I missed it so damn much.* I let the sun soak into my skin, warming me to my core. Donney runs out in front of me. Why he's so excited, I'll never know.

I follow him, running out into the sunlight. He keeps walking until he's into the wall of trees and then stops in an area surrounded by trees. There is enough room to fit a whole other house here and have room for a big deck in the back yard.

"What are we doing here?" I shout across the field. Donney immediately runs towards a lonely oak tree and starts running around it with his head down. He scans the ground, mumbling to himself.

"There!" he yells as he dives to the ground to pick something up. I squint to see him holding … a ball? I walk up to him and he stays still. "I knew I saw it out here on the walk over."

"The point of the ball is …?"

Donney's shoulders slump with disappointment. He then jumps back to a smile and snaps his fingers as if an idea just came to him. He runs back into the trees and comes out with a large, thick stick.

"Now do you get it?" he says, holding both the ball and the stick.

"Ah, yes. I get it now," I acknowledge, and his smile grows. "My favourite game, Stick and Ball."

"It is baseball, and you know it," he says through gritted teeth.

"Right, my apologies. My favourite *sport*, Stick and Ball." He glares at me and holds up the stick in a threatening manner.

"Do you want to go back now or later?"

Thinking of my cement-lined prison room and my lame cot and the *stupid* chessboard, I shiver.

"The later, the better."

He smiles as if he's won. "Perfect, do you know how to play?"

"I mean this with a hundred percent honesty: no."

He looks disappointed again. *It's like a freaking rollercoaster with this one.* He shakes it off. "No problem. I can teach you." He takes his time explaining the game and I think I understand it.

I raise my hand "I'm pretty sure you're supposed to have a team for this game."

"Yeah, well, no offence, Tal, but no one wants to play with you right now."

Rude. "Offence taken but also understood." He throws me the stick. "Ready?"

"Do I have an option?" The stick is filled with dirt, which I rub off onto my shorts.

"Nope."

"I'm not sure about this." My hands are sweating already.

"You'll be fine. Ready?" Before I get the chance to answer he's throwing the ball at me. I jump out of the way with a shriek.

"What the hell, Donney?" He wipes his face with his hands.

"I could not have been clearer. Hit the ball. Use the stick." He gestures to the stick in my hand. "Now, you missed, so you go find the ball."

I march off in a humph. "Maybe don't throw it *at* me next time!" I yell back.

"That's how you *play the game*!" I look until I find the ball in the grass. Thankfully, he didn't throw it a mile a minute, or else we'd never find it.

I lift the ball over my head while wiping the sweat from my brow. I throw it back to Donney and it lands a few feet in front of him, he lifts a sarcastic thumbs-up.

"Ready to try again?"

"Just throw the ball!" I place myself back in front of the home base, stance wide, open, elbows up. Donney throws the ball and I connect. *YES!* I look over to him to see him already running after it.

Right, run. I run to get around first base, the wind in my hair feels amazing. Running to second base, Donney stands in my way, waiting for me. I slow down my running as he stands there, ball in hand. The second I stop he places the ball on my shoulder.

"You're out!" He laughs and tosses me the ball. "My turn." He saunters over to the home base and picks up the bat.

"Just so we're clear, I still got one point." I take my spot next to the pitching mound.

"We are very clear on the fact that you only got one point." He takes his stance.

"Don't think I didn't notice that you added the word 'only' in there." I take a good throwing stance.

"You were meant to notice." I wind up and the ball leaves my hand, heading towards the bat, and he swings and connects and … the ball soars high over my head. I immediately run to grab it. I see it bounce off a tree towards the back of the lot, so I know exactly where it landed. I run and grab the ball. By the time I turn back around, he's already I second base. I barrel to home base, hoping to cut him off.

I keep my eyes on the target and I see him moving towards it as well. *I must beat him.* The wind burns my eyes, forcing them to water. I finally reach home base and he's right there next to me, reaching it at the same time.

"Ha! Only third base. That's three points!" I toss him back the ball, which he catches gracefully.

"What are you talking about? That's six. I made it home before you!" I pick up the stick from where it was dropped.

"No way. I made it here a split second before you. You only get three points." We scowl at each other for about thirty seconds, neither of us willing to back down. He thinks he made it home. I know he didn't. A minor difference of opinion.

"Wanna call that a practice round and start over now?"

Donney is already marching back to the pitching mound. "Yup!" He stands tall in the middle of the field. "Play ball!"

I roll my eyes and laugh. "Throw the ball!"

We play for a solid hour until we are both too exhausted from running to even move. I plop down in the grass and he sits down a few feet across from me. His brown hair blows with the strength of the wind. I can only imagine how messy mine must look.

Note to self: Ask Clary if she knows how to braid.

Final score: Donney: 36, me: 12. But it was a *good* twelve.

"We should probably be getting back before they realize that I'm gone and throw some sort of parade." I rip out a handful of grass and throw it up in the air. He laughs, only to go immediately silent as the crack of a twig sounds from around us.

The blood rushes from my face. He holds a finger to his mouth, telling me to be quiet, and gestures for me to lay down in the grass. He does the same. If I wasn't sweating before, I am now. What could've made the sound? Did the Silver Men find us? Is it someone from the squad ready to kill me? That'd be a sight. My heart is beating out of my chest, so much that it's making my chest move with it.

I try to focus on my breathing again, but I just can't shake the feeling that we're being watched. *In ... out.* It's going to be okay; it's going to be fine. Just keep taking deep—

"*Cluck ... cluck ...*" Donney and I both sit up at the same time. We share the same confused look on our faces. We look over to the owner of the sound ... it's a chicken. A stupid wild chicken. With its feathers small and stupid and its stupid little beak. We both break out into laughter, scaring the chicken away.

I guess we know where dinner keeps coming from.

"I think it's about time we head back. Don't you think?" He smiles at me before standing up. We make our way back in silence.

When the house is in sight, I look to Donney. "Think we can play again tomorrow?"

He smirks. "If we have time. Sure." I smile back to him and we continue to the house.

CHAPTER

22

Inside the house, dowsed in sweat, I start making my way back to my prison. I hate having to be so locked up after being so free, but I can always go back. I stop at my front door, which Donney blocks me from.

"Where do you think you're going?" He sticks his chin out at me.

"I'm going to rest. I'm tired, I need a nap."

"No, what you need is a shower." Donney pushes me along past my room and to the bright-white washroom. He pushes me in, grabs a towel from the closet, and throws it at me. "You smell like shit."

I glare at him. "Was that necessary? You don't exactly smell sweet either." He smiles and takes the opportunity to reach in and shut the door.

Fine, whatever. I can always nap after I shower. I take off my clothes and turn on the water. I let it warm up for a minute, as one does. I lift my arm to see how ... *very bad. I smell very bad.* Yeah, I'm taking that shower now.

I hop into the shower and look around for something I can use to wash the days-old grime and sweat off me. I find the remnants of a soap bar that looks like it's down to its last few uses. I quickly use the soap to wipe down my body and hair. I'm rising off as Donney knocks on the door.

"Hurry up! You're not the only one who enjoys hot showers." I roll my eyes and take an extra minute or two to spite him. Only when the water threatens to turn cold do I get out.

The mirror has steamed from my shower. I wipe off a streak to see my face. I look tired. I use my hands to squeeze my cheeks. I grab the towel and dry myself off before wrapping it around me.

Donney opens the door and strolls in. My mouth falls ajar. "Oh good, you're out."

My face turns red with both embarrassment and anger. "You can't just walk in like that! I could've been naked!" Donney looks me up and down in my towel, then to himself in the mirror, the door, back to himself, then back to me. He looks like he was falsely accused of something and is hurt and shocked.

His smile grows bigger. "And what a treat that would've been."

I reach up and smack him in the arm. He laughs as he rubs the spot where I hit.

"I did *not* deserve that. I was a perfect gentleman."

I huff. "Gentlemen are just perverts with a fancy name."

His eyes soften. "I forgive you for both your mean words and your violent tendencies. I left you some clean clothes on the bed, and for the last time, the underwear is *new.*" He sticks up his nose. I go to add something to his points, raising a finger, but he's not worth it. I drop my hand and leave.

I hope the water's cold, you bastard.

I make my way back to my room and close the door behind me. I drop my towel and turn to look for the clothes Donney left out for me, only to see a rat sitting on my cot.

"Montey, what the hell are you doing in here?" His lip twitches in disgust. His hair is a mess. He harbours huge bags under his eyes, insinuating that he hasn't slept well for a while. He turns away and throws the clothes at me.

"Do us both a favour and get dressed."

I slip on the black sports bra, pink tank top, and blue jean shorts, but I still don't trust the underwear. I throw them onto the floor next to Donney's chair.

"You can turn around now. Or better yet, just get out." I point to the door, but he stays firm.

"I have so many better ideas, Talia, many better than my leaving." He shoves a hand through his hair only for it to get stuck about halfway.

"For crying out loud, Montey, what do you want?" He stands up and marches towards me until we are only a couple inches apart.

"I want you to leave. Leave the squad, leave the base, leave and never come back." His words snarl through his teeth like poison from a snake.

"And why the hell would I do that?" He takes a step back, interlocking his fingers.

"Why would you stay? No one wants you here! Literally no one."

My mind flashes to Donney and Doc standing up for me and Clary and I playing card games for hours. "There are people who want me here."

"No. There aren't, really, if you think about it. Everyone would be better off if we never found you. Not only that, but we would be better off if you left now. We would no longer be a target for the Silver Men since you won't be here. So, if you think about it, Donney would be happy that you're gone, since his sweet little sister would be safe, and Doc would be happier once everybody stopped fighting."

His words loop around in my head. He's not wrong. Everyone would be safer. *Everyone would be safe.* That is, unless they aren't. Besides, I'd have nowhere to go. I'd probably die out there on my own.

"I'm not going, Montey."

He mimics strangling me. "Yes. You are." His hands ball into fists. He takes a deep breath and releases the grip on his hands. "Yes, you are. Because I'm going to make you. For the safety of my family."

"Oh yeah?" I step up to him. "And how do you plan on doing that?"

The devious smirk on his face does not give me a good feeling inside. No, more like rotting slime is swirling around my heart just waiting to cease hold of his face and crush it in my hands.

"How? Well, my dear Talia ... I'm going to lead them here."

CHAPTER
23

"Lead who here?" Montey's smirk grows wider. "Montey! Lead *who* here?"
"I'm going to lead your old squad directly to us. If saving my family means putting us all in danger, then so be it!" He throws his hands up in the air.

"Montey, that's psychotic. You aren't that insane."

"I'm at my breaking point, sweetheart. They will come, they'll take you, and they'll leave us alone. We'll not only be free of you, but we'll also be more than fine to return to our home sweet home rather than this hovel."

"Montey, that's not how it's going to work, and I think you know that. They will kill *everyone* they come into contact with. They don't care. They tried to kill me already too! Remember?"

"Yes." He turns around and lifts a finger. "And I have a theory for that too. I don't think they meant to do that. I think they were just going to kill everyone they saw; I think they knew that you were going to be okay."

"And what are you going to do then? Huh? What are you going to do once they kill everyone? *Because they will.* How will you live with yourself?" I ask, and Montey's eyes soften for a split second to the boy I used to know.

"I couldn't stop her ... she ... she found a radio and told them where we were again. Oh my God, she killed everyone!" His smile twists up his face into something more crooked than ever before.

"That's insane, Montey. Don't you hear yourself?"

He points a finger in my face. "Leave tonight, at midnight. Or else. Nod if you understand."

I want to punch him in the face. I nod. "Good."

He moves around me and is reaching for the doorknob when Donney opens it from the outside and punches Montey across the jaw. "She's not going anywhere.

Do you understand me?" Donney stands tall over Montey while he straightens his back and spits blood onto the floor. He turns around to me and gives me a big bloody grin. He looks back to Donney and leaves the room without another word.

Donney is over-taking the doorway, his face scowling and tight. He turns around to follow Montey out the door to do who knows what.

"Donney. Don't. He's not worth it." He freezes. His hair is sopping wet and dripping down to his t-shirt. He turns back around and slams the door shut.

"I think it's time we get some rest. Go to sleep." I nod and climb over to my cot, where I know I won't sleep. Not when I have an offer to contemplate.

CHAPTER
24

I think I've made up my mind. No matter what Donney says. He and everyone else will be safer once I leave. I'll leave at midnight. Not because of Montey's threat. Like Donney said, he's a coward. He wouldn't do something like that and risk his own life.

No, I'm leaving because whether he leads them here or not, they'll most likely find us eventually, and only because they're looking for me. If I go back, they might stop, or maybe if I'm not here they won't bother with them; they'll be just another squad.

Yeah, I've made up my mind.

It's for the best.

It's definitely past midnight now. I think. Donney's been asleep for a couple of hours, and no one has watches. Let alone me. I take a deep breath and stand up.

I move closer to the door, careful not to make a noise. I tiptoe past Donney's chair with my hand on the doorknob.

"Back to bed," he says without opening his eyes. *HOW?*

"I can't use the washroom?" I say, red-faced with embarrassment, not that one could tell in this darkness.

"Not while you're a flight risk. I have zero faith in you doing as you're told." He moves onto his side, still not opening his eyes.

"So, you want me to just hold it for eight hours?" He finally opens his eyes and sits up. He looks up to me, arms folded. "Tal, you're not doing anyone any favours by leaving. They can't just treat every stranger like they treat you. They need to learn how to deal with … *problems* as they arise." He stands up, walks over to the door, and flicks the light on. I'm startlingly blind for a second until my eyes adjust. He looks like he hasn't slept a wink. His blue eyes are rimmed with red.

"You don't know anything, Donney. You like it that way. Now, close your eyes and forget that I'm leaving."

He throws his hands up. "What could he have possibly said that would make you want to leave this place? You're screwed out there, Tal. What are you hoping for? To find a new squad? To find your old one? They're long gone!"

"Would you keep your voice down? I can't have anybody waking up, okay?"

"Talia, what did he say?" he says in a loud whisper. He looks deep into my eyes, searching for an answer.

"Donney, you're going to have to trust me when I say that it's better if I go." I turn so we aren't face to face.

"Think about everyone here that is on your side. Are you really going to abandon them? Leave them in the dust without so much as an explanation? Just disappear in the night?"

I take a deep breath. "Just let me leave. It's safer for everyone. You have to trust me. I *have* to go." My heart could beat out of my chest and I'm on the verge of tears. My eyes are pleading with him.

"You don't have to do anything you don't *want* to do."

"You don't know what he said he'd do if I don't."

"Then tell me what he said."

I shake my head; I can't tell him. It'll only cause more problems than it would solve. They were happy before I came here. *Most importantly: they were safe.* "I won't."

His tired eyes beg. I didn't even think he would know how to. He's desperate …

"Please?" he asks softly.

I close my eyes. I try to pretend I'm anywhere but here. I'm on the tree with James, I'm free. But like all good dreams, you eventually have to wake up.

I open my eyes to see Donney still waiting on me. "He said he'd bring them here. He threatened to kill everyone. He's going to make it seem like they came here for me so I wouldn't get out of it." The words sink into him as the anger flexes in his forehead. His lips twist and he looks genuinely terrifying.

"Why would they come for you?" He is shaking, vibrating with rage. "That doesn't even make sense."

I blink before answering. "He thinks they are my old squad."

"That ... that ..." He holds up a finger and laughs darkly. "That really is insane. I saw them try to kill you."

I try to put my hand on his shoulder, but he recoils instantly. "He has a theory for that too, actually."

He holds his hands out to stop me. "He's an idiot and a coward. He'll never hurt anyone. He made me slaughter the chickens growing up because he couldn't stomach it. He wouldn't kill his entire family just to get rid of you." He lets the words sink into his head. He takes a deep breath, grabs my shoulder, and pushes me down onto the cot. "Sit. Stay. I'll deal with him in the morning."

"Donney, I–"

"Enough!" He closes his eyes, composing himself. "Go to sleep. And that's the *last* time I'm telling you." He walks to the light switch, flicks it off, and sits back in his chair. He doesn't close his eyes, though; he just sits staring at the ceiling. I sit on the edge of the cot, staring at the door. Maybe I should make a run for it? He'll be glad in the long run.

He doesn't care. Sit down, you're a coward too.

"On second thought ..." Donney's back straightens so much that a ruler would be jealous. Then, as if being pulled by a wire, he stands, turns towards the door, and practically rips it open.

My heart could jump out of my chest. I stand to follow him out. My cheeks pale with fear, my stomach ready to give up the little food I've eaten.

"Stay here!" he yells back at me.

Fat chance. I follow him through the door as he sets his tirade down the hall. I swear the walls shake with every step.

"Donney, what are you doing?" I ask hurriedly.

"I told you to stay in the room, Tal." He continues down the hall, opening every closed door and sticking his head in every open one. He turns around at the end of the hall to search the rest of the house, but he bumps right into me.

"Donney, think about what you're doing. Please!" I try to hold out my hands to stop him, but he brushes them aside, refusing to meet my eyes.

"You can't read my mind, don't pretend to. I just want to have a few words with our friendly neighbourhood devil." His words drip poison, and his muscles are tense.

Montey sits peacefully in the wide-open living-room space on the ugly green-velvet couch, with his nose in another book. This one with the cover torn off.

"Hey! Bastard!" Donney yells when he sees him. Montey looks up to see Donney hurtling towards him.

Montey throws the book down and stands up. He looks completely petrified, from his pale white face to his extended fingers. Donney grabs hold of Montey's collar and lifts him against the wall.

"Donney, what the hell has gotten into you?" Montey's face contorts into confused anger.

"You weren't going to do it, were you? Tell me you weren't really going to risk everybody's lives just cause a girl wouldn't let you get into her pants."

"I was *housekeeping*. I'm getting rid of the cockroaches. The thing that doesn't seem to want to die."

"For crying out loud, Montey. We saved you! We gave you a family here. When NOBODY wanted you. We took in another orphan because we wanted to give you the family you lost."

"Oh, *piss off*. Don't act so high-and-fucking-mighty. Like I'm just some filth you found on the street on the bottom of your shoe. *You didn't have a choice.* That's not how it worked. Yeah, I was a little late to the party, but at least I wasn't a part of some elaborate smash and grab with a sister who couldn't care less if I lived or died. *Oh, wait.*"

Donney shoves his arm under Montey's neck, choking him. "You're a bastard, you know that?"

"I …" He forces a breath in, " … wouldn't have it…," his voice is hoarse from the air being forced through, "any other way." Donney sees that Montey is about to pass out and elects to not let him go that easily. He lowers him to his feet and looks him dead in the eyes.

Montey lets out another cough. Catching his breath is painful, and I have to hide a smile.

"Donney." Montey's eyes look soft as if what just happened was nothing more than a familiar disagreement. "I want to offer you a solution. You seem to know what I plan on doing. I'm sorry to say that I will. Unless she …," he points around Donney to me, "leaves tonight." He pats Donney on the back. "So, why don't you just let the little princess go, and we could forget about all of this. Go back to being brothers."

Donney pauses, and his shoulders fall in defeat. He looks over to me. I don't think I do a good job of hiding my feelings. I feel a teardrop fall and hit my hands that are held eagerly out in front of me. He looks at me with an apology in his eyes and I know his answer. I want to tell him that it's okay; that family has to come first.

He looks back to Montey, solemnness in his eyes. "I know better than to make deals with the devil." He lifts an arm and knocks Montey in the jaw.

I freeze with shock. *What just happened?*

Montey spits the blood onto the taupe carpet. *That's going to stain.* "You're going to regret that. I'll make sure of it." Montey takes a visible deep breath and yells, "Help! Help! I'm being attacked!" He smiles at us until a pair of footsteps make their way down the hall. Montey's face falls to fear as Doc and Bea show up in the threshold.

Doc looks furious immediately, whereas Bea looks consoling.

"Does someone want to tell me what is going on here?" Doc asks through gritted teeth.

"Come on, Talia. We're leaving." Donney pushes past Doc. I turn to follow him, only for Bea to stand in my path.

She gives me a pained smile and steps out of my way, gesturing for me to follow him. I run to catch up, but neither of us says anything until we reach the room. I close the door behind me. Donney stares into nothing while contemplating kicking the wall.

"I should leave." I know this is for the best, but the look on his face tells me that he disagrees.

"No, you shouldn't." He looks like I just put a knife in his back. "What do you think that would solve?"

"It could ensure the safety of the children that live in this house. It could keep everyone safe."

"Honestly, if they can't vote to keep a person like you safe, then I don't think they deserve to be safe. Excluding the kids, they don't have a choice. But don't worry. If I've said it once, I've said it a million times." Donney places his hands on my shoulders "He is a coward. Now, go to sleep." He pushes me towards the bed and flicks the lights off for the last time tonight.

I guess when nothing is certain, the only thing you have left to do is sleep.

CHAPTER
25

The next day comes quickly. Nothing is too off-balance. The air tastes the same, stale, and bitter, as it always does. Which surprisingly feels great.

Donney sits on the chair, curled up onto his side, holding his small blanket completely wrapped around himself. I'm careful not to make a noise as I step around him. I do a little quick prayer that the door doesn't squeak when I open it.

Not willing to risk it, I only open it enough to squeeze through, and thankfully, it doesn't squeak. *Whatever works.*

My skin prickles from the cool morning temperature. I'm dying to take a nice warm shower. I walk down the hallway, looking through all the rooms as I pass. I see Clary and two other girls squished on a queen-sized bed, with a black blanket being claimed by the little blonde girl in the middle.

These kids will stay safe, I tell myself as I push past the doorway. The bathroom is only one door further.

I reach for the doorknob to open it, but it's locked. Quickly, the door springs open in my face. Montey steps out and a puff of steam follows him. His eyes meet mine with shock. "You're still here," he says in disbelief.

"Yeah, and I'm sorry but I'm not going anywhere. And honestly? You can't make me," I challenge back.

"You bet your ass I can." He steps out of the steam-filled room to stand face to face with me in the hall. His hair is sopping wet, and his skin is so dewy, he looks annoyingly beautiful.

"I don't even get it, why you want me gone so badly. Why is my very existence a threat to you?" I force my eyes to look away towards the crown moulding separating the old wood from the walls.

"Talia." His voice is soft and surprising. I look back to see him staring right into my eyes. "I've already told you. If they come back here for you, they'll kill everyone." He grips my shoulders, too tightly for a second, before letting go and balling his fists at his sides. "And I won't lose my family again. If I can't have them, no one can."

"Montey, that's psychotic."

"Then call me crazy."

"Believe me, we do."

"I'm just trying to do what's best for everyone. You understand that, right? If you're gone, they are all safe. No matter what."

I think for a second about his proposition, it's a hard decision. Should I stay or should I go? I don't think I've ever truly decided. I don't think I ever can. I guess this is our stalemate. "I'm sorry, Montey, but I'm staying." *At least for now.*

His face contorts to a scowl. "You should've left when I told you to." He pushes past me. "Now, whatever happens, it's on you."

He leaves. The air around the room leaves no trace of the conversation that happened. The bathroom has no more steam, and the mirror is not even fogged, albeit it's cracked a little. But what's a crack in a world that's filled with them?

I stare at myself in the mirror. The single dim light bulb is the only source of light in the room, making my skin look greener than it is. *Or maybe it's just my skin.* The air does feel sticky today, an ugly humid that makes my hair frizz.

I splash cold water on my face and turn to leave the bathroom, only to see Clary standing on the other side of the door.

"Oh! Hi, kiddo, how'd you sleep?" She looks chipper and refreshed as if she just had a hundred-year nap. *I don't think I've ever been more jealous of a child before.*

She smiles widely at me. "How am I supposed to know? I was asleep!" I stare at her for a second. *She's too witty for her age.*

"Oh, is *that* all?" I joke.

"No. Julia kept stealing all the blankets. It was a cold night." I chuckle and move out of the open door, allowing her to slide in. "What are you doing up so early? I'm used to being alone this time of day." She whispers, "Except for Lucifer."

I roll my eyes. "Wait, what time is it?"

Clary shrugs and answers, "I don't know but the sun is only up about a thumbnail ... so ... early."

"Got it. Well, I'll see you later, kiddo." She gives me a mock salute and closes the door.

I walk to the living room where Donney confronted Montey last night, with the ugly green couch and the half-emptied bookshelves. I take a seat on the couch, and it's soft and comfortable despite its obvious age. I twiddle my thumbs, unsure of what to do with myself. I don't want to sit in my prison cell much right now, and while everyone is asleep, I don't have much to lose.

I stand up to investigate the shelves. I caress the stained wood, which removes a streak of old dust from the edge. It looks so much better like this that it almost makes me want to clean all of the shelves.

So, I do.

I remove the books one at a time, using a tattered old throw blanket to dust them off before placing them back on the shelf. I just can't decide whether to do it alphabetically or by colour. There aren't many colour variations, so I guess alphabetically will have to do.

By the time I'm done, at least an hour has gone by, but the shelves and books look brand new. Not a cobweb in sight. *No spiders were harmed in the dusting of this shelf.* I step back to admire my work.

I'm pretty impressed with myself. "Nice work, Tal," I say aloud.

"I agree." I snap my head around to see Clary standing in the archway. I laugh at my fear.

"How long have you been standing there?"

She shrugs. "Honestly? A while. You're fun to watch. Like our old movies." I laugh and throw my hair over my shoulder.

"Hey, wait a minute. I've been meaning to ask! Do you know how to braid hair?"

The smile on her face grows ear to ear. "Absolutely! Bea taught me when I was younger, after seeing the monstrosity that Donney called hairstyling." *Now that's an image that is fun to imagine.* "Sit!"

I kneel in front of the couch and she climbs around me, pulling every piece into perfection. I don't let the smile on my face loosen. This feels so right. *Painful,* but right.

"There! All done." She pats the top of my head and swings around to look at the front of it. She holds out a hand for me to take, which I grab graciously. She helps me up, in spirit ... she's very tiny.

I follow her back to the bathroom, where she pushes me in front of the mirror and turns on the green light.

I like it. My hair is separated perfectly evenly into two braids falling and reaching the middle of my ribcage.

"I love it," I say, fiddling a braid through my finger. "Thank you." She grabs my waist and pulls me into a hug. I don't know why I hesitate, but I do, and I also hug her back. It feels right.

She pulls away. "I'm going to go do some more exploring of the area before Donney wakes up and tells me not to." She turns to run out.

"Stay close to the house!" I call back to her.

"Sure thing, *Mom.*" She keeps running until she's out of my sight.

I have no idea what to do now. Should I go back to my cell, hang out in the open? As if on cue, my stomach growls. *Right. Breakfast.*

I walk towards the kitchen. The room seems quiet, minus a little light chatter of people playing cards. I don't think about them. *Food* should be my only thought until I get back to my room. I reach to the counter to grab a piece of bread, seemingly baked fresh this morning, ingredients brought over from previous government aids. I notice that someone from the table is moving towards me. I glance over my shoulder to see Karen standing right behind me.

"Hi?" I say quietly.

"What do you think you're doing?"

I turn around to face her. "I'm just getting food … I'm hungry."

"We're all hungry, Talia, and we're rationing because we have one more mouth to feed that wants enough food to choke herself."

Okay, Talia, I think it's time to go back to our room now. I try to move around her, but she moves in my way. "Hey, I'm going, okay?"

"Yeah, you're going, alright. Back to your murdering family." It's at this point that I realize the sharpness and poison on her tongue. Her eyes are twitching, her hands itchy to do something.

"I'm going back to my room now." I keep my voice calm, my hands out in a non-threatening stance. "Please."

She reaches onto the counter and swings something at my face. I lift my hands to protect myself. A sharp sting hits my arm, and I grab it with my other hand and squeeze over it. I push as far to the back wall as I can. Everyone else at the table just watches as if it's Sunday football.

Karen walks towards me, a deranged look on her face, a bloody knife in her hand.

Bloody knife covered with … my blood? I close my eyes as I bring my arm around and open them to see that the blood from my arm isn't being contained by my hand at all.

Call for help!

No one will hear me.

"Go back!" Karen yells as she steps towards me again. I try to move past the table, but someone sticks out their leg and I trip. Karen stands over me. She pins me down, her knees to my shoulders, and holds my arm over my head and places the knife over my fingers.

"When I say leave, I mean LEAVE!"

"No." The panic turns into tears as I plead, "Please! No!"

"Karen. Stop!" The booming voice snaps Karen's attention up to Doc, giving me enough leeway to wiggle out of her grip and stumble to the archway, dripping blood along the way. Too much blood.

I run through the hallway, stumbling all the way to my room. I fall into the doorway and Donney is nowhere in sight. *Now?! Now is the time he chooses to leave me alone?*

Even still, the prison has never felt safer. I shut the door behind me and shove Donney's chair in front of it so they can't get in. Frantically, I look around the room for anything to help stop the bleeding. *God, this is a lot of blood.*

I look at my pillow. I trip over to the bed and rip the case off. Then I try to rip it in two, but my hands are too sweaty. I finally find a torn edge, wrap my hands around it, and pull. It fights me, but it eventually gives.

I wrap one half around my arm and tighten it with my teeth. *This isn't going to work.* I'm already bleeding through the case. Using my other arm, I tighten it more. *More!*

I reach for another piece and start wrapping it too. Sweat is dripping down my forehead but I feel so cold. I start shivering, unable to tie the knot.

Come on, Talia, I'm not ready to die yet!

I grip it with my teeth and finish the knot, throwing myself into the far corner of the bed. I squeeze my bad arm with my good until I can't feel either.

Can't give up. Not now.

At this point, who even cares? What should I care for? For living here? Running away? Waiting for it all to return to how it was pre-war like the rest of this god-damned country?

Let it burn, for all I care.

My room gets much brighter and then much darker. Voices are stirring outside the door, and some people even try the door. Just trying to finish me off, I'm sure. They won't get the satisfaction.

The door finally breaks open. Let 'em try me.

I'm so cold. I'm so damned cold.

Sleep now, Talia.

CHAPTER
26

I dream again. Not like last time; this doesn't involve James or any of those other blurs I saw last time. Everything around me is dark until I see a spotlight fall on me. It's so bright, nearly blinding. The air is stale and cold enough that I can see my breath. I feel goosebumps popping up all over my body, and when I look down, I am wearing a loose blue hospital gown.

In the distance, another spotlight appears, and under it stands a Silver Man. Its soft, flowing metal shines against the light, making it look like the most beautiful thing in all of creation.

I try to walk towards it, but my feet feel like they're weighed down by a whole bucket of cement.

What is this place?

I look around, trying to see anything else, but everything is black. I squint, but it doesn't help. I hear the click of another spotlight turn on behind me. I try to turn around, but I still can't move. I can feel eyes burning on the back of my neck as my hair stands on end.

My stomach drops and my heart beats faster than humanly possible when I hear footsteps approaching me from behind. I turn my head as much as possible to each side. The … whatever it is, is hiding perfectly in my blind spot.

I take a deep breath and fog pours out of my lungs like a puff of smoke. The thing's footsteps grow louder as they get closer, a soft clacking noise like high heels in an empty hallway.

My heart feels as though it will pound out of my chest. I'm still not able to move, but I suddenly feel as if I've just run a mile. They're directly behind by now, as I can feel their warm breath crawling down my spine.

Icy air surrounds me as I breathe in, freezing my lungs to the point where a slight tumble could make them shatter.

I look down at my clothes and suddenly I am in nothing but blue tattered jean shorts and my red sports bra. I feel so bare to the cold air as it hits every piece of my exposed skin.

I swing my arms around myself, attempting to provide more coverage, but my arms feel colder than the air around me as if they are bricks of ice themselves. I shove them back down to my sides, which arguably feels so much worse.

I don't like it here. Get me out of here.

I reach around to try and grab the person behind me, and it's like my hand is touching glass. Cold and thick, like an icicle hanging off the roof of a tall building. I recoil from it.

Why can't I move?!

An icy glass finger slides up my bare arm. I try to swat the hand away, but it grabs my wrist. Its grip is tight, crushing my wrist. My hand looks to be turning white as I try to fight it to let me go.

I turn back to look at the Silver Man, but he's gone. The spotlight is there, but nothing. I look around to try and see if I can see it anywhere, but it's just *gone*.

Comforting.

A sudden booming sound grows around me: gunshots, drums, sirens, alarms, bells, whistles, and pretty much anything else you can imagine. The sounds burst through my eardrum and scrapes against my brain.

The noise must have also scared the thing behind me, because it let go of my arm. I grab my hand and hold it to my chest, attempting to provide the most amount of warmth possible. Everything goes silent.

Comforting.

A sudden gust of warm wind blows towards me. It's strong enough to push me off my feet. I fly forward and manage to catch myself with my hands before my face hits the ground.

I jolt up. *I can move.*

I turn around, trying to get a glimpse of the ice creature, but it's gone too.

I look around in a circle, but now the Silver Man's light has gone out as well, leaving my light the only one on for who knows how far.

I hear the thud of another spotlight turn on behind me.

Turn around. It's better to know than to not know.

Yeah, like hell.

My curiosity takes over, and I turn around to see Green. He walks towards me, hand outstretched, with a big smile on his face. I walk towards him, carefully considering every step.

I crouch down so I can meet his eyes. "Thank you," I attempt to say but nothing comes out. He puts a finger to his lips and grabs my hand. His hand is as warm as pure, golden sunlight, which for once I don't think I mind.

He pulls me along behind him at a slow pace, which makes it easy for me to keep up with him. He turns and curves as if he can see where he is going. He slowly guides me through the darkness. No more spotlights turn on. Just the empty darkness around us.

He reaches his hand out and stops. He pulls my hand and places it onto a cold doorknob. I twist and push. He lets go of my hand. I want to turn around. I want to tell him to hold on, but he's gone. Completely out of sight.

I look back to the door and I pull it open. Light pours through, filling the room behind me. I don't look back. Sometimes it's better just to leave monsters to the darkness.

CHAPTER
27

I awake, blinking hard. I swear I can hear every eyelash bat as I force my eyes open. Eating the shine of the light bulb like it's their last meal. *God, my head kills.* Where am I? *Right.* Wait. Did I survive again?

It's official, I'm freakin' immortal. Either that or someone bigger than me is playing quite a few sick jokes. I'm not counting anything out yet.

I lift my head enough to take a look at my newly bandaged wrist, which is about 75% of my arm covered by gauze.

I push myself so I'm sitting up. I'm still in my prison, where I was when I … fainted? I pick at the tape holding the gauze in place and start unravelling it. Believe me, I know I'm going to regret what I do next … I turn over my forearm to see bruised skin surrounding black string holding my arm together.

I look next to my bed, where someone has conveniently placed a bucket, and I empty my stomach contents, or lack thereof, into it. I wipe my mouth with my good wrist and spit one last time into the bucket before placing it back down.

I look over to the wall farthest from the bed and rewrap my arm without having to look back at it, or else that bucket is going to get a little fuller. I look back at my arm once I'm satisfied that my wrap job means I won't have to look at that ugly thing again.

The door creaks open, and my heart skips a beat before his voice pops up. "Don't panic, it's just me, okay?" Donney. The door opens the rest of the way and he slides in and shuts it behind him.

He strides over to the bed and sits down. His stupid maternal look is smothering his normal sly grin. He meets my eyes, and the look he gives is so damn patronizing. *What did you do now?* I'm sure he wants to ask. He leans over and looks at the contents of the bucket. My face turns red, but he smiles at me, his normal slyness returning.

"Ha! Doc owes me his dessert." He notes the confusion on my face and expands ... sort of. "He said no one throws up from stitches while they're knocked out. I knew it wasn't going to be the pain that made you toss your cookies." I go to punch him, but he dodges. "Hey, hey, now. Don't pull out your stitches. I worked hard on those."

"You put in my stitches?" I lift an eyebrow at him.

"Well, yeah. Doc was busy on crowd control. I'm the only other one that knows how."

"Seems like a flawed system."

"Sweetie, have you seen the world? The whole thing is a flawed system." I laugh. We both fall quiet, neither of us knowing what is supposed to happen next.

He stands, arms crossed, in the middle of the room, looking around at anything but me. "I should probably clean that." He gives a sickly smile at the bucket, and I think I know what he's thinking.

"Donney, I want you to dispose of that properly, like a toilet, or in the forest or something, okay?" He looks over to me and grins that mischievous grin I'm so used to by now.

"I choose 'or something.'"

"If I hear screaming, I'm barricading you out of this room again."

He laughs. "You know the reason you're not dead right now is because that didn't work, right?"

I bounce my head from side to side. "Fair ... fair." I shrug and gesture fawningly to the door. "Do what you will."

He smiles and glides out of the room.

I look around. You'd think I would've gotten bored of the room by now ... I have. There's nothing to do in here, but at least I get to play games with Clary and Green.

Woah.

My dream comes crashing back at once. The Silver Man, the freezing ice *thing* that sends a chill down my spine thinking about it now, and Green.

That last one makes little to no sense. What would he have to do in a room filled with such darkness? *Dreams, man, who knows?* Fair play.

Donney skips back into the room, happier than when he left. Not returning with the bucket is suspicious enough, but he brings me a glass of clean water. He hands it over and I down it in about three seconds flat. I hand it back to him, and he looks at the empty glass, forehead squished in a confused smile, and places it on the ground.

"So," he says, leaning against the far wall. "I have good news and bad news, which do you want first?"

I hate both options quickly, knowing full well that neither of them will be remotely ideal. "Good."

"Karen won't be bothering you anymore; in fact, no one will." I blink quickly, trying to hear what he just said.

"That's good, isn't it?" I am now extremely suspicious of the "bad" news. "What's the bad news?"

He purses his lips and takes a deep breath; one I mimic to prepare. "No one is allowed to see you at all. Excluding me." His head falls to the side. "And Doc, if necessary. But no Clary, Greg, or anybody. You're on complete lockdown." *Greg? Green?*

I feel my cheeks burning all the way down to my feet. I throw myself to standing. "What do you mean, I'm on lockdown? I did nothing wrong! I was trying to get breakfast!" I'm shaking, itching to hit something, to *smash* something. *Anything.* At least before I could get myself food. Albeit, it didn't go over well, but I at least had the *option.*

Donney places his hands on my shoulder in an attempt to calm me, but I throw them off immediately, along with shooting him a warning stare that would kill him if given the chance.

"It's Montey, isn't it? He's opening his mouth when he shouldn't again. I'll kill him."

"Not that I'm not digging this new murdery side of you, but do you think that's wise?"

"When have you been concerned about being wise?"

"I'm the wisest damn person you know. And don't forget it." He pokes my forehead. "But, on a more depressing note, Montey is like their child; they aren't going to take your word over his or Karen's. So, for now, you are enemy number one, and she was justified. Unfortunately, Tal, no one is going to believe you."

"You believe me."

He goes quiet for a second, working his way to his chair. "Yeah, I guess I do."

CHAPTER

28

"So ...now what?" I have no idea what is supposed to happen next. *Lockdown.* Great. I'm literally a prisoner now, as opposed to a metaphorical prisoner before.

Sort of ... I'm sure if I tried to leave, no one would stop me. Excluding the parties who already have. That being said, my options at this moment seem to be: leave for good *or* pretend I don't exist. I don't think I'm going to be too good at either option.

"Now, you rest."

"Donney, I swear, if I have to rest for another minute, I'm going to go stir crazy." That is if I haven't already.

"Then don't rest. Sit in here and do jumping jacks or something. I would love to let you roam around and dust a shelf or two ..." I shoot my eyes to him and he cracks a smile.

"Clary told you ..."

"Yeah, of course, she did. There's nothing that happens here to talk about, so of course, the weird new girl dusting old books at six in the morning was going to come up."

"I'm sure everybody else has been saying a lot of different things about that same weird girl ..." I let my head bow down.

Donney exhales a whine. "If you wanna throw yourself a pity party, would you mind keeping it to yourself?"

He's got a point. "Yeah, okay, my bad." The look on his face tells me he did not expect me to say that. "But seriously, I'm not just going to rest. I'd rather shoot myself."

He gives an exhausted exhale and gets up. He turns to leave the room.

"Where are you going?" I ask, and his response is an eye roll that moves his entire head.

"I'm going to get you a gun." He leaves and shuts the door behind him, only to re-enter less than thirty seconds later with a deck of cards in his hands. "I couldn't find a gun."

"Ha! I win again," I say triumphantly. His chair is pulled so it's facing the bed. It makes him much taller than me, and it makes me much more secure in hiding my cards.

Donney huffs, "I let you win." He tosses his cards on the table and sits back like a young child refusing to eat his broccoli.

"Four times in a row?" I laugh.

"Nah, the third time you cheated."

I scoff at his accusation. "*Cheated?* I barely know how to play this game."

"That's what makes you a good cheater."

"You do realize that makes no sense." I gather up the cards and put them into a neat pile. I shake the deck in my hand "Want to play again?"

"We just played four times and you want to play again?"

"I prefer to beat people in odd numbers and stopping at three was too soon."

Donney lets out a simple *ha.* "Fine, one last time. This time I'm not going easy on you."

"You can go first this time," I say, holding my cards close to my chest so he can't see them.

"My, my, aren't *we* feeling generous today." He laughs before continuing "Do you have a six?"

I look down at my deck and see that I have two sixes. I immediately slump my shoulder and hand him the cards.

"Why, thank you, dollface. I don't suppose you also have a jack, do you?"

A bit of time passes, with suddenly game after game of him beating me. There's no way his luck just turned around like that. Man, if he has some luck magic and is wasting it on a game of cards, I'm going to be *so pissed.*

"Got any twos?"

"Nope." I pick up a card from the messy pile on the tiny kitchen bench in front of us. "Got any queens?"

My shoulders slump as I hand over the card. "You're cheating."

"How on earth could I be cheating when you're guarding those cards like the damned silver gates?" *Zap.*

I'm electing to ignore that. I narrow my eyes and purse my lips. "I don't know. All I know is that you haven't let me take a single one of your cards since you started 'not going easy on me'."

"Call me intuitive." He winks at me over the cards that he holds tightly against his nose.

"C'mon, Don, admit you're cheating." He pulls down his cards to glare at me, and I know exactly what I did because I did it on purpose.

"Don't call me that."

"Yeah ... why is that again?"

He reaches over and taps his cards on my head. "Nonya business. Just don't like it."

"So, what *can* I call you?"

"You can call me Donney, dear."

"Okay, *Donney dear.*"

He freezes for a second and starts nodding. "I ran into that one, didn't I?"

"Like a blind man running a hurdle race."

He laughs and I join him. We laugh for a solid minute, and I don't think it was even that funny. Maybe we're both stir crazy. "Hey Donney, can I ask you a question?"

"Will you ask it anyway if I say no?"

"Yes." He gestures his hand, telling me to go ahead. "Does Clary's friend, I think you called him Greg earlier, have a past before the government squads?"

"Okay, first things first." He holds out a finger, stopping me from asking anything else. "You've known him since, what, your second day with us? And you don't know his name?"

"No one ever said it!" I throw my hands up in frustration.

"You didn't think to ask?" He laughs. Yeah, I don't have an answer to that. I shrug.

"And my second question?"

Donney shakes his head at my ignorance. "Yeah, he does, but don't we all?" He goes quiet.

"Do you wanna talk about it?"

"About myself? I'd rather cut out my tongue." He doesn't sound like he's kidding.

"Fine, can you tell me about Greg then?"

"All I know is that his father was a piece of shit. Killed his mother before the Silver Men got him." Donney laughs to himself. "Maybe the only good things those things ever did."

"Besides end the war, you mean?" I ask.

He shrugs. "The war was just a bunch of people trying to survive." I'm taken aback. The Wastelanders were taken care of. We fed them, they got greedy and wanted more than their fair share.

"Yeah, if they can't survive then no one can. Right?" I throw my cards down and glare at Donney.

"Hey. Don't be like that. There're a million sides to every story. I tend to see a few of them. A trait that *you* should be grateful for." *He's got me there.* I take a deep breath and nod. "Good, I think it's time we take a break from this for a little bit. Despite what you think, you still need rest."

"We were in the middle of a game!"

"It's not like you had any more interest in playing it, and you know that." He moves the table back against the wall and places his chair next to it.

I exhale sharply. "Why do you always want me to get rest?"

"I don't want you to do something stupid and rip my beautiful stitches out. I worked hard on not letting you die; don't make my efforts good for nothing."

I scowl at him but quickly give up and lie down.

"Good girl," he says jokingly.

"Bite me," I say, slightly less jokingly.

CHAPTER
29

Time seems to roll by like a minute is a second and a day is an hour. I have nothing to do but sit in my room and read the books that Donney brings for me. I finish one and he brings me another. I'd say that it was like clockwork but there have been a few times I've been bookless.

It's not like it's the end of the world when I am without reading material. I feel like I need a little bit of time to mourn the book I've just finished and the characters that I'll never hear from again before I jump right into another one.

I've been in this room on lockdown for a week now. I'm not allowed to see anybody but Doc and Donney, not that I've seen much of either. Donney comes in to bring me food, and to ensure I don't get murdered in my sleep, but our conversations have been limited to that. Doc I've only seen twice. He checks in randomly. I'm not quite sure what he's checking for, but I hate it.

At least I have books.

My prison room is cold, and I have to keep the door closed, which just makes it colder. Donney brought me new socks last time so I could at least change those. These are warmer, anyway. I keep my blanket wrapped around myself at all hours, which just makes me hot, then I have to take it off again, but then I'm cold, and thus begins the vicious cycle of temperature regulation.

I gasp as my door shoots open. I sloppily shove my current book underneath my pillow, worried that someone might try to take away my only source of entertainment.

Donney stands in the doorway. I exhale in relief. He strides over to the side of my cot carrying gauze in his hand, and he kneels in front of me, placing the gauze on the floor beside him.

"Howdy, stranger," I say with a tip of my hat.

"I should've never given you *Riders of the Purple Sage*. Give me your arm," he says sharply, clearly not willing to play along.

"Say 'please'," I say in a childish voice, holding my arm to my chest. He stares at me as if I'm the biggest burden on the earth. I wait an extra second, roll my eyes, and give up my arm. I speak next in an old southern accent. "'Where I was raised, a woman's word was law. They just don't get it anymore.'"

He says nothing in retort. He grabs my arm and slowly removes the gauze that covers my stitches. He takes a wet cotton ball and rubs it against my wound. I try to retract but he has a firm grip on my wrist. "I'm almost done."

He picks up the new gauze from the floor and wraps it around my arm until it's completely covered. "Done," he says as he picks up the cotton ball and the old gauze, and he turns to leave.

"Wait," I call, and he turns his head to look at me over his shoulder. "What?"

I didn't think I'd actually get this far. "Can we play cards or something? The silence of this room is killing me. I need something to do."

"Did you already finish the last book I brought you?"

"Well no, but I–"

"Tal, I can't stay right now, okay?"

I shoot up off the cot and stand behind him. "Why the hell not?"

He sighs unnecessarily loudly. "Because I have a huge mess to try and clean up." He finally turns to face me. "Everyone out there wants you gone now more than ever. The food rations are shortening, and we barely have enough to go around, never mind having to feed a mouth that everyone would rather see starve. So no, I can't stay. I'm going to go, and I'm going to try to defend you as much as possible, but for now, please, for crying out loud, just stay quiet and stay in your room."

I nod and fall back onto my cot. He stops for a moment and drops his head. He looks almost disappointed, but he shakes his head and heads out the same way he came in.

Not that it matters. I'll see him in a couple of hours anyway.

CHAPTER
30

Another few days pass, with conversations limited to about thirty minutes a day, if I'm lucky. Donney is coming back into the room later each night. I feel like I've abandoned the hope of seeing sunlight again.

Not exactly a negative, though …

I sit on Donney's chair for a little variety, reading what he brought me last: *Sherlock Holmes.* Can't go wrong with a little mystery. Although between these mystery novels and the one that I read by Agatha Christie, I think I prefer the one written by her—much less banter.

My stomach grumbles, acting as my internal clock telling me that Donney is late for lunch … again.

I know, I know. He's fighting for me to keep a place here; I know everyone is going hungry. Still. *I need to find that boy a watch.*

My door creeps open, and I take back everything I said. What a punctual boy. *Lunchtime.*

Although, rather than food, my stomach eats my heart as Montey pushes himself in, quickly shutting the door behind him.

"What are you—" I start. He hushes me to stop talking, and it only boils my blood further.

His face changes again like he's a master of disguise with a million different masks. "Long time no see, Talia."

"Get out," I say sharply as I stand fast to face him. *Bad idea.* I straighten my back to try to hide the fact that I'm seeing stars.

"Where's the guard dog? I haven't seen him today," he says, ignoring my demand.

Answering him might get him to leave faster … "He was by this morning."

He points to my bad arm. "How is that, by the way?" He snags my bad arm and twists it. I yelp.

"Ow! Dude, what the hell?"

Using his grip on me, he drags me closer and whispers into my ear, "Hey." His breath rolls down my neck like a bead of sweat. "Remember the old deal? Leave now or else I bring them here."

"We've established already that you're a coward, remember *that*?" I try to pull from his grip, but he digs his nails in.

"That was before we were starving. That was before keeping you here was hurting people directly." His words are forced through gritted teeth, and he pushes on my cut harder. Blood starts seeping out of the bandage and onto his fingertips. "I will do it, Talia, dammit! This is your last chance. Leave now."

Tears are fighting to burn down, but I'll hold them off as long as I can. I close my eyes and take a deep breath. "Donney will never let me leave."

"Then it's a good thing I don't plan on telling him." He lets go of my arm. I pull it back and protect it behind my back. He lets out a sick chuckle and continues, "He's not in right now, and he won't notice you leave."

"He'll be back at lunch," I say, trying to find an excuse to scare him off.

"It's eleven-thirty." He leans in close. "Run."

I look him dead in his exhausted, pretty green eyes.

What the hell happened to him?

His blonde hair, once soft and curly, is now crazed and being pulled in every direction. His bottom lip is bleeding like he hasn't stopped biting it. His overall look is dishevelled and concerning. A real rock-bottom energy spewing out of him. I know that right now, at this very moment, he means what he says.

"Talia, think about the kids … Clary, Greg, Julia, Emma, and think about Donney. They will all *die*." I pause and stare at him. "DIE, Talia!" he yells as he grabs my shoulder and shakes me until the stars come back.

"Okay!" I cry out so he stops. "I'll leave," I say because I mean it.

Montey throws me back and steps aside, creating a path for me to walk out of the room. I know I have to shake off whatever pride I have left. I fold my blanket and tuck it under my arm, grab my book from under my pillow, and I walk past Montey into the hallway. He follows me closely out of the room.

Where can I go?

Just pick a direction and start walking. Sooner or later, I'll come across … something. Hopefully.

I have to force every step towards the front door, my legs begging to collapse, my eyes begging to cry. I push forward until I'm there. I turn around to look at Montey.

"Please, don't do this," I beg.

He looks almost as if he's pitying me. "I want you to know that I don't want you to do this. I want you to live. Really, I'm rooting for you. In fact–" He holds up a finger and runs around the corner and comes back with his hands behind his back. "This will help you last longer." He holds out the bag of Raisin Crumbs.

Of all things— "Good to know you haven't lost your sense of humour along with your sanity." I grab the box from him.

"I think it's time you go now." He nods solemnly.

I turn to grab the door, but it opens with my hand an inch away from the knob. Donney stands on the other side.

His face bends from confusion to anger faster than I've seen before. He sees me, then Montey, then the blood on his hand, then my wrist. His eyes immediately fix on Montey.

"Talia, are you okay?" Donney says as calmly as possible, without removing his fixed eyes from Montey.

"I will be," I say.

He sticks out his arm for me to grab and, when I take it, he swings me behind him. "Okay. Go back to your room now, I'll be there soon."

"I don't think so," Montey interrupts, wagging a finger in the air. "Talia was just going for a short walk, weren't you, dear?" He bends to look around Donney. His eyes scream out at me, telling me that it's time for me to go. Now.

I'd like to think I have a choice.

But I don't.

I look up at Donney, whose eyes are still fixed on Montey, and let go of his arm. He turns to look at me, as much as he can with me directly behind him, his brow furrowing.

I can see Montey's face fully, his malicious smile growing. Donney turns around and meets my eyes.

I don't l have a choice. This isn't my home, and I'm ruining it for those who can call it that.

I take a deep breath and look back to Donney. "I want to go for a walk." I take a step back, instantly greeted by the sun.

"Tal, no," Donney says, trying to reach for me. I step back so he can't.

"Donney ... " I pause, and a sneaky tear manages to slip down my cheek. I wipe it away immediately. "Fresh air is good for the lungs, right?" I force a painful smile.

"I'll come with you!" he says quickly. "Just a small walk. I suppose fresh air is a good idea!"

"She wants to go alone," Montey cuts in.

Donney's face hardens, every feature turning to stone. He looks down at my bloody arm and straightens his back.

"Wait here a minute, okay, Talia?" He turns on his heels and faces Montey. "Hello, Lucifer." His voice is cold and emotionless. In other words: *terrifying*. "I am going to ask you one simple question."

Montey attempts to mimic Donney's composure, but his face cracks after a second into a burst of dark, rolling laughter that makes me sick to my stomach. "I'm sorry." His laughter turns into a deep belly laugh. "Lucifer? Really? The angel who was the true favourite until he cared too much and was willing to sacrifice everything to prove his love for his father?"

"Montey, I'm only going to ask this once. What happened to her arm?" Donney doesn't lose his composure even for a second.

"Lucifer? The angel, the best angel? The most perfect being in history, who was too overwhelmed with love that that very love became hatred over something else." He pauses and straightens his expression to stone, matching Donney's perfectly.

Montey advances a step toward Donney and says in a husky whisper, "I needed her full attention, and she wasn't willing to listen. So, I might've grabbed her arm, and I might've shoved my fingers underneath her skin, and I might've allowed her blood to warm my fingers. And man ..." he leans in closer "... it was *empowering*."

A blink of an eye is all it takes, and Donney has Montey by the throat and throws his head against the wall beside him. His head leaves a dent in the wall on impact.

Punch after punch, Donney feeds Montey his words as I do nothing but watch from the open doorway. To the gut, to the jaw, to anywhere he can reach, and Montey doesn't even pretend to fight back. The whole thing only lasts a minute.

One full minute.

Donney relentlessly wails on Montey for what seems like forever, only to be portrayed by sixty seconds. When he is finally done, he tosses Montey on the floor and Montey is laughing with a bloodied grin.

Donney spits on Montey and repeats maliciously, "*It was empowering.*"

CHAPTER
31

Witnessing what I just had, I don't think I will have a sleep without a nightmare ever again. The blood splashing, spitting, oozing out of Montey. Donney's face seemed like it had never known an emotion that wasn't pure anger.

It made me sick. More importantly, it made me terrified.

Montey lies on the floor, gasping for air, and with every breath he gets, he seems to waste on sick laughter. It only makes my stomach hurt more.

Is this what I have to live for? Is this what I have to stay for? Trading one murderer for another? Seems like I traded James for Montey and Montey for Donney. I should've seen the signs.

Montey was quick to hurt anybody. He made decisions that were certainly going to hurt someone. He told me where I was found, ripping away my peaceful ignorance. That should've been the first sign. His stupid *Art of War*, the chess games, his anger at losing. I don't want to forgive myself for not seeing these things sooner.

Donney was no different. What was the first thing I heard about him in this house? *"He needs his privacy so he doesn't kill us all."* Or his secret past. Now, this?

I do not have a good track record with whom I choose to place my trust...

Solution: Never trust again.

Donney's face turns to me. He is still huffing and puffing. He has a small splatter of blood below his right eye. He tries to wipe it away but only ends up smudging it.

"How are you?" He doesn't wait for a response, which is probably for the best since I wasn't going to give him one. He grabs my arm softly and investigates my soaked gauze. "Let me fix it."

"It's fine," I say, taking my arm and hiding it behind my back. "I should go." I refuse to meet his eyes for two reasons. One: I can't take my eyes off Montey, and two: I know he can convince me to stay. But that this is not the end. Montey is beyond the breaking point. He's *broken*. And he's willing to break a few toys, so he doesn't have to play alone.

"Tal, you can't." He tries to find my eyes, I try to avoid them, but I find them all the same. "Please." His pleading eyes are a gorgeous blue that just stares into my soul. I force myself to look away.

"Donney, I have to." I somehow manage to pull myself together and I start marching towards the door. I am leaving. For his safety. For everyone's *safety.*

"Talia!" I jump. His voice is dark and hardened, anything but hollow. "Don't you dare walk away from me." I pause and turn around to see Donney's face stern and serious. Honestly alarming. I take a deep breath to regain my composure.

What's he going to do anyway? Tackle me?

I'm through with being scared. "Donney," I say matter-of-factly, "I am leaving now, and you can't stop me."

He looks pissed, more than pissed, he looks furious again, but this time it's at me. A small vein pulses out of his forehead and his cheeks turn a bright red. He runs his hands through his hair, which makes it stand up in little spikes.

And he *laughs*. The redness fades, the vein subsides, and he laughs. Not a crooked laugh, not a maniacal laugh, but a laugh, like someone said something hilarious. I just stare at him, confused as I can be.

Donney lets out one large sigh before calming down, his perfectly straight face like none of it ever happened. "Yes, I can."

"Wait, can what?" I ask, confused while trying to sound as strong as possible as if I can't feel the blood from my arm dripping onto the floor.

"Stop you," he says bluntly as he picks me up by my waist and flings me over his high shoulders.

"What the hell, Donney?" I try to squirm out of his grip but to no avail. "Let go of me!"

"Sorry, Tal, but I don't see that happening." Donney carries me to my prison, throws me on his chair, and leaves.

I can't believe I didn't just run. I had literally a full minute. He would've stopped the second I left. *I'm such an idiot. I wasted my chance, and I don't think I'm going to get another one for a while.*

I sit here muttering to myself until I remember that I am seventeen years old and I know how to stand up. I reach for the doorknob and open it. Donney is standing on the other side holding a roll of gauze and a small medkit.

He doesn't look disappointed; in fact, he looks almost amused. "Can I bandage you up now?" he asks in an exhausted, pleading, *please, for me* kind of way.

I look at my arm and it's only now that I start feeling it. My body reminds me of the travelling fingers that Montey had digging around in my forearm. I can still feel every single digit as if it were present. "Yes," I say as I back into the room and fall back onto his chair.

Donney kneels in front of me with the medkit placed on the table beside him. "Ignore whatever Montey said to you." He looks up into my eyes, only to let go and shake his head. "Ramblings of a madman. Whatever he said, like I've said a million times before: he's a coward." He looks back to finish bandaging up my arm.

"Donney," I say and wait until he agrees to look me in the eyes. "I don't think he has anything left to lose."

"Montey is a coward, no matter how dishevelled he may appear. He won't hurt you, or anyone else, for that matter, he just isn't capable."

"I don't know." I want to shake him until he understands that we can't mess around with Montey right now. I *have* to leave for the safety of everyone.

"Trust me," he says, like it's that easy like he hasn't already lost my trust. He offers me a shy smile and claps his hands loud enough to startle me. "Lunch?"

CHAPTER
32

I have to pause and think for a moment before joining him. I'm still on lockdown, and if today's actions have said anything, it should be that I should make myself as unnoticeable as possible, but Donney waits patiently at the door for me to follow, so I do.

I crawl out of the prison, looking both ways before deciding that it's safe. I follow a little too close behind him. I can smell the soap he used this morning. He smells like freshly cut grass and something that is familiar but isn't. *Zap.*

I decide to focus on my own hair. My braids are still in from when Clary put them in nearly two weeks ago. They're messy now, of course, with hair falling out, but I keep them in when I shower and when I sleep, so it's to be expected.

I think I should be paying at least a little bit of attention to where I'm walking. Donney stops unexpectedly and I crash right into him. *Yeah, I saw that coming.*

I can really smell the soap now.

He chuckles in front of me and glances over his shoulder to see that I'm fine before continuing into the kitchen. We walk in as a united front and smile to Emma, the young Picasso, eating at the table. She gives us a gleaming smile so big that we can see the food stuck in her teeth.

"I'm starving." I smell the food boiling on the stove. I sigh with disappointment when I realize that the food must belong to someone else. "Donney, are you sure it's okay that I'm in here?" I look up to him and see his profile more defined than ever from this angle.

"I'm almost positive that everyone heard what had happened. I don't think they'll try to mess with you while I'm right here." *Yeah, surprisingly, that doesn't make me feel better. Wonder why.*

He looks down at me and crooks up the corner of his mouth in a halfway smile until it fades. We simultaneously feel the presence behind us and turn around to see what it is. I am terrified to see who might try to give Donney his second round.

For a pleasant surprise, Doc stands in the doorway, with a concerned smiling. He looks different, almost hollow.

He nods to me. "Talia, nice of you to join us for lunch. Donney, a word?" Donney looks at me, nods, and strays off into the hallway. Doc follows him a second behind.

I move over to the fridge and open it to see sparse vegetables, enough to feed everyone a few times over, but not much more than that.

I grab a thin piece of lettuce, a tomato, chicken meat, and I forage through the cupboards for bread. I find a nice loaf of brown bread and piece myself together a beautiful sandwich. I take a huge bite out of it without bothering to sit down.

I think I would marry this sandwich. I haven't exactly had five-star meals in my lockdown. Don't get me wrong, Donney made sure I didn't starve, but he wasn't a great cook.

Donney comes back into the room alone. He points to my lip, which has a drop of tomato on it. I lick it up immediately. *I'm enjoying this sandwich too much to give even a crumb of it up to gravity.*

He roams over to my side and begins to make a sandwich for himself, modelling it after mine, of course. I finish my bite and swallow to ask, "What was that all about?"

I didn't listen in, but that doesn't mean I'm not still nosy.

"He just wanted to know about a certain snake in the garden."

I pause for a second to think. "What do you know about snakes? In what garden?"

Donney sighs and knocks his head into his hands. "Never mind."

"So, what was that all about then?" I shove another bite into my mouth.

"Lucifer," he replies, taking a bite out of his sandwich.

"Ah," I say through another bite. *So tasty.* "Gotcha."

"Hey, do you want to go hang out with Clary for a bit later? Remind yourself that there are more good things than just me in the world?"

I snort out a laugh. "Donney, dear, I don't think I ever would've classified you as *good.*"

"Ouch." Donney grasps at his heart as if I just shot him. *Oh, the melodrama.* I roll my eyes. "Talia … sweetie … darling. I've never been anything but good to you … in the last hour."

"I would love to see someone other than you for a change. When can we go?" I finish off the last bite of my sandwich. *Pity.*

"Okay, how's thirty minutes?"

I'm so excited that I want to go now. "Sounds good!" As soon as I speak, I regret my words. I look like a mess, my hair is in tangled, weeks'-old braids, and I feel like I'm giving off a *malnourished-child-who-has-lived-in-a-basement-her-whole-life* vibe.

I need a shower. Desperately.

I jump in and out of the shower and then dry off. Donney has placed my fifth outfit since I arrived with this squad on the sink. It's a grey cotton tank top with a daisy on it and more jean shorts. I slip into them and open the door to see Donney at his post at the door, where he always is.

I use my fingers to untangle my hair. I take it out of the braids, which makes me sad, but I know that I can just ask her to do them again. But for now, I think it's best that I pull my hair back into a ponytail.

"C'mon! Let's go," I say impatiently, waiting to leave the doorway. He gestures for me to step in front, which I graciously accept.

"You look like a huge dork, by the way," he calls from behind me. I respond by showing him my favourite finger. The boy can't dull my sparkle right now. I'm on the freakin' moon.

I pause to look down every hallway to make sure no one is down the hall waiting for me.

"I see what you're doing. Calm down. The Boogie Man isn't coming to grab you today," he says, half-jokingly.

"That's what you think," I huff. "He already has."

CHAPTER
33

Donney jumps in front of me and slowly opens the door to Clary's room, which makes me irritated. I'm overflowing with excitement. *He's teasing me.*

"Open it now, before I hurt you." I glare at him. He shuts the door completely.

"Well, if you're going to behave like that, maybe I won't take you to see my little sister."

"Donney, I swear, if you don't open that door right now, I swear to God I will–" The door opens. Clary's bright smile and strawberry-blonde hair lights up the door frame, highlighted by the stupendously pink walls behind her.

"Talia!" she yells, and it makes me think she is almost as excited as I was. She jumps into my arms, her arms wrapping around me. I wrap mine right back and squeeze. She lets go a second later, but I'm not done yet. "Talia," she coughs, "can't … breathe."

I wonder where she could've possibly learned such melodrama.

"Sorry, sweetie." I let go and she just smiles back at me. "I just missed you a lot."

"I missed you too," she replies as if it's obvious. "But seriously, what is up with your hair?"

Of course, she would point it out. "I … I didn't have a brush."

"Silly, I do. Let me do your hair. Please?" I look over at Donney, and he nods.

"I'll skip out on the stereotypical girl fest today, but thanks for the invite. I'll be in the hall if you need me." Donney shoves me into the pink room and shuts the door behind me.

I sit on the edge of the bed, my legs folding over each other until they go numb and I have to shift them. Clary is just finishing brushing my hair, but the room is anything but silent. She is telling me about everything she does in her free time, and stories of how she swears Greg is cheating at checkers. Here's the best part: she recites off all kinds of ways that he is cheating... from secret cameras to telepathy.

She tells me about the garden, and how they don't think they'll get enough to last the winter without having to go back to their original base to get the rest of the canned food in the basement—that is, if it isn't already gone.

"How's that?" She gestures me to the old desk sitting behind her in the corner. She shows me how she folded my long hair into two beautiful braids, not a single strand loose.

"I love it," I say fawning, over them like they are a newborn baby. "You are amazing!" She smiles and rushes for the door and whips it open. Donney stumbles backwards. I try to hold in a small chuckle.

"Donney! Look! Isn't it pretty?" Clary points to me.

Donney takes a long time to answer, bobbing his head from side to side. "I liked it better matted."

"Jerk!" Clary yells and shuts the door in his face. She turns back to me with a cheeky smile. "I think it looks wonderful."

"As do I."

For the next fifteen minutes, Clary continues to tell me stories about going outside and the animals she's seen in the trees and different coloured birds and animals that made her run in the opposite direction despite doing nothing but existing. She is a bit of a scaredy-cat.

The door pushes open quickly and without warning, startling both of us.

"Time to get going, Tal. People are getting tired of staying in their rooms, which means it's time for you to get in yours." I nod. Clary hugs me one last time. Nowhere near as long as the first one, and I don't fight.

I follow Donney to the doorway and Clary shouts out for me, "Maybe we can hang out tomorrow? A picnic outside, just the four of us?"

"Four?" Donney says a bit too quickly.

"Duh," Clary responds, eyes narrowed like the answer should've been obvious. "You, me, Talia, and Gregory."

"Oh, okay," Donney huffs back. "Sounds like a party. Talk to you later, kiddo."

"Bye!" She says quickly as he pulls the door shut behind us. God, what I wouldn't do for that girl.

CHAPTER
34

I march with Donney back to my room at a quick pace. Once we get in, he hastily shuts the door. I fall back, sitting on my cot, realizing I must've left my book in the hallway or kitchen, or something. Point is, I don't have it now.

"What now?" Donney asks, seeing the look of dismay on my face.

"I lost my book," I say, adding some extra pout to my voice. "I think I left it on the kitchen counter."

"I'm not going to go get it." He falls back into his chair.

"Fine, if you're not going to get me my only source of entertainment then will you stay here with me and play chess?" He looks like he's weighing his option.

"Yeah, okay. It's not like I'm wanted out there that much after laying into the Golden Boy." He picks up the chessboard sitting behind his chair and places it over the table, pushing his chair so it's facing my cot. "Me first." *Ever the gentleman.*

We play a couple of rounds for a few hours, Donney humouring me with embarrassing stories of Montey when they were kids. Everything from him forgetting pants to him eating a worm on a dare. He tells me stories of other people, too. Like Doc trying to dance, or when Emma drew on her bedroom walls the one time she was left with a marker.

The stories make him genuinely smile, which is nice to see. Around dinnertime, he leaves to get us food and comes back with a couple of plates of boiled veggies and chicken again. But for once I don't care about the food, because after he hands me the plate, I can see that he's holding my book.

"Yes! Thank you! Where was it?" I grab the book from his grip and hold it tightly to my chest.

"On the kitchen counter, like you thought. It did have a little bit of blood on it, which might explain why no one bothered to try to move it." I pull it away from my chest to inspect it for blood, and after seeing none I pull at my shirt, but no blood there either. "I already wiped it off."

"Thanks." I look at the book when the meaning sinks in. "You're leaving again?"

His lips press together in a thin line and he nods. "Only for a couple of hours. I'll be back tonight, like always, and we'll have that picnic in the field tomorrow as I promised, Clary."

I can't help but feel disappointed. I liked spending time with him, but I understand that he has to go out there for the greater good and well-being of me and everyone else that may rely on him. I nod and sit against the wall.

I sigh. "Donney?"

"Yes?" he asks with his hand already on the doorknob.

"I also forgot my blanket. No rush, but can you try to find it when you come back tonight?"

"Sure," he replies and leaves.

Great. Now I'm bored again. At least I have my book. I open it up to where the crinkled-up tissue paper is holding my page and start reading again.

CHAPTER
35

I don't remember falling asleep, or Donney coming back, but I wake up with him in his puffy leather chair, with my blanket covering me. I genuinely feel more awake than I have in a while. Much use that's going to do me when I'm stuck in this room all day.

Wait.

No, I'm not.

I get to have a picnic today with my favourite people in the world. I stand up and flick on the light bulb, but Donney doesn't stir. I consider kicking him, like, *I'm hungry. Go get my breakfast, food monkey.* I quickly decide against it because, while I am hungry, I'm not really in the mood to be left alone again.

I don't even have that much left in my Sherlock Holmes novel.

I look at his face, and he blinks awake slowly, peacefully, until he sees me standing at his feet, then he jumps back a mile. "Jesus, are you trying to kill me?"

"Let's face it, if I wanted you dead, you'd be dead."

He rubs the sleep out of his eyes and sits up. "I'm too tired to be witty. Go to sleep until I've had enough sleep to snark you back."

I do kick him this time. "I'm hungry. Go get my breakfast, food monkey."

"You are officially starving forever now."

I run around to the side of his chair where his head is currently lying, and I place my face right next to his. "Is it because I called you my food monkey?"

He opens his eyes to see how close I am, and it doesn't even faze him. He blinks and puts on a childlike frown. "Yes."

I sigh. "If I apologize, will you go get me breakfast?"

He rolls onto his other side. "Yes, but you have to mean it."

Guess I'm starving forever. "Fine, Donney dear, I'm sorry I called you my food monkey when you are clearly a food gorilla."

He jumps up off the chair, knocking me back. "Forgiven. I'll be right back." He saunters out the door.

What just happened?

I fold my blanket and tuck it onto the corner of my cot. I look at my book to see that I only have thirty pages till the ending. I am *not* ready for this to be over. I want to savour it, but I'm also excited to see what book I can read next. A romance? A tragedy? A mystery? Another western? My mouth drools at the endless possibilities of books left on that shelf.

Although one day I'll run out. And how many books are left on that shelf anyway …?

On second thought, I'll savour it.

Donney kicks the door to get me to open it. I oblige; opening it for him is pretty normal when he brings me food. The door has to remain closed, but his hands are filled with our dishes. I scarf down the canned breakfast beans until I am scraping the spoon on the walls of the bowl trying to get the rest of the sauce.

He finishes before me and waits for me to finish before taking my bowl. Before he leaves, he turns back to me. "I'll come get you when it's time to leave for the picnic, okay?"

"Okay, I'll be here." He shakes his head at the joke that I've made about fourteen times too many.

Okay, now that he's gone, I have two options with what I can do with my time—one: read and finish that book or two: *not* do that. Personally, I think I'm feeling the latter today.

I go over to Donney's chair and pull out the chessboard from where we hid it, and I play against myself, which I think takes something out of the thrill of knowing something your opponent doesn't, but whatever, it's just a game.

I play for long enough, and then I end up finishing my book anyway. I feel like there has to be more to the story than that! It can't just be *over!* There're more stories here, I know it.

Ah yes, the post-book depression. I know it well.

I look around my room and try to figure out what I can do. My brain will explode if I try to play chess again. So, I guess I'll just keep staring at my ceiling until I die of boredom.

My door opens and I look over to see Donney with a wooden picnic basket in hand. *Great. I was hoping he'd let* me *make the sandwiches.*

"Ready?" he asks, lifting the basket.

"I am beyond ready." I pounce off the bed and rush towards him, well, toward the basket, desperate to see what awaits me.

He pulls it out of reach. "Nu-uh. It's a surprise."

I scoff at him. "Any food made by you is a surprise. Whether it's good or bad is the question."

"Bite me."

Tempting? No.

Hungry? Yes.

Now tempting? Still … no.

"Whatever, can we go now?" I try to push out the door but Donney has his arm blocking me from leaving.

"I'm still not sure this is the greatest idea …"

I roll my eyes. "C'mon, Donney, what's the literal worst thing that could happen?"

"The world could end."

"And I'd rather die anywhere but this room."

He shrugs and moves his arm, allowing me to pass. He follows on my heels as we head to where we're meeting Clary and Gregory, which is the small lot in the front of the house. Then we will walk to where Donney and I played baseball last time we came out here together.

When we open the door to outside, the kids come into view. I can see that they are playing a game of catch. Kind of—they are no more than three feet apart, throwing the ball back and forth. *No, they're catching the ball. This is catch.*

"No need to practice," Donney calls to them from behind me. "I'm going to beat all of you, no matter how much you toss a ball back and forth."

Clary rolls her eyes and pretends to whip the ball at Donney … also me, who is currently standing in front of him. I duck out of the way, a poor reflex that leaves me more embarrassed than protected. She giggles.

"Sure, laugh at my suffering," I call out with a smile. "I'm sure I've got enough of that to go around," I mutter and Donney smacks me in the back of the head. *Fair.*

"Shut up," he says simply. "All right, let's go!" The kids take off in a run. Donney looks at me with a smile and shrugs as if to say *kids, what canya do?*

He gestures for me to walk through the door, bowing like one would at a princess.

"Shut up," I say.

"I didn't say anything!" he says with slight disbelief in his voice, along with a bit of a whine.

"Maybe not out loud," I correct.

Donney follows a step behind me then speeds up so he's beside me. We walk through the trees in silence, except for the random childish laugh-screams that come from Clary as she weaves through the thick bush until we finally reach the wide-open space where Donney and I were last time.

"PLAY BALL!" Donney yells, a bit too close to my ear, ensuring that I will never be able to hear from it again. I follow him to home base as he briefly re-explains the rules, as per my request.

CHAPTER
36

We split the team Women versus Boys, to which no one protests. The only difference between now and when Donney and I originally played together is that now I pitch to Clary, who plays with me, rather than at someone who plays against me.

I eventually figure out how to pitch it so she can hit it. Although, I do kind of throw away the first couple of rounds. *My bad.*

After a few rounds of me playing in the far-field, *a mess, by the way,* I finally get a turn to hit the ball. Donney insisted I waited for my turn so we didn't waste all our energy on running to get all the balls I was going to miss. *Asshole.*

I take my spot at home base, *check,* elbow up, *check,* shoulder back, *check,* eye on the ball, *check. Ready.* Clary, at the centre plate, gives me a nod. I nod back to tell her that I am ready. And just like that, the ball is flying towards me. I have my large stick, or bat, if you will, in hand, and I swing as hard as I can.

I'll call this a surprise because the ball goes flying. I shake off my shock and start running. I make it to first base, laughing so hard that it's almost impossible not to topple over. I keep running.

I yell through whatever breath I have left as I step around the second stick acting as a base. "Eat ...," *Pant ... pant ...* "my," *pant ...* "dust!" Donney gives up watching Greg run after the ball and runs to cut me off just as I am rounding third and heading home. I dig my heels into the ground, trying to slow myself before I crash into him, but instead of moving, like a vaguely intelligent person would, he bends down and throws me easily over his shoulder.

Donney takes a deep breath and looks over to the kids, who are just now returning with the ball. "Lunch?" he says while I pound at his back.

"No fair! I was almost there! That counts! Donney, I swear to god. Put. Me. Down." I wiggle as hard as I can, trying to get free, but he has a tight grip around my waist, making all resistance futile. That doesn't stop me from trying.

"God, Tal. You're like a child who's been given way too many sweets ... and then turns murderous." He chuckles as he puts me down under a big tree. I pull his neck down to the dirt with me, causing him to fall, hard. I *clearly* didn't think this through, because of course, as *I'm* the one pulling *him* down, he crashes onto me, landing us both in pain.

I grunt as I hit the ground. Donney chuckles, lying on top of me. "Get off," I mumble. He rolls off me and we look over to see Clary and Greg, who have seen the whole thing. They are rolling through laughter. Their laughter, being as contagious as it is, gets me laughing too.

"What the hell was that?" Donney asks through a chuckle as he lays laughing on the ground next to me.

He asks good questions; too many that I don't have an answer to. "I just wanted to show you that I'm stronger than I look, so if you tried that again, you'd know what's coming for you."

Donney's blue eyes look over to meet mine. He rolls over back on top of me, pins me down by my wrists, and grapples his legs on the sides of my waist, successfully keeping me from moving at all. "How'd that work out for you?" He smirks.

I scan him up and down. He should be sweating in that black shirt and in this heat, yet not a single drop appears on him. His hair falls so softly, which is highly uncharacteristic. *Did he use conditioner?* He's still smiling at me but looking more and more curious by the second. I am realizing now that I have forgotten what he asked. I swallow. "What?"

Donney laughs and releases me. He stands up and reaches out a hand to help me to my feet. I grab it, get up, and get pulled up into him. He doesn't even smell sweaty. *Boundaries, Talia, boundaries.*

"Didn't you say something about lunch, Donney?" Clary says, tapping her belly impatiently.

Donney laughs. "Yeah, I guess I did." He ducks behind a tree and comes around the other side carrying the wicker basket. He gestures to it like it's a prize to be won. I roll my eyes.

"Cut the theatrics, I'm hungry," I call, and the kids nod in agreement. Donney pouts and puts the basket down in the shade of the big tree.

I sit down between Donney and Gregory. Clary whips open the basket and pulls out four plates, glasses, small bowls, sandwiches, and two cans of corn that, thankfully, have a pull tab, so no can opener is required.

Donney grabs the cans from in front of Clary and opens them, pouring the juice out. He empties the cans into the four bowls and puts them down in front of us. "Thank you," Clary says, placing her fork in it immediately.

"You're welcome, Tater Tot." He smirks, and she looks downright offended.

"What did I tell you about calling me that?"

Donney's smirk doesn't even flinch. "I don't know. I couldn't hear you over all of your tater-totness." He giggles as he hands Gregory his bowl. Gregory nods in thanks, and Donney nods back and diverts his attention back to Clary, who doesn't seem to be finished with her objection.

She huffs. "Dammit, Donney!"

"Language!" Donney says, perhaps harsher than he meant to be. Clary bows her head and seems to have calmed down.

"Whatever," she says underneath her breath. Donney rolls his eyes and hands my bowl to me.

"Thanks," I say quickly, before tipping the bowl over to pour the corn into my mouth.

"You're welcome, Tal."

Clary stands up. "Oh! I see! She gets a nice nickname, but I'm Tater Tots?! I'm a potato snack? I'm a ... a ..." Donney reaches over and grabs her. He pulls her into a hug.

"You're my favourite girl." He holds her tightly until she agrees to hug him back.

I stop myself from awing sarcastically, then I realize I could get my sandwich from the other side of this hug. So, I let them finish.

"And I guess you're pretty cool too," Clary says to Donney, just as he releases her.

He tucks a piece of her soft hair behind her ear. "Thanks, Tater Tot," he chirps quickly.

"That's it!" Clary yells as she starts swinging for Donney. Gregory is quicker, though. He has her by the back of her shirt and then by both arms. "Let me at him! I can take him! Call me that *one more time!* I dare ya!"

Donney bursts out laughing, and I don't think he's going to stop. He rolls onto his side and holds his stomach as if it could burst. I find myself laughing with them. I can't stop laughing either!

She looks redder than a chipmunk whose nuts were stolen. Donney laughs louder, which only makes her angrier. Gregory can't hold her back any more; he gives her what she wants and lets go of her arms.

She goes flying towards Donney. She's punching him with all her might, and he just keeps laughing, as do I. I am laughing so hard my sides are hurting. I can't help it! Donney pins her arms down in another hug, holding her so tight I can see her hands and face turning red from the constriction.

Good day.

I look to Gregory and I nod to the sandwiches that are easily within his grasp. He nods back and grabs two and tosses one to me. I nod to him again in thanks.

I open the bag, no longer paying attention to Donney and Clary. I immediately smell the chicken. Still cold, somehow. I pull the sandwich out of the plastic container and notice that it is made the exact same way as my sandwich was last night. I look up towards Donney. He and Clary have separated and she's now catching her breath next to him. I have no idea when that happened, but he shoots me a wink. I hold the sandwich up in thanks and take a huge bite.

Perfection.

Donney smiles at me. He has such a nice smile, with little dimples that hang around on both of his cheeks. I don't see him smile much.

Smirk? Yes. Smile? No. What a waste. It's almost suspicious. "Do I have something on my face?" I ask.

"Yes," Donney says, smiling even bigger. He leans over and puts his hand on my cheek, using his thumb to wipe away … a crumb, maybe?

"Ha," I mumble, taking over the de-crumbing. "Thanks."

I hear a loud bang from behind us. Donney and I jump up and run to the middle of the field and look around for what could've made the noise.

"Look!" he shouts. I turn around to see what he does: a bright, streaming light shooting straight up into the sky, then falling back down.

A flare.

CHAPTER
37

Donney and I both look terrified, a look I hadn't known him to possess. A second flare shoots up, showing anybody that heard the first one exactly where they were. *Montey upheld his promise.*

I run around Donney and stand right in front of him. I look up to his eyes and see a single tear roll down his face. A realization of what's happening must be sinking in. He won't look away from the flare. Not even for a second. I grab him by the shoulder and start shaking him. "Donney!" A tear starts down *my* face. I wipe it off and continue shaking him. "Donney! Dammit, snap out of it!"

He finally looks down to me, sincere and stoic. "We have to leave."

"Where would we go?" I shake my head in disbelief.

He grabs my arms right back. "I don't have time to figure that out. We need to run. *Now.*" He looks over to Gregory and Clary.

"Donney, we don't have time to stand still, you said it yourself. Get the kids, we have to go." We nod in agreement and rush towards the kids.

"Donney, what's going on?" Clary asks, a calm seriousness in her voice.

"We are leaving."

"Like, going back to the base?" she asks, her brows furrowed and her eyes slowly growing more panicked with every passing second. I don't answer her.

"No, we're not going back there for a while," Donney says, trying to make her understand quickly.

"But my clothes! My, well … everything! I need it."

"Not as much as you need your life," Donney says with white fire. It leaves her speechless. She nods and grabs his hand.

"Let's go." I grab Gregory by the hand, and we hurry into the forest.

Our pace quickens with every step until we are practically running, jumping over and dodging every fallen tree branch and poorly placed root.

I feel woozy. *Come on, Talia, keep it together!*

I think back to Donney and the solitary tear for everything he's ever known, the only family he's ever had, and for all of that being over. I lose myself in my thoughts and end up tripping over a branch. Donney keeps running.

"Go," I say quickly to Gregory, who stops with me. "I'll be with you in a second." He nods and runs.

We have no idea where it's coming from. Which way is danger? Is it following us? Or are we closing the gap? Hell, I don't even know if we're being chased. That doesn't change the fact that if we stay still, we are probably screwed.

I pull my leg out from under the large branch to see that a twig is now sticking out of my shin. *Great.* I pull it out and blood comes spurting out. I could pretend it didn't exist for now if it wasn't for the pain. *Crap! Push it down, Talia, we can deal with it later.*

I need to run. Catch up with them, at least.

I push myself off the dirt and stand on my own. The throbbing pain hurts like a bitch. *I need to keep going.* I run until I catch up with Donney, who seemed to have slowed down his pace to wait for me.

"We've been running long enough. We need a break," he says through broken breaths. We approach an open space and rest under the shade of a huge tree. Running blind won't help us anyway.

I lower myself on my newest wound, carefully applying pressure with my hand to block it from the dirt, weighing the pros and cons of telling Donney.

Pros: he might be able to help. Con: he would insist on helping even if it meant staying out in the open for longer. *No thanks.*

"What are we running from?" Clary says to Donney. They are both standing in front of me.

"Danger," Donney replies while scanning the surrounding area.

"What kind of danger?" Clary persists, stepping up against him.

"The dangerous kind."

Clary rolls her eyes. "I want to go home."

"Me too, but we can't go back there. It's not safe."

"I said," Clary shoves Donney, "I want to go home!" She shoves him harder, so much so that he falls right onto me.

I yelp in pain. I guess fate has decided *"Screw the pros and cons list. This is happening."*

Donney whips his head around to me. I shove him off to relieve the pressure. He grabs my arm. I look away from him, not daring to meet his gaze.

"Hey!" he yells at me and grabs my face with his open hand. "Look at me." I meet his gaze and smile through the pain, my eyes not cooperating with my smile. "What is wrong?"

"Donney, don't worry. Keep going, we should start up again. We can't afford the lost time."

He grips my arm tighter. I fight against yelping at that pain too, although, by comparison, his grip is a picnic. *Pun not intended.* "Like hell. Talia ... what is *wrong?*" I move from my leg. The pressure being taken off makes the blood flood out faster. I don't dare to meet Donney's gaze. "Shit. Tal." He falls backwards, a bead of sweat rolling down his creased brow.

Blood still pours out, more and more every second. I rip off my shirt and use it to hold pressure for as long as I can. *Thank God for sports bras.* Donney jumps over and puts his hands on mine. He looks at me and sighs. "Look, Donney, I meant what I said. Leave, take the kids as far away from here as you can." My voice is hard and rushing.

"And I meant what I said. *Like. Hell.* We are *not* leaving you." He forces my hands away from my leg, and now I am completely relying on him to keep the pressure on my leg. "Not now. Not ever."

Out of the corner of my eye, a shining spot appears in the forest about a couple hundred metres in front of us, and of course it's where we were running towards.

A bright glimmer of light has never been a symbol of darkness until now. I look at Donney. "Donney, please, listen to me, even if now is the first and only time you do. I'm not joking. Run. While you still can."

"Funny, Tal. I'm not going anywhere."

I grab his face and force him to look at me, tears filling up my eyes. "Donney." He looks at me, like, really *looks* at me. He scans my face, now looking just as terrified as I am. He tries to turn around. "Don't look," I tell him, refusing to let go of his face. "Just look at me. Grab Clary and grab Greg. Run back as fast as you can, run sideways if you don't want to go back, just keep running. Okay?"

"Talia, I'll carry you," he says as he takes away the pressure from my leg and tries to stand up, but I just tighten my grip.

"No, you won't be able to run fast enough. I'll stay here. I'll buy you time."

"You won't. You'll come with us, you can run, come on, slugger, tough it out," he says, trying desperately to convince me.

"Donney." I allow him to stand. "You're running out of time. Now go. Run. For Clary's sake, if not for your own!" I yell, trying anything to get him to leave. I can see the hurt in his eyes when he realizes that he has no choice.

Without taking his eyes off me, he yells, "Clary, Greg, come here." They both find themselves at his side. "You guys want to go back? Let's go."

"We can't go back. It's not safe," Gregory says. We all turn to look at him.

"Okay, then," Donney says, getting them back on track, "then we go sideways, and we'll figure it out. We always do. Let's go. *Now.*"

I look over to where I saw the glimmer, and I can see it now in its entirety. The Silver Man. My heart sinks, and I know what happens next.

Donney tightens his shoulder, doing his best to be the brave big brother Clary needs. "Donney," I call as I push myself onto my feet. "*Run.*"

CHAPTER
38

Donney runs as he's told, staying a small step behind the kids, sure to keep them in his line of sight. Once he reaches the edge of the forest, I can't help but hope he turns back, even though I know he shouldn't. When he doesn't, I feel emotions are mixed.

Good. He runs right into the forest and doesn't stop for a second. *It's for the best.*

My leg makes it hard for me to stand, but I need to buy them time. *Every second counts.*

I fight myself not to look down, to not look at the blood I'm losing every step I take. I push on, further and further to the middle of the field. The Silver Man's liquid-metal body glides closer too.

Wait.

What did I do to the last Silver Man I touched? What happened to him? *Could I do that again?* Or would I die? *I'm dead either way.* I could keep running circles around it. Maybe that would make it dizzy. *Do Silver Men get dizzy?* Probably not. Not that I could really run, either. I look down at my leg. *Big mistake.* I can feel my consciousness floating away. Black dots appear in my vision. I can't shake them away.

I'm within a few feet from the Silver Man. So close I can almost touch him.

Why don't I? I'm dying anyway. I'm not going to escape.

So, that's it. *That's* what I'm doing. I don't think I'm on a roll for good ideas lately.

Worth a shot.

I reach my hand out, and like a mirror, it does the same thing. Who's controlling it, I wonder, or is it here alone?

It really does not matter.

"Talia! No!" I look to my left and see Donney standing at the edge of the forest. *Idiot.*

"I said—" I don't get to finish my sentence before my body lights on fire. Electricity spurs through me, forcing me to throw my head up in a howl. I can't hear myself scream, but I can feel the soreness in my voice. A strong force pulses in my body and drains me of *everything*. Everything hurts … everything.

♟

White noise fills the air around me, voices pulling through the silence. Different voices. Donney? He had nothing to come back for. *I swear to God. If he put those kids' lives in danger by coming back here, I'll kill him myself.*

"Come back." I hear the voices ring and echo in my head. Some sensation is coming back to my body, I can feel a strong pressure on my chest. It's a constant, heavy pressure. I try to move my arms to stop whoever is doing this, but I can't move anything.

"Talia Witson, you had better come back to me right now." *A different voice? Or the same, I really can't tell.* The pressure relieves and then stops. "That's it. Keep it up." Now yelling *loudly*? I can't make out a single thing. It is two people fighting. Then the yelling stops. The pain in my stomach doesn't ease up. I force myself to open my eyes, and I mean force. This is easily the hardest thing I have ever had to do.

A soft groan leaves my lips as I lift my head off the ground. I push my good arm under my body to help me sit up. Of course, the first thing I see is Donney exchanging punches with someone.

"Donney?" I say softly, but it's enough to get his attention. He shoots his head over to me, leaving himself open for a punch. He gets knocked down right in front of me. I pull myself into a sitting position. It's all I can manage.

"Who are you?" I scream to the other person. My vision is unbelievably blurry. I can't make out the attacker. All I can see is the bright blond hair. "Montey?"

The figure comes over and places his hand on me gently. I can see him studying my face right before I finally see him. "James?"

A tear runs down his face as he pulls me into a hug. "That's right, Tal, it's me." I don't know why I start crying, but I hug him back.

Donney seems pissed. He shoves him off me and pulls me to my feet. I wrap my arm around his shoulder on instinct, so I don't fall over.

"Tal, he tried to kill you." I feel confused and sick, with a feeling in my stomach that seems to branch over my every nerve.

"What?" I say, trying to look over to James.

James bows his head, not even trying to deny Donney's claim. "I swear, Talia, I didn't know it was you."

"Then exactly who were you trying to kill?" I say sharply, trying to knock Donney off me, but I'm way too weak.

James looks up to meet my gaze. "Not you. *Never* you. I lost you twice already. I wasn't trying to risk a third."

"Well, she should be dead!" Donney says, pulling me behind him like he's my shield. "No one should be able to survive a touch from a Silver Man! It's a *bloody* miracle she survived."

James looks confused. He looks around Donney and tries to meet my gaze. "You didn't tell him?" He's smiling as if we're children hiding a secret from our parents.

"Tell him what?" I ask, honestly having no idea what he's referring to. Donney's shoulders clench. I place my hand on his back and he relaxes, but only a little.

"She didn't tell you," I swear I can feel the smirk on James's face as he lifts a finger to point and laugh at Donney.

"I didn't want to know … I *don't* want to know. I don't care. She's alive, that's all that matters." Donney never did favour the truth.

My heart drops and I swear it stops beating. "Where are the kids?" I ask, frantically looking around.

Donney turns to me. "Well, I told them to run, so …" He pauses and looks to the forest. "Clary, Gregory!" he yells, and they immediately pop their heads out from around a tree. "I knew they wouldn't go, but at least they stayed hidden." The kids rush over.

"Talia," James presses. "Tell him."

"I don't know what you want me to tell him!" I yell back.

"There's no reason to hide it now, Talia. We all know."

"I can't tell him what you want me to tell him because I *don't remember anything.*"

"What do you mean you don't remember?" The question was asked to me, but he's glaring at Donney for the answers.

"She was found with amnesia," Donney replies softly.

"Bullshit, then how does she remember me?" Donney looks back to me, his soft blue eyes staring into mine with concern.

"Donney, I …" I have no idea what to say. Anything I say will make me seem like a liar now, not that he's ever wanted to know. "I remembered a little bit of my old life. Just after the attack at the house. During my seizure."

"Okay. Then, that explains it." He looks back to James, more ferocious than ever. "Your friend is alive. Please leave us alone forever with that knowledge." He holds out an arm, pushing him to leave.

"I'm *never* leaving her again," James says, and I can hear in his voice that he means every word.

CHAPTER
39

"Look, you said it yourself. You can't go back to where you came from," James says. "So, just come back to our base. After an attack a while ago, we have a lot of spare bedrooms and tons of food to go around. Plus, we all like Talia."

"What about the kids?" Donney closes his eyes and I can see he's preparing to swallow his pride.

"They can come too. We don't have any kids around their age, but we're a young squad, and no one will have a problem." James is clearly willing to bargain to get me back. Yet, for some reason, I don't get a vote.

"Okay, but the *second* there is a problem," Donney says sharply, through gritted teeth, holding a finger to James, "I'm taking the kids *and* Talia and we are leaving."

James looks pissed at the suggestion. "Bullshit. Talia will stay with us. We are her squad."

"*We* are her *family*." My heart does a little flip when I realize that they *are* my family. They have cared for me when everyone else was against me, and they risked their lives to bring me back.

"We were her family first," James retorts quickly.

"Then where were you when we found her?" Donney knew this would shatter him, and it does. James runs his hand through his hair. The softness of it makes it look messy. His lower lip is quivering, and his eyes are avoiding looking at everyone.

I speak up, loosening myself from Donney's grip to stand on my own. "That's enough." I waver back, almost falling back down, and Donney wraps his arm around my waist to provide me with the exact support I need but am annoyed to receive. "It doesn't matter. We just need to go. Let's go with James. If he says it's safe there, then I trust him." Donney looks down at me and his lips press into a thin smile, but his eyes don't follow.

He nods. "Okay, we'll go. But I meant what I said. I will take you with me. If anything goes sideways,"—he looks to James—"I won't hesitate to get rid of *anyone* in my way."

"Let's go then," James says, starting the walk back.

"What about … *that?*" Clary asks, gesturing to the Silver Man that looks like it had been set on fire.

"Don't worry about that," James says, smiling. "We have plenty more where that came from."

Comforting.

James gestures for Donney to lead the way into the forest. Donney picks me up and carries me on his back. I wrap my arms around his neck, and his arms lift my legs. He leads the way. Clary and Gregory follow behind us and James is just behind them.

After the first thirty minutes, James races up to me and Donney. "Let me take her for a bit," he says.

Donney refuses him outright. "No."

"Come on, buddy," James calls out, and Donney stops immediately. The kids murmur behind him. Donney stands against James like a challenge. James takes a step back, not wanting to start another fight. He gestures to me. "Lemme take her. You've gotta be getting tired."

"Back off, buddy. I'm *fine*," Donney says sharply before tripping over a loose branch, hitting the ground, and bringing me with him.

"Ha! You both totally ate dirt there!" James cracks while helping me up. I lean on him for support again.

"Donney, are you okay?" I ask.

"Aside from my pride, yeah, I'm fine. I just tripped." He dusts off his shirt and keeps moving forward. I stifle a laugh.

"That settles it. You're a danger. I'm taking Talia now." Before I can object, James has my arm and hoists me up onto his back, just as I was with Donney. My legs fall comfortably in the space between his arms and ribs. It's weird; it's almost as if I fit better here. *Metaphor?*

Donney sulks off with a little blood dripping from a scrape on his knee; nothing he plans on caring about. "If you hadn't distracted me, I wouldn't've tripped!" he says. He looks ready to take a swing but looks at me on James's back and seems to vote against it. Donney huffs and lets James take the lead following in the rear with the kids.

We walk for what feels like forever, which has probably only been an hour or two. Not that I can complain, I'm not walking anywhere. Plus, it's nice to be with James again. My heart kinda grows when I remember I'm with someone who loves me and has loved me for my entire life.

"Are we almost there?" Clary chirps from behind me.

"Yes," James replies, looking around the trees.

"How much longer?" she whines.

"Not much longer, little one. We should be able to see it …" He pauses as we move around a big rock. "Now."

We all look over to see a house made of beautiful red bricks and great green vines that seem to be holding the whole thing together. *This is the place from my dream.*

An old, rusted swing set sits sturdily beside the house. To the right of it seems to be a fenced-in garden. Vines stretch all over, making it look like a tiny jungle. *Makes me hungry.* I barely got to finish my sandwich before … everything.

James carries me to the front of the house before setting me down next to Donney. He is quick to throw his arm around me to keep me standing. The reflex makes me smile.

James swings open the front door and sings inside, "Honey! We're *home.*"

"Who's we?" some girl yells back.

James rolls his eyes. "Come and see!"

"I'm comfy! Just tell me!" the voice whines.

"Jenna, I swear to God. Come here!" There is a thud, and footsteps move inside another room.

"Fine!" The girl, Jenna, has long, fire-red hair, freckles like mine that are sprinkled all over her body, and is very meek-looking. When her eyes land on me, she stops short. She blinks hard and shakes her head. She mutters something for her ears only and leans in to look closer. "Is it …?" She moves a strand of hair out of her face. "Is it really you?"

I smile at her. *I have no idea who you are!* I want to tell her, but she seems too excited. She jumps forward and throws her arms around me, taking me from James' grip.

Part of me wants to hug her back, the other part of me wants her to let go. Although, as usual, I'm not sure which part to listen to, so I just keep still.

"Talia?" Jenna asks, stepping back from me, eyes narrowed. I fall to Donney, and he catches me easily. She snaps her head over to James. "What did you do?"

"Me?" James asks, touching his hand to his chest, almost angry at the question.

"I'll tell you what happened!" Donney snarls. "He attacked her with the fucking *Silver Man!*"

Jenna looks at Donney as if she didn't know he was there until he spoke. Her eyes then trail to the kids as Donney tucks them further behind him. She looks confused but she shakes it off and looks back to James. "Tell me you didn't. Tell me you weren't this damn reckless."

James takes a few steps forward and grabs her arms. "Jenna, it was an accident, *I swear.*" Jenna looks like she could kill him. I'm almost convinced she would if there weren't witnesses. Instead, she lifts her hand to his face and slaps him. His eyes are in shock and his blond hair is messier than before. Donney chuckles.

"And who the hell are you?" Jenna seems to be overflowing with anger. *I like her already.*

Donney puffs out his chest like a gorilla and gestures to himself. "Let's get this out of the way, should we? Me: Donney. You: Woman. Now that we've established that, my dear friend Talia here has amnesia. She can't remember jack shit. Except for this douche." He gestures towards James.

Clary steps forward. "Yeah! So back off and leave my brother alone!" I can't help but laugh as Jenna throws her hands up in surrender.

"Alright, well, I guess y'all will be staying with us for a bit." She turns to look at James. "Have you talked to Bethany yet?" Donney's grip on me tightens.

"Who's Bethany?" He sounds unnecessarily nervous all of a sudden. I look up to him, and his eyebrows are pressed together.

"She's our elder," James says nonchalantly. Donney's grip and his face relax. James turns back to Jenna. "And no, I just got here. I haven't spoken with her yet, but I don't think she'll say no. We could use the extra hands, and you know it."

Jenna nods then shrugs. "Alrighty then, come on in."

CHAPTER
40

J enna holds out an arm for us to officially enter the house. The air is cooled instantly, like an air conditioner that no one should be able to have right now. *Consider my attention piqued.*

I have no idea what to expect inside this house. It already seems to be as perfect as I expected. People are glad to see me, and it even smells nice, like sweet oak and something I just can't place, something that smells like a memory I can't access.

The first thing we see is two kitchen tables that seem to be pushed together to make a long table and wooden benches for people to sit at. The fridge looks like it can hide at least two dead bodies in it.

Why would that thought be in my head?

I shake the question off and keep taking everything in. The rest of the kitchen is nice, plenty of food on the shelves, and the cabinets look clean and dust-free. The floor is a shiny brown wood like someone had just washed it. Jenna marches us right past a set of stairs into a grand open living room with three couches, one on each wall, excluding the one with the television on it.

Something doesn't feel right here.

"Hey, where is everyone?" I ask, studying the room. The couches are all black leather and look beat up from use. The television is big and black as well, and the walls are wine-red. The coffee table in the middle of the room is big, round, and wooden, and also at prime height for shin-smashing.

"They're around," Jenna says, turning down a second set of stairs leading to a basement.

"Around where?" Donney presses.

Jenna stops at the bottom, letting us all enter another open room, this one much colder than the rest. There is a grey-carpeted floor, and dark-grey paint

162

covers the walls. A single red couch sits against the wall, and a glass shelf filled with board games is fastened to the wall. Jenna glares at Donney before turning her attention back to me. She smiles at me like I could break any second. "What do you remember?"

"Nothing. I only remember James, and that's only from a weird seizure-induced dream." I smile softly back at her. "But I know what happened."

James looks at the clock on the wall and looks at Jenna and nods.

"The first time you had your seizure. How long after the Silver Man was it?" *How does he ...?*

"I don't know," I say quickly. Why?"

"About two hours," Donney answers.

"This way." Jenna leads us down yet *another* hallway, to a big room with three beds on the wall. They are all made up, with the corners tucked in.

James looks at Jenna. Something about the look makes me feel sick to my stomach. "James?" I ask softly. "What's going on?"

James smiles sadly. "This was ... *is* your room. I figured we got here just in time."

"Just in time for what?" I ask before the room starts spinning and I start to shake.

"Talia!" Donney yells. "What did you do to her!?" His grip on me tightens, stopping me from falling to the ground.

"Relax," James says, lifting me out of Donney's hands and carrying me into the room. "This has to happen. She'll be fine." The room turns a hazy white and then everything does. The light is so blinding that I have to close my eyes.

I don't want to open them again.

I just want to ... sleep.

CHAPTER
41

I feel like I'm walking through a fog. Ghosts of my past graze my skin as I walk through. My heart skips a beat with every touch. They all feel unnatural, like a knot twisting in my stomach. I keep walking as if I'll die if I stop, even though my feet feel like they're being weighed down by cement.

Another ghost bumps into me, knocking me off balance, but I catch myself quickly. A hand grabs onto my wrist, steadying me. I look to see what could've caught me. A woman with raven-black hair and blacker eyes stands before me, and I know her instantly.

"Hey, Bethany," I say as if the words have crossed my lips a million times before. She smiles back at me.

"Hey, brat, maybe watch where you're walking?" Her words seem candy-coated, sweet as sugar despite the words themselves.

"Can you help me get out of here?" Another ghost bumps me from behind.

"You're not here, Talia. Come on! Use your brain! You're there. While you're here. Confused? Doesn't matter. I guess it's my turn to exit the fog." Her voice is deep and gentle.

"Has anybody ever told you that you have a flair for the dramatic?"

"Only you, but like, a million times." Another ghost crashes into me. Bethany grabs my wrist again to stop me from falling.

Dammit, what's the point of these damned things?

"Ready to re-enter the world of the living?" she asks with a sick smile.

"Do I have a choice?"

"Nope!" Bethany says as she shoves me backwards, and it seems like I'm falling forever. Falling through ice-cold air and grey clouds until I hit the ground.

The fan on the ceiling seems to be spinning, and I can't tell if that's because it's on, or because I'm outrageously dizzy. My head feels like it has been soaking in ice-cold water for a week. I pull my hands up to my face to reorient myself.

I look around the room and see Donney sitting on the bed next to me. "Donney? What's going on?"

He quickly kneels beside me. "You've been out for over an hour; you had a seizure. *Again.*"

"Whatever, you know I'm tougher than I look, I can handle anything."

"I know. You're like a freaking cockroach, but that doesn't mean we need to test it." I force myself to sit up, wincing through my body aches, which are, by the way, *EVERYWHERE.*

I look at my leg to see that it's been bandaged up. I look up to Donney, and his hair is out of place like he's been running his hands through it repeatedly. I nod to him in thanks.

"C'mon, everyone is waiting for you upstairs. I'm sorry, but this is probably going to be very awkward." He helps me to my feet. Black spots cloud my vision, and I try to blink them away. Donney waits for me before continuing.

We follow the same path we took to get here, going upstairs to the kitchen, where five new people are seated, along with James and Jenna. They seem to range from early teens to mid-twenties, and they are all staring at me. My heart beats hard.

I am not ready for this.

I hold onto Donney for support once again.

♟

"We've all missed you," a brunette girl on the other side pipes up. "I guess now that you're back, you'll want your old room back, huh?" She lets out a breathy laugh, but I don't think she really meant it to be funny.

Their words go over my head. I feel like I'm lost in the fog again. Ghosts of my past are all here in front of me. Donney reads into my nervousness, steps in front of me, and ensures that his face is the only one I can see.

"Talia, you can go rest if you want." He flips my braid over my shoulder. "We know that this is stressful. If it's too much, we can try again later."

"At least let us finish our introductions … or reintroductions, I guess," the brunette says. Donney looks at me as if waiting for an answer. I don't want to be here, but I feel like I owe it to them. I nod to Donney and he reclaims the place at my side. "I'm Cat. I was your roommate, along with Lily." She gestures over to a petite girl with dark-brown hair that almost looks black, who replies with a small wave. I nod back to be polite.

"I'm Eldon," says a boy with olive skin and arm muscles bigger than both my arms combined. "Good to see you again, Pip."

"I'm Nick," says a short, dark-skinned boy with dark-brown curly hair tied back into a bun. "I'm also the only person here who can dance better than you." He laughs, and Cat smacks his arm. Donney looks over to me.

"You dance?" He sounds surprised. *I not sure I even know how to walk half the time,* I want to say, but instead, I shrug.

"Oh yeah!" Nick says. "She's the second-best dancer I've ever seen!" Cat elbows him this time. "Ow, calm it, would ya? I'm only jokin'"

"How is she supposed to know that?" Cat says, elbowing him again.

"Knock it off, *Catherine*." She punches him in the arm … hard. I can't help it, I laugh. *Mistake.*

They all turn to look at me, and I strongly wish I could turn invisible. I halt my laughter, and a silent lull fills the room. Instead of saying anything, they all burst out into a grand chuckle. I join them. Laughing with them just feels *right*. I can't help but wonder if maybe I have finally found a home.

Doesn't hurt to try to find out.

No, I guess it doesn't.

CHAPTER
42

I sit down with them at the long table. Donney takes the spot across from me. The people, *my squad*, stare at me like either I'm a brand-new present or like I'm an ice sculpture and it's 40 degrees out. All except for Lily, who seems to be looking around at anything else.

"I remember when you were a kid," Eldon says, "and you would try to climb to the top of every tree in the yard. I swear you fell more times than you'd care to admit. Although, I say fell ..." *Zap.* He holds up his hands and shrugs.

"You didn't always fall," James chirps in, and everyone shares a little giggle.

"What? What's so funny?" I ask.

"You would jump," Eldon finishes. "Sometimes you would get stuck and not know how to get down. You figured jumping and risking hurting yourself was easier than dealing with the embarrassment of asking for help." *Zap.*

"That explains *so much.*" Donney laughs across from me, and I kick him under the table. A *thud* rings in the room, making everyone laugh more. "Don't let that stop you. Please tell more stories," Donney says, ready to eat up every word.

"Well, there was all the celebration days where we would pick a CD out of Carlisle's old set and make a dance to show everybody," Nick says with a cocky grin on his face. "Don't get me wrong, we were pretty young. But I've gotten better since then; you still suck the same." *Zap.* Realization sets in as he turns to stop Cat from hitting him. "No. Don't."

She relaxes in her seat. "If you know it's coming, you know you deserve it." She quickly reaches over and punches him again.

"Dammit, Cat!"

"Who's Carlisle?" I ask, and everyone is suddenly sombre.

"He was our elder. Died of pneumonia a while ago."

"You guys seem to have it good here. How could someone die of pneumonia?" Donney asks, and everyone looks at him like he shouldn't have.

"We had to fight for what we have. Our elders weren't skilled, so we didn't get enough government support to sustain everyone, and Carlisle thought it was important that whatever care we got went to us." Eldon's head lowers at the thought. Everyone seems to be quiet for a minute. All mourning a loss. It's kind of messed up to think, but this is technically my loss too, and I can't even mourn with them.

I don't think I've ever been angrier at this *stupid* amnesia.

Cat stands up, breaking the silence. "Who wants lunch?"

Lily cooks at the stove. I don't look over at what she's making, but it smells delicious. We sit around and they tell more stories. Thankfully not just about me. The moral of the stories seem to be the same: We're all stubborn idiots.

There is the story of how James and Cat used to fight fist to fist over which movie to pick, or the one where Eldon and Nick would race around the house until one of them nearly passed out. My personal favourite is the one where I tricked our elders into celebrating Lily's birthday three days before her actual birthday because we all *really* wanted cake.

There are some sweeter stories too. Like how I once ate some poison berries on a dare and Jenna stayed up with me all night to make sure I didn't die, or how when they were kids, Cat was stung by a wasp and James and Eldon went out in search of the little bug to get revenge.

All these stories are accompanied by that little *zap* I get when I look for a memory that I'm not allowed to look at. The stories are worth it, though; they are all endearing, or at least funny. I know I was in good hands here, and I feel like I will be again.

"Lunch is ready!" Lily sings from the kitchen, bringing over plates for each of us and a couple extra. "Maybe go find where your munchkins have run off to," she says to Donney, who nods and runs outside.

Lily places a plate down in front of me. She smiles, but when I smile back, she looks away quickly. *Okay, then.* She heads back to the kitchen and comes back with two plates with quesadillas stacked higher than my hand. As she places them down, Donney comes back in with Clary and Gregory.

"Wow! I didn't know that food could smell this good!" Clary says, smelling the pile in the middle of the table. Lily smiles and sits down. Clary sits down next to Donney, and Greg takes the spot next to me.

"Well then, dig in," Jenna says, and no one seems to need to be told twice.

Everyone sits in a murmuring silence as they eat their chewy, cheesy dinner. I'd love to hear more stories, but this is just too good to pass up. Everyone quickly eats all of it, not even leaving a slice for the birds.

"Can Greg and I go explore more now?" Clary asks in a loud whisper. Donney smiles and bows his head. "Sure." Clary nods at Greg and they both get up and run out the door.

"So, where are all of your elders?" Donney asks.

"Bethany will be back soon," James says.

"Yeah, but other than her?" Donney persists.

"There are no others," Cat adds.

Donney looks up and around, thoroughly confused, looking for an answer in someone's face, but no one gives. One thing I have learned to appreciate about Donney is that he never asks a question that he doesn't want to know the answer to. "Okay, then," he says simply.

"She's out with Noah and Eliza right now. They're gathering supplies," Nick adds.

Now Donney looks more confused. "Your elder goes to gather supplies?"

"Oh!" exclaims Eldon. "I get your confusion. She ain't old." Everyone looks like they're fitting pieces into their puzzles too.

"What do you mean 'she ain't old'?" Donney presses, seeming less patient.

"I mean, she ain't old. All our elders died, so Bethany took over. She's the oldest by a few years, so the G-men put her in charge. After a reduction in our resources, of course, but we weren't willing to be split up again."

Donney looks terrified and sad at the same time. "Does she have black hair? Like … like a raven?"

"Yeah … How did you …?" Eldon is cut off with Donney rushing towards the door.

"Donney! Where are you going?" I yell, my heart pounding out of my chest. "You're scaring me."

"Talia, come on, we're leaving."

Everyone yells at the same time, "No!"

"You are not taking her from us again," James states matter -of-factly.

Donney runs back and grabs my arm. I follow him instinctively. We both rush towards the door and whip it open, only to see Bethany holding Clary by the shoulder.

"Bethany," Donney accuses with poison on his tongue.

She looks Donney up and down as recognition slowly pours into her eyes. "Don?"

CHAPTER
43

"Let her go," Donney demands. He reaches for Clary, but Bethany moves her out of reach, passing her on to the man standing behind her. He looks like an Igor, but I think they called him Noah earlier. *I don't like it.*

"Now, is that any way to greet your long-lost sister?" Bethany asks, and the voices behind me seem to blend into nothing but vocal vibrations.

"If you could be lost a little longer, I'd appreciate it. Now let go of Clary," Donney spits out angrily. Bethany's eyes widen, and she smiles as the realization sets in.

"This is the baby? Holy shit! This is the baby that you freakin' adopted. You … you are a real Mother Theresa, you know that?" She wags a finger at him. "Speaking of long lost, good to see you, Talia. I knew James would find you eventually; a little obsessive, that one."

"Hey!" James chimes up from behind me.

"Bethany, let her go, please," I ask.

She sighs, disappointed. She takes an extra couple steps inside to close the door behind her. "So, how did *you* two find each other? Please, don't spare any details," Bethany asks, trying to prod Donney. Clary, in the hands of Noah, is crying silently. When we don't say anything, she presses harder. "I'm sure I can put the pieces together myself, but I'd rather you and Don fill me in."

"Don't call me that! And you'll give her to me if you know what's good for you."

"You know? I think I'd rather keep her for a while."

"That's not what you said eight years ago."

"I was a different person then. I'm a family gal now. A mother to all of my children." Her eyes narrow and she smiles. "And my children do love their mother."

Donney lunges forward and takes a swing at Bethany, connecting with her jaw. She pauses, spitting out blood, and smiles.

"My turn."

Clary is released from Noah to Eliza. Noah marches past Bethany and grabs Donney by the shoulder. He tries to shake him off, but James has his other arm. Bethany takes a swing and strikes him across the face.

"No!" Clary yells.

Clary shakes free from Eliza and runs to jump in front of Donney. I grab her arm before she can. She fights me, and I pull her into my chest. *Donney can handle this, but not if Clary gets hurt in the crossfire.*

Bethany takes another swing … and another, relentlessly whaling on him. Clary cries out, and I squeeze her tighter.

Donney yelps and I don't want to look, but that won't help anyone. I turn to place Clary behind me and I straighten my back. "That's enough!" I yell. Bethany keeps swinging. I take a step forward, and as she winds up for another one, I grab her wrist. "I said that's *enough!*"

Bethany stops and looks over to me. She smiles and shrugs as if nothing happened. James and Noah drop Donney onto the floor. Clary is quick to run to his side.

"Take him away," Bethany says to the boys, who quickly pick him back up off the floor.

"Hey! Where are you taking him?" I demand.

"Relax, Tal. We have plenty of beds in this place. He just needs to rest a little." She winks at me. "We both know he'll be fine."

She gestures for the boys to take Donney away, and Clary follows on their tails, quiet tears still dripping down her face. I look outside to see Gregory hiding behind a tree. I wave for him to come inside. *He's not in any danger,* I tell myself.

When he arrives at the door, Bethany turns around, taking in the sight. "Now, *we* have never met before. What's your name?" Greg just looks over to me before running into my arms. Bethany doesn't have the most welcoming face.

"He doesn't speak," I say, and Bethany laughs.

"Well then, he's officially my favourite one here!"

CHAPTER
44

What hurts the most right now is that I can't even trust the memories I do have. In them, James would never hurt a fly, let alone *murder* or allow someone to beat someone half to death just because that someone snapped their fingers.

My memories of Bethany seem to make more sense. *Sisters in arms.* No one crossed her, least of all on my watch. We fought tooth and nail for this goal, and it seems like they have it, whatever the goal was. They have food, and no one seems to have even a sniffle. They seem to have it good.

If what Eldon said was true, the government support should not be enough to get them all of this. *So, where are they getting it from?*

I have a feeling I'll regret that question later.

"Talia, come with me," Bethany says, gesturing for me to follow her. I can't explain why I do. Call it pure curiosity, but everyone knows it'll get me killed one day anyway.

She leads me downstairs to where my bedroom is, though she walks past it, continuing to a different door. She smiles at me and I smile back. *Sisters.*

She knocks on the door and a bunch of random things seem to clatter to the ground. There is a voice exclaiming, "Dammit!" I look to Bethany, asking a question with my eyes, and she just shrugs.

"Open the door!" she yells, and there is still a symphony of loud banging coming from behind the door.

"I'm coming!" the voice yells back. The door creaks open and a guy with curly orange hair steps out. He looks up to me and pauses immediately. "It's you." He shakes his head as if imagining it. "Is it really you?" He looks over to Bethany for confirmation.

"It's really her. Can we come in?"

"Uhm, uh, yeah!" The boy fumbles backwards over something on the floor. The more he opens his door, the more we can see that there is hardly a spot *not* covered by a metal thing or an open textbook.

"Talia, this is Charles."

Charles rolls his eyes. "She obviously knows who I am, Bethany." He stops short, turning to point an accusing finger in my face. "You do know who I am, don't you?" I shrug in response. He smiles like a kid in a candy store. "Oh! Okay, what do you remember?" *Again, with these damned questions. I should get these answers put onto a t-shirt.*

"I know Bethany and James, and that's only because of a weird seizure-induced dream."

"Well, that makes complete sense, except for the fact that you touched a Silver Man twice."

I pause, completely taken aback. "How'd you know that?"

He waves me off like I asked what one plus one was. "Well, when you survived the first time, it made complete sense to us. The memory thing is a little bit of a setback, but if you can remember anything, then clearly there is only one possible answer."

"And that answer is?"

"Not important." He waves me off. I huff.

"Okay, if you're so smart, tell me this: How did the Silver Men break in the first place?"

"Oh man, am I going to have to try to teach you basic computing again? I know you don't remember, but here's a hint. Last time, you threw a book at me."

He probably deserved it.

"Then put it into words that I'll understand."

"No."

He definitely deserved it.

"Why not?" I kick one of the metal things lying on his floor, and he looks at me with disappointment.

"Because the last time I did that, *I had a book thrown at me*," he says through pursed lips.

"Do I look like I have access to a book right now?"

He pauses, studying the area around each of us before finally sighing and explaining. "It's called a buffer load error. When we no longer needed them, we went to turn them off, but it's not as simple as an on/off switch. It must be done through a series of complex calculations. When this was done for the Silver Men, someone must've been off by a decimal, and since computers like this don't exactly

understand what a negative number is, it goes to its system's absolute maximum."
I look over to Bethany, who stands nonchalantly, as if to say, *been there, heard that.*

"I see why I have thrown books at him in the past."

Charles groans. "Good to see you again, Talia. Please leave me so I can get back to work." He hurries us out of the room and back into the hallway.

"Barrel of laughs, that one is," I say, and Bethany laughs.

"You don't know the half of it."

CHAPTER

45

Bethany opens a door to show me Clary sitting next to Donney, who seems to be almost passed out on a bed. Clary holds an ice pack to Donney's head. She turns her head at the sound of the door opening. She gives me a clipped nod to tell me that he'll be okay. I lift my chin in response. Bethany reaches across and closes the door again.

"Why did you show him to me?" I ask.

"Weren't you curious to see if he was okay?" She tilts her head.

"Yes, and frankly I still am. You could've killed him. I honestly don't have a reason why we shouldn't get up and leave right now."

She smiles sweetly but she doesn't seem to be being sweet. "Because we both know full well that you would already be gone if you had anywhere else to go." I feel like it shouldn't make sense how smart everyone is here, but I suppose if they lasted this long without government support, they have to be good at something.

"I think I should stay in there with them for a while," I say as I try to push back through the door, but Bethany stands in my way. Her obsidian hair falls gracefully over her shoulder. "Please."

Her smile seems a little more genuine now. *Genuinely full of pity.* "You're no good to him here. Come, let's get you changed," she says, holding out an arm and leading me down the hall, away from Donney.

He'll be fine. He's always fine.

"Changed?" The word strikes in my mind. I look down at the raggedy clothes draped over my form, which were torn to bits running through the forest. A week ago, I would've sworn I'd be buried in this red shirt and shorts. *Now, all of a sudden, I have a wardrobe?*

"Yeah, I convinced everyone it would be best if we got rid of every trace that the others had ever been here, to begin with, to help with moving on. Y'know? But James somehow convinced me to let him keep your clothes until he was ready, and after he saw you at that *other* place, we both knew it would be best if we kept them handy." She walks me over to my bedroom and leaves with a wave of her hand. "I'll send James down to see you."

I creep into my room, and now that I'm not dizzy, I can look at the things sitting around. Pictures upon pictures hang along the wall. They make me smile. There are some of me and James, and of James, Bethany, and me. Our smiles look so genuine and pure.

I wonder what happened.

I look over and grab the frame on the bedside table. A little girl sits on a man's lap, with a woman sitting peacefully next to them. The girl has his eyes and her smile. These must be my parents. *Zap.*

I don't think I've ever hated that stupid zap more.

A knock on the door makes my heart skip a beat. I run to open it and see James and his goofy smile standing on the other side of it. I immediately feel the anger rise in my cheeks.

"What the hell were you *thinking*? Why would you just let her nearly kill him like that?" I punch him in the arm.

"We do as we're told, something you'll remember eventually. I'm sorry your friend got hurt. *I am.* But he did take the first swing." He pushes past me into the room.

"So, it's only fair that she takes the next twenty, right?" He keeps walking, back facing me. He shrugs and turns to me.

"*We finish what others won't* ... family motto." He smiles at the last part. I'm still steaming. *How could anyone think that?* The end does not justify the means.

He grabs my shoulders and forces me to look him in the eyes. Such annoyingly brown eyes and a really *punchable* face right about now.

"Hey, look." He waits until I agree to meet his eyes. "I'm sorry. I really am. I never want to hurt you, okay?"

I feel like if I try to respond, I might get kicked out of this house anyway, so I just nod. He straightens his back like he just had an idea.

"C'mere." He leads me to the closet and opens it to reveal a large blue tote. He yanks it out, causing things to fall. He looks at me and shrugs a *what canya do?* I try not to laugh, but a small *ha* slips through.

He opens the lid to show a ton of clothes, from pink dresses to teal crop tops, all the way to the ugliest cargo shorts I've ever seen.

"These are mine?" I'm too excited to breathe until I get an answer.

"They're all yours." *Breathe*. He watches me beam as I rummage quickly through the clothes. I pick out a sparkly silver shirt and beige short shorts. *Perfect.* I look up to James, holding the outfit against my body.

"What do you think?" I move my shoulders like I'm posing for a cover shoot.

"Fitting," he says with a sarcastic smirk. I lean over and punch him. He punches me right back.

I forgot how hard he punches.

I refrain from rubbing my arm, not willing to give him the satisfaction.

"Now, go shower. You stink."

I'm tempted to punch him again, but he punches back hard, and I've yet to recover from the last one.

CHAPTER
46

I jump out of the shower and dry myself off with an unnecessarily fancy towel. The steam floods the room so much that I can barely see my hand in front of my face.

Maybe I overdid it with the hot water.

I toss on the silver top, which sticks to me as I try to drag it over my torso. It eventually complies. I even got underwear this time. *My own underwear.* Finally, a pleasant thing happening to me. I smile as the heavy fog dissipates until I can see my faint outline in the blurred mirror.

I drag on the shorts and look down at the cut on my arm. The stitches have fallen out, but it looks like, if I don't do anything stupid, they should be fine.

I open the bathroom door and allow the fog to roll out. The bathroom is upstairs, which means there isn't much up here at all. There are some doors, but only a couple look big enough to be bedrooms given the space that seems to be available.

Operation Curiosity Killed the Cat *is underway.*

I walk over to the big heavy wooden door and open it. Inside is a big bed that looks like it hasn't been slept on in forever. The room smells awful, like must and mothballs, so I close *that* door about as quickly as I opened it.

The next door is the same, big and oaky, so of course, me never having learned my lesson, I open it. This room seems to be oddly empty, and weirdly clean like it had just been wiped down by an expert and everything was burned five minutes ago.

Comforting.

Next door is a broom closet. Potentially the most normal thing in this house.

The final door. This room is as seemingly plain as the rest, and when I open it, it has a big table in the middle and maps hung up as wallpaper, making the room look much smaller than it is. I stroll inside.

The room is hot. There is a fan in the corner, but it's dainty considering the other lavish items they have in this place. The maps on the walls are old, like, *really old*. Places that the new world has long since forgotten, let alone the new *new* world in which we currently reside. I can't explain how I know that these maps are real and not just something from a nerdy tabletop game. They just *feel* real, I guess.

I want to stay in that room longer. I want to study each map. I just want to know all the places from before. I guess I want to know what the world was like before the Final War.

Pfft, so much for Final.

I back out of the room slowly, holding my breath and hope no one is watching me snoop. I'm not really in the mood to get reprimanded by a bunch of strangers.

I look both ways before deeming it safe. I continue to the end of the hallway, where the only thing that lets any light in is a large, pointed-top window covered with so much dust that I can't see through the glass. I take a hand and wipe off a streak.

That was … so gross.

I wipe my hand off on my shorts and look out the window. It looks like there's nothing but trees for miles. A sparkle of sunshine catches my eyes, and I look over to see what's reflecting it.

A small nail on a wooden cellar door catches my eye.

Operation Curiosity Killed the Cat *continues?*

"There you are!" James shouts from the other side of the hallway. "I was starting to think you drowned or something."

"In the shower?"

"I've learned that it seems like anything is possible when it comes to you." I laugh, and he points to the glass and my heart jumps.

Have I been caught?

"You touched that? Gross." I let out a breath I didn't know I was holding and hold out the hand I touched the glass with, trying to wipe it on James.

"It's only dust. Here, high five!"

"No! You keep that hand away from me." I push towards him, and he takes off in a sprint down the hallway and down the stairs. I *of course* follow him.

"What's a hug between friends?" I yell, chasing after him.

"Suffocation!" he yells back. He dips and dodges around the tables and into the living room and around the couches. "Stay away!"

"LOVE ME."

"I'll die first!"

"Oh, I know! I'll just pin a Silver Man after you!" He stops dead on the other side of the coffee table.

"Too soon …" I jump onto the table and lunge at him, causing us both to fall back onto the couch. I wipe the hand over his shirt and face while he screams in protest. "Stop! Oh, my God, stop!" Or my personal favourite, "That went *in my mouth!*"

So worth it. I roll over and fall onto the floor, which only makes me laugh more.

We both lie here laughing for a solid five minutes until the final laugh breath leaves our lungs. He helps me to my feet, using my other hand, and I smile at him.

"I really missed you." He smiles sadly. "I'm glad you're home."

Honestly, I'm glad I'm here with James. "Me too."

CHAPTER
47

After roughhousing with James, the cut on my arm opened. I recognize that this qualifies as me being an idiot. I run back up the stairs to the bathroom in hopes of finding some gauze or a first-aid kit or something. *Nothing. Damn.* I head back down the stairs, which creak with each step. I didn't notice this when I was flying down them earlier, and they don't do this when you go up.

James is watching me from the bottom of the stairs, smiling at me with every step. I put my weight on the handrail, which doesn't help since it also seems to be very unstable.

"Yeah, you didn't like those before either; there's a reason that your bedroom is in the basement." He chuckles to himself.

"And you never thought of getting them fixed?" I yell down, trying to not fall over the rail or, quite literally, through the floor.

"We would, but this is too damn amusing. We used to watch you do this every time you showered. It's better than reruns of old cartoons!"

I roll my eyes. "Assholes!" I say through a smile.

I drag my way to the bottom, where James is waiting.

"Does anybody here know how to fix stitches?"

He looks confused. "Why?" he asks. *Right,* he's never seen my arm; it's been covered in gauze this whole time. I turn my arm around to show him the gash.

"Turns out my jokes aren't well-received with the older crowds," I offer, shrugging with a smirk. James doesn't seem willing to laugh. He's too encapsulated by my injury.

"Tal, what happened?"

I pause. How do I answer that question? *With whatever will make him hear it.*

"You killed their family." I tuck my arm behind my back, forcing him to focus on my face. "You came looking for *me*. So, I was the easy target of their anger. I was the noose to tie, and they didn't tie it tightly."

"You left me that message! You wanted me to find you!" He steps forward and I step back.

"I didn't know who *you* were, or that you'd bring an army of murderous robots with you!" I didn't notice until now, but we have a crowd. Eliza and Jenna sit at the kitchen table in the next room staring at us. "Can I help you?" I yell at them, and they just turn away.

"Tal, please, I didn't mean to hurt you."

"No, I know. It's not your fault, it's mine. I called you, I had Sara and Mary killed, I lied to everyone. This isn't on you. It's on me." I turn around to walk away.

"Talia, that's not what I meant."

I wave a hand back at him. "No, I know, don't worry. I'm sure I can just re-string it myself."

"Talia, we both know that's your bad hand and that you aren't doing anything with it."

"Relax! I'll survive. I always do. I'm going to check on Donney." I make haste for the basement, and he doesn't try to stop me. I feel like I desperately need to get away from that conversation. A tear wells in my throat but I hold it down.

Now is not the time, Talia. Now is the time to be strong.

CHAPTER
48

The basement stairs are less steep and less downright awful as the ones leading from the upstairs. I immediately find my way to the room where Clary and Donney were earlier, only to find neither of them there.

With my brow furrowed, I take a few steps into the room to take an extra look around and see Donney sitting alone on the floor next to the bed. His knees are pulled up to his chest and his head is buried in between them. I turn back to close the door before seeing if he's okay.

"Donney?" I whisper cautiously. He groans and stirs his head up; my breath catches in my throat as I can finally look at him. My stomach is twisting.

I didn't expect to see him in good shape, but *this*.

His lip is cut, busted, and bleeding, and one of his eyes is swelled shut. I can even see a bruise on his collarbone. I kneel in front of him. I place my hands on his knees and persuade them to lay straight, and he does so with ease. They seem to be the only part of him that isn't sore. I take my place in between them.

I put my hand on his chin and rotate his head to get a better look. He doesn't protest much, but his face gives up how much pain he's in.

"Hey," I whisper, "are you okay?"

"Better question,"—his voice is raspy and sore—"what the hell are you wearing?" I look down at my shirt and punch him in the arm. *Unfair? Yes. Deserved? Also, yes.* He falls into the hit. "Ow?"

"I meant ..." I take a deep breath, reminding myself to be a little bit more compassionate. "What are you thinking?"

"That I hate your shirt."

"Thanks! Glad to see that she didn't knock you into another personality."

"She'd have to punch me a lot harder for me to like sparkles." He laughs, which turns into a cough. Which, of course, makes me laugh.

"I'm sorry about all of this. What can I do?"

"Well, if it really is my dying wish…" He pauses and looks at me longingly. "Burn that shirt." Screw injured; I punch him again. "Hey!" he says, rubbing the spot that I punched. "That hurt. Good job!" He gives me a thumbs-up, and I wind up again. "No! Wait!" I hold off and shake my head. *What a buffoon.*

"Wait, where's Clary?"

"Gregory came down, and I didn't want them both here, so I told them to go play outside and to scream and run if any of your *family* tried to come near them." *Sounds about right.*

I shrug. "Probably for the best." I place a hand on his shoulder as I stand up. "I'm going to get you some ice for that eye. While I'm gone, remember that I hate you."

"Hurry back!" he says like a princess.

I flip him off and walk out the door.

I take the stairs back up. I turn the corner to see James and Bethany in a heated conversation, and I, being the cat that I am, hide in the staircase to hear as much as I can.

"Yes, because that was the first thing on my mind," James says sarcastically.

"Maybe it'd be better if you didn't have anything on your mind at all?" Bethany throws back like a dagger.

"I'm not risking losing her again. Let her remember us. Let her remember why we're doing this. She was on our side before, and she will be again." My stomach twists. Why was I on their side before, anyway? Why would I ever be team *Murder*? Then again, I don't even know if they're talking about me or not.

Obviously, they are.

OR … *maybe I'm just a little bit of a narcissist.*

"She would have no memories of what we lost, no pain, and without that, she won't understand." *Yeah, no, this is definitely me.*

"You know we have the means to make her remember all of it," James whispers. I have to strain my ears to hear what he's saying.

"We are not wasting that many men. Okay? Besides, you don't call the shots here, I do. It's better for everyone if you didn't forget that again."

"How could I forget when you remind me *every five minutes.* Compensating much?"

"Why are you pretending that you don't know what this means? The Children are out there. Worst of all, she's one of them. We can't let her know everything; she'll turn eventually. I am *not* losing this war."

"Do you even *hear* yourself? This isn't a war! This is a myth, a fallacy, it's just a kid's story. The Children, even if they do exist, would not know what they can do. They're just people. If you're worried, just have Charles start the upgrade."

"So, you want to ensure that she doesn't get her memories back now? Pick a side." Her words spit poison. "Besides, I tried, he won't do it until we're sure."

"Finally, someone with a brain." She punches him. "Ouch! Dammit, Bethany, she'll be fine."

"I don't know. You've almost killed her twice with a Silver attack, and you want to ensure that she dies this time?" *Yikes, I don't like how this conversation is going.*

"You know damn well that those were accidents!" James yells back. *I think I've heard enough of this.* I tiptoe down the stairs and stomp my feet as I climb up, ensuring they hear me.

"Hey guys, just grabbing ice for Donney." They both look like they're trying to cool down. "Everything okay?" I ask, and James forces a smile.

"Yeah. We're fine," he says, and Bethany follows suit by nodding.

"How is my long-lost little brother?"

A chill falls down my spine. I grab the ice tray from the freezer and crack a couple out. I straighten my spine before turning back to her.

"Don't call him that," I say, and Bethany looks mildly taken aback. "You lost the right a long time ago. The jury's out on whether you ever had it in the first place."

"Hey! I took care of that kid like he was one of my own. If anyone can call him family, it's me." She steps towards me, and I turn back to the ice, wrapping it in a dishtowel.

"You always beat your family half to death?"

"Tal," James warns.

"I didn't come up here to start a fight, I'm just trying to get some ice. Care to stop me?" She takes a deep breath, looking like she wants to fight me, but ultimately decides against it and steps out of my way. I grab the ice-filled cloth and make my way downstairs. As much as I want to turn back, I know it'd seem suspicious if I did.

What the hell is going on in this house? The thought makes me want to run and never look back, but I don't think I'm ready to leave yet. Bethany is right, I have nowhere to go.

Screw that. That's just an excuse. I've made it work before, and I can make it work again. I'm not stuck here.

I'm not stuck here.

I'm not. But I don't want to leave James. He's my best friend, and if I leave this time, I might never see him again.

I refuse to lose him again.

CHAPTER
49

When I get back, Donney is standing in the middle of the room with his shirt off. He is pointing to each bruise and scrape.

"Donney." He turns to face me. "What the hell are you doing?" He smiles like a giddy little child.

"Counting," he says as if it was obvious. "I'm seeing how many I owe her."

"No," I say firmly. I step up and push the ice on his eye, making him wince. "No more fighting. I overheard something …"

He takes the icepack from my hand to hold it in place himself. "I'm shocked," he quips.

I stare at him, like, *really, dude?* "Do you wanna know what I heard or not?"

He throws up his free arm. "No! Do you know me at all?"

"Fine, highlights then." He rolls his eyes. "They're hiding something from us."

"I could've told you that."

"Do you know anything about children?" I ask, and he looks at me like I started speaking Vietnamese.

"That is potentially the vaguest thing I have ever heard come out of your mouth." *Yeah, he's not wrong.*

"Right, long story short, maybe we should keep personal details to ourselves."

"Carry on as normal then?"

I roll my eyes and turn back towards the door. "I just hate how they're hiding something from me!"

"Christ, Tal. Why is everyone always hiding something from you? You're not special."

"Thanks," I shoot back sarcastically as I turn to him. "Except I survived a Silver Man attack, somehow, *TWICE*! I'm just saying, what they were saying up there was—"

He sticks his fingers in his ears. "Lalalala! I can't hear you!"

I bow my head down. *What a child.* "Real mature."

Donney still has his fingers in his ears as he squints at me. "WHAT?" he yells.

I pull his fingers out of his ears and push his icepack back onto his eye. "Have you ever heard of the phrase 'knowledge is power'?"

"I have. I just figured I'm powerful enough without it." He uses his free arm to flex.

"Oh, yeah? Big tough guy?" I push on the worst bruise on his body, the one right below his ribcage. He bends over in pain.

"Bitch!" he curses.

"So powerful." I laugh.

With the snap of a finger, he throws the icepack onto the bed, grabs my shoulder, and pulls me backwards into his chest, throwing his arm around my neck. "Power isn't never getting hurt. It's knowing you're going to get hurt and kicking ass anyway." He releases me, and I turn to look at him.

"Then why didn't you fight back?" I'm louder than I want to be, but I can't quiet down now. "You are stronger than both those guys ... easily!" I shove him. "You know Clary was right there? Do you not give a shit about scaring her? Imagine how it would've affected Clary if Bethany killed you."

Donney's face hardens. "She didn't."

"She could've!" I yell back. Donney's arms fall, and the side of his mouth turns up in a pity smile.

Why is he pitying me? Hit him so he stops. I punch him in the arm.

He looks thrown off. "What was that for?"

"Your face. I don't like it."

"Thanks?"

CHAPTER
50

Dinnertime rolls around quickly, and the smell of meat comes down the stairs, bringing me and Donney to attention. We leave the room and find ourselves upstairs quickly. The only meat we've eaten in almost a month has been chicken, and this is definitely *not* chicken.

I find Clary and Gregory sitting at the long table with Lily and Cat. Donney shoots Clary a look, to which she shrugs in response and gestures to Lily. Lily turns softly and gives a nervous smile to Donney. Donney repays her by not acknowledging her. Which, given everything, is very kind.

Eldon, Nick, and Noah step in from outside.

"What were you guys doing out there?" I ask.

Nick smiles at me. "Just looking after the garden," he replies. He looks over to where Jenna is standing in front of the stove.

Noah shoves his way around Nick. "Smells amazing."

"Thanks! It's a new soap I'm trying." Nick punches him in the arm.

Jenna turns around, laughing. "Thank you, Nick. I figured I should make something nice for Talia's first day home." I try not to cringe at the word *home*. Instead, I smile.

"It's very kind of you to think of me," I say as Eldon marches over to me and throws his arms around me, taking me by surprise.

"We really missed you," he whispers into my ear. I hesitate, but I wrap my arms around him.

"I'm sorry," I say quietly. Suddenly all eyes are on me. Eldon pulls away, hand still on my arms, his fingers fitting into the grooves that Montey left me. I grimace and pull away, which only pulls more attention to me. Donney quickly notices what happened and claps his hands to direct the attention away from me.

Love that jerk.

"What's for dinner, anyway?"

Jenna rolls with it and nods. She turns back and grabs a plate with patties stacked on top of each other. "Burgers!" The room makes celebratory noises, including Clary. I can't help but smile at her. Jenna places the plate down in the middle of the table, and Eldon grabs a stack of plates from the cabinet and places one down in front of everybody.

Donney turns to me before sitting down as everyone is digging into their dinner. He points out my stitches or lack thereof.

"Remind me to fix that later." He looks into my eyes. I notice the deep blue of his eyes. I quickly look away. "Okay?" he asks. I don't know what he's talking about now, but I feel it's not the stitches.

I take a deep breath. "Okay." We take our seats at the table.

This meal is filled with as much conversation as the last one. People are telling stories about me and funny stories about everyone; there are stories of Bethany and James that I can vaguely remember. I have mixed feelings about them. I am feeling almost closer to them, knowing some more personal parts of the stories, but I also feel like a stranger sitting outside a big glass window.

"So, what's the plan for the rest of the night?" I ask, shoving another bite in my face.

"Do you think we plan out every evening?" Bethany replies.

"Well, no, but you have, haven't you?" I stare her down before she finally gives in.

"Yes, we have," Bethany says, turning to look at James. "James is going to take you to the cellar, then we are going to talk."

I look over to Lily, and she looks worried, which is odd because everyone else is focused on their food. No one seems to care about our conversation. "Okay, sure, how's eight?" I ask, and Bethany's head shoots up.

"Why eight?"

"I want to wander around the house a bit more, and I don't want to feel rushed. It's what?" I look over to the old clock on the wall. "Six-thirty now? Yeah, eight sounds good."

"Works for me," James chirps in.

"Fine. Go at eight."

"Thank you?"

We eat the rest of the meal in silence.

Eight o'clock rolls around, and the only thing I did in my wandering time was look through my old clothes and listen to some music with Nick. The music was nice.

Donney was wandering around outside with Clary and Gregory, scoping out the area. I warned them to not get in trouble. To which I got nothing but three shrugs.

I meet up with James at the front door like I said I would. He stands there with his arms crossed, staring at his feet.

"Wake up," I sing from across the room. He looks up, smiling.

"I wasn't sleeping," he says through a smirk.

"Then why were you snoring?" I say as I reach his side.

"I wasn't … I don't … *ugh*. Let's go." He opens the door and gestures for me to go first. He leads us to the tree door I saw from the dirty upstairs window.

It looks more secure from up close. It's a thick wooden door with two iron bars on thicker latches.

Comforting.

James lifts the bar from the hinges and swings the doors open. Inside it's pretty dark; the light shines in just enough for me to see a row of six or seven flashlights hanging on the wall. James grabs one and passes it to me and then grabs one for himself.

"Follow," he commands, leading forward down the wooden stairs. I make sure to only fall a step behind him. My throat is in my stomach. *I feel like I'm going to throw up.* Especially since I know what I'm going to find. He rolls down the dark hallway like it's something he's done a million times. He shines a light on a steel door. He undoes a latch and slides it open.

On the other side of the door is exactly what I knew I was going to see. Ten Silver Men standing. "This is how we get all our supplies," he says nonchalantly.

It hits me like a brick. "You kill for it."

"No!" he scoffs, offended by the accusation. "We just use these guys to intimidate. We only take what we need, then we leave, and we don't go back to the same place twice."

My heart seems to be palpitating a million times a minute. "I need to go." I spin on my heels, eager to get out, but James grabs my arm.

"You can't leave. We just got you back." He closes his eyes and takes a deep breath, steadying himself. "Please."

"I'm not leaving. I just … I can't be down here anymore." The cold air is starting to reach my bones. The coolness is refreshing from the murkiness outside, but with the mixture of cold air and sweat, I just want to throw up. Definitely not because of the near-dozen murderous fluid robots in front of me.

Yeah, definitely not that.

I take a last look at the beautiful monsters in their cage before turning back the way we came.

"Talia, please! We aren't villains here."

"Tell that to Sara and Mary!" I yell back. He seems to stop following me, as the sound of his footsteps no longer seems to be approaching. I run back up the stairs, looking out into the trees. It's dark outside now. I tuck the flashlight back in its port on the wall and push forward and march into the trees. I'm not running. I'm just not going back right now.

I find a nice tree. I can't explain why I define it as nice. I climb as high as my arms will allow me. The branches get thinner the higher I go. The breeze up here is chilling, but it's a more welcome chill than the icy cellar, and aside from a few hundred leaves, I have a pretty good view of the stars from here. The moon looks like a fingernail, and I hold my hand up, acting like it's a part of my hand. Just the idea of it makes me smile. I find small star patterns that I can remember, my favourite being the Big Dipper.

I know I should probably be putting more thought into the whole *everyone I know is capable of murder* dilemma that has recently been raised, but I like the shape of the moon and I'd be damned if I didn't think of the little things when my life has gotten as difficult as this.

How long have I been up here?

At least an hour.

I don't want to go back yet.

I could just live in this tree! I don't have to go back. I'll just be the friendly neighbourhood tree-dweller.

Clary and Gregory.

Yeah, I have to go back.

I nod a quick thanks to the moon and stars before climbing back down.

CHAPTER
51

When I get back into the front door of the house, no one is in sight. I let out a relaxed sigh before making my way back down to my room.

I take my time heading downstairs, and I still don't see anyone. *Where is everyone?* I head back to my room and grab one of the totes out of my closet. I start folding my clothes and placing them in empty drawers. *Am I moving in?*

I immediately drop the shirt I'm folding like it's covered in rat poison. I fall back onto my bed when Donney shows up in my doorway.

"Oh, hey," I toss out, and he looks back to me, astonished.

"Oh, hey?" he says, mimicking me. "Where have you been? Everyone is looking for you." *I forgot about that for a minute.*

"Right. Why are you still here?" I sit up.

He tilts his head and sighs. "I was not about to invite Clary and Greg to go out in the dark with your *family.*"

"You can stop calling them that anytime." I roll my eyes and fall back down. I grab one of the pillows that was so neatly tucked below the headboard and hold it over my face, contemplating screaming into it. It wouldn't solve anything. I'm just so tired.

His lips press into a thin line. "Are you okay?" he asks quietly, even though I'm sure it's just the two of us here. I'm grateful for his whispering.

I lift the pillow off my face enough to make eye contact. "Do you really want to know?"

He gives me that stern motherly look that he does so well. "Yes," he says, the concern never leaving his voice.

I pull the pillow completely off my face so he can hear me clearly, but my stare never moves from the ceiling. "I'm sick of my *home* being stuffed with foes disguised as friends." He picks up a pillow from the foot of Cat's bed and throws it at me. "Hey!"

"If you want to leave, we can leave. Screw the idea that we will die out there alone. I lived for years without government support." He throws his arms up as if to say *I turned out fine!*

"I don't think raising Clary in a world of looting is exactly what you wanted, is it?" I press, even though I know the answer.

He looks down to his feet, considering the option and slowly letting it die in his mind. "No."

"We're fine here until we aren't. At which time, we can leave. I don't think they're going to hurt us. Or at least until we can find a safe, *stable* place to live. Sound good?"

He comes over and sits on the corner of my bed. "Sounds good." He smiles and lays down, with my feet at his head. "Do you think we should tell them that you're here? Like, they're all still looking."

I stare at the ceiling and take a deep breath, weighing my options. "Maybe in an hour or two. Maybe Clary and Greg would want to play a board game."

"I think they would love that," he says, smiling. He walks over to the foot of my bed and reaches out a hand for me to take. I look up to meet his eyes. I grab his hand, and he yanks me up so hard that I almost fall into him. I reward him with a punch for his efforts.

"Let's go see the kids, jerk."

CHAPTER
52

"Yes! Ten again!" I shout as I move my piece.

"Wow, at least there's one version of life that you're good at," Clary says. I pause, absorbing the massive insult she just hurled at my head, leaving the rest of us in shock too. I can't help but burst out laughing. *She's just mad because I'm winning.*

"Clary! Be nice," Donney says, spinning the wheel for his turn. Three. "Never mind, I'm with Clary." He points an accusatory finger at me. "You're cheating."

I throw up my hands. "I literally just learned this game. You guys are quick to burn the witch." Donney and Clary share a quick nod before Donney stands up, lifts me over his head, and runs around the table in a circle, bouncing me up and down in his arms.

"BURN THE WITCH! BURN THE WITCH!" they chant as Clary joins him in running. Greg shrugs and joins them, pumping his fists above his head all angry-villager-like.

"Put me down!" I laugh. "Donney! Put me down!"

"BURN THE WITCH! BURN THE WITCH!" Donney stops short. He puts me down and we are greeted by the rest of the squad standing at the bottom of the stairs, all seeming pretty pissed off. We can't seem to stop giggling, and their faces only make us laugh louder. James steps out to the front of the crowd.

"Where were you? We have all been looking for you." He is talking to me, but his angry eyes keep flashing to Donney.

"I've been around." I shrug. "We're just playing a board game if you guys wanna join. We still have a couple rounds to go, but we could end it early if these guys wanna just call me the winner."

"Nu-uh!" Clary yells from behind me. "We aren't calling you anything but a cheater WITCH!" The four of us burst out laughing again. The rest of the crowd doesn't seem too amused.

"We were worried," James says, clearly trying to get me to apologize or something. I take a step closer to him. Donney steps up with me, and James's eyes flash a dare to him. I hold up a hand to tell Donney to wait behind me. I walk as close as I am willing to get and narrow my eyes at James.

"What would you have to be worried about, James?" I challenge. He presses his lips together and shakes his head before backing away and running back upstairs. Bethany's eyes follow him before turning back to me. She looks *pissed.*

"Everyone go back to your own business. You,"—she points to me—"come with me, you owe me a chat."

I follow Bethany up the stupid creaky stairs. I watch each step, but I just tell myself that if they haven't broken yet, today probably won't be the day that they do. I follow her to the room with the maps on the walls.

"I wasn't hurting anyone. I just was climbing a tree," I say as I take a seat on the other side of the table, right beside the spinning fan. I don't know why I don't sit in front of it. It'd be cooler if I did, but it just feels wrong. Bethany smiles at the uncertainty on my face before taking a seat across from me.

"You're not in trouble, Talia. I know you don't remember much, but you were my number two. You were the only one I trusted in this house to do what's best for everyone." Her black eyes look intensely into mine.

"Then what are we doing here? What did you need to say to me in private?" I uncross my arms and lay my hands down on the table.

"I need you to trust me. I need you to have faith in the idea that I'm doing what I'm doing for the safety and security of our family and nothing more."

"Dammit, Bethany, give me a reason to!" I lean onto the table to get as close as I can to her, pleading for any reason to not hate this place. Any reason to not have nightmares when I go to bed tonight.

"Okay, one reason. One story. If you'll let me." I straighten my back, re-cross my arms, and gesture for her to continue. "You were about thirteen when I got sick with pneumonia. Our elders, Eleanor and Carlisle, weren't sure if I would make it without the medication. We weren't getting any more support. We had used it up for the year. The heat was turned off; it was the dead of winter. I was

a lost cause. Y'know, it's funny, you were the only one who didn't come to say
goodbye. I guess, in hindsight, I can see why. Everyone came in with tear-filled
eyes, ready for me to bite the big one. I was never going to make it until you came
home that day.

"It was the coldest day of the year. The mercury from the thermometer was
spilling out onto the snow. You left sometime the day before, and while some
insisted on finding you, Eleanor and Carlisle knew we couldn't risk another
person. You came back nearly frozen solid with the medication we needed; the
medication *I* needed. You came to me immediately with the pills and practically
forced them down my throat. Ready for the twist? Both your hands and the pill
bottle were covered in blood. You refused to tell anyone, including me, where you
found them.

"I know this doesn't mean much to you. Or maybe it does, but if this is your
come-to-Jesus moment, maybe put it off for a bit. I trust you with my life because
you've proven you would ensure my safety, and I would ensure yours the same
way. Do you see now? Why I will keep you safe? I will make sure that no harm ever
comes to you. You are my family. Take that for what it means because it means
everything to me."

The words stir in my brain, making me dizzy. Too many questions. *What the
fuck did I do?* being the biggest one. Does this make me trust her? Knowing that
I would go that far for her even before the elders died? I honestly have no idea. I
can't help but feel ... more connected to her. Like there is some shared past that
makes everything a little better. I hate that I want to trust her after everything
she's done.

Or is it that I'm a hypocrite? I was the first person to kill someone in this
house. I paved the way for a house filled with murderers.

We don't know that that's what happened, or even if that story is true.

I remain on guard for the rest of the conversation. "Is that all?" I ask, refusing
to meet her eyes.

She sighs. "No, I'm also sending you on a supply run tomorrow, to see that
what we do isn't that bad. We aren't the heroes of this story, but Talia, you have to
understand that we aren't the villains either."

CHAPTER
53

Bethany filled me in on the details of the supply run. We essentially will go to some poor sap's house and flex them our murder machines and politely demand their food. And yes, I'm paraphrasing.

The mission, so to speak, will consist of Eliza, Noah, Silver Man One and Two, and myself. We are going to Squad Base 59, which is about a four-mile hike. Noah will be the one controlling the Silver Men, as he's most familiar with the remote.

I was told to not worry about it for tonight, but that's like putting a marshmallow in front of a four-year-old and telling them not to eat it. Some things are inevitable.

Like my overwhelming anxiety.

I head back to my room to see Donney and Lily talking. Both their faces read serious.

"What's going on?" I ask.

"Talia, we have a problem," Lily says in a rushed whisper.

"You're damn right, we have a problem. You guys are keeping almost a dozen Silver Men right below our feet!" I say, my voice loud and strong.

"Keep your *damn* voice down." Donney stands up and looks at me warningly.

"Wait, you know?" The realization hits me like a brick. I meet his eyes and his ferocity turns soft.

"Lily was just telling me."

Lily stands up and joins us in the middle of the room. "We need you, Talia. There are a lot more than a dozen down there—try *hundreds*," Lily says quietly. I turn to look at Donney. He holds up a hand to tell me to wait.

"Just listen," he says and looks back to Lily.

"Talia, you should know how you survived the attacks."

"Yeah, are you going to tell me? Getting almost killed twice kinda sucks, especially when you don't get why you didn't. I survived two attacks and I think I deserve some answers," I press.

"Three," she corrects.

"I beg your pardon?"

"You survived three attacks. The one that took your memory was the first. It was a Silver Man, and you'll have to trust me when I say it was an accident." She waits for my agreement before continuing. "The second was at Donney's squad's base. The one that helped you remember James. The third was this morning." It feels like forever ago. "The one that helped you remember Bethany."

"Okay, so tell me why. Why did I survive when so many died? *Tell me,*" I demand.

"Literally what do you think I'm doing? God, calm down," Lily says through an exasperated breath. *Okay, that's fair.*

"Tal," Donney interrupts. "Are you sure you want to know? Ignorance is bliss and all that crap."

"Donney, this is *my* life. Just because you want to live in the dark doesn't mean I'm willing to do the same. Knowledge is power."

"No, power is power, knowledge is a burden," he quips back.

I look back to Lily. Her hazel eyes shine under the light of the overhead lamp sitting in the corner of the room. "Tell me."

"Well, for starters, you have been told about the war, right? How the government barely managed to lock up all the Silver Men so they couldn't hurt anybody again?" *Duh.* I nod. "Well, Bethany let them out. All of us did. But then, in a freak rainstorm, we lost control. They killed thirteen of our people before we managed to regain control. It was James who ran back to get the remote right after he saw you ... well ... die. Or so we thought. Charles managed to fix it, but it was too late for many of us."

"I mean ... that explains some of it," Donney says.

"That's not even the half of it," Lily replies.

"Continue," I urge.

"When James heard your voice on the radio it was pure luck, believe it or not." *Not.* "We had to try to convince him it wasn't you, but when we didn't find your body, it was the only thing that made sense."

"It made sense that I survived the un-survivable?"

"Would you be quiet? I'm getting to that bit," she says sharply. I have to hold back a giggle at the idea of little Lily getting mad.

"Would you just tell me what I want to know?" I ask firmly.

"God, you're impatient. I'm getting there!" Lily chirps. "Fine, long story short. You're immune to the Silver Men."

"Thanks, genius," I quip sarcastically. "I got that bit, what I want to know is why."

"Because, Talia, you're one of them. You're a Silver Man."

CHAPTER
54

The room stays silent for a solid thirty seconds. Everything is whipping around my mind. Nothing makes sense. *I am not, nor have I ever been, a metal man.*

"Do I look like a Silver Man to you?" I joke. This is a joke. I can't stifle my laughter anymore.

"Would you take this seriously? I'm being serious!" Lily practically yells before remembering where she is. "I'm serious."

"This is a waste of time. She doesn't know anything. She can't help you," Donney says as he grabs my arm, preparing to pull me out of the room. Before he can, Lily speaks again.

"I know it's hard to believe, but it's true. It'll take some explanation, but please, stay." I look at her and truly study her. She stands tall, which would almost be oxymoronic if you saw her.

"You have five minutes," I snap. "Be quick."

"Fine, quick version. You are what's known as a Silver Child. You are a part of a secret government project that took young children and turned them into weapons against the Silver Men. There wasn't enough of you to stop the war before the Silver Men attacked the scientists creating you."

"Bullshit, I wasn't 'created,' I was born," I interject.

"Yes, but it's what happened after your birth that matters. You were selected to undergo a procedure. The scientists put a microchip in your hippocampal gyrus in your brain. The chip magnified your natural electricity that every human has. This type of electricity is of a different form than the Silver Men. To put it simply, they're allergic to the energy you can produce."

"Humans aren't electric," Donney says.

Lily sighs, slumping her shoulders, almost defeated. She straightens back up before pressing on. "Yes, you are. On average, every human produces a hundred watts of electricity. The chip amplified that, well, *a lot*. This makes you stronger than any Silver Man. Makes you able to take them down. Your memory loss has been an unforeseen symptom. Your extra electricity is working on readjusting your synapses so they can speak with your long-term memory again."

"Why are you telling me all of this?" What does she have to gain from me knowing this?

"I'm telling you this because we need you."

"Who's we?" Donney hisses.

Lily swallows and looks directly into my eyes as she says, "The Silver Children."

CHAPTER
55

"There is a group of Silver Children. All around your age, boys and girls alike, all who want nothing more than to bury the threat of the Silver Men once and for all," Lily explains. She sits on the bottom of a bunk bed while Donney and I sit on the bed across from her.

"Bethany would rather die than let that happen," I say, remembering the story that she told me earlier. *She'll protect her family until her last breath.*

"They know. They don't plan on hurting anyone; quite the opposite. They want to make sure everyone stays safe."

I remember the conversation I overheard earlier about the Children. Bethany and James know about them. As much as I would love to trust my best friend, I don't. He knows what I am and didn't want to tell me. *Or couldn't tell me.*

"How do Bethany and James know about the Children?" I ask, and both Lily and Donney's eyes are on me. *Did I forget to mention that? Oops.* Lily shakes her head before responding.

"Charles figured it out after managing to use an old computer network to get into a backdoor security program for the military. Apparently, when there's less than one percent of the population than there was thirty years ago, they stop caring too much about genius hackers." She laughs to herself. "They've known about the myth for a while now, but you have come back from the dead, which pretty much confirms it. The only thing they don't know is how many of the Children are aware of who they are."

"Well, are you going to make us guess?" Donney asks.

Lily smiles slyly. "At our last count? Eighty-seven out of the supposed two hundred that were involved in the program. And they're all together."

"Wait. What?"

"They live together. All safe, all training for a fight that we all know is coming. The real question is, will you fight with us?"

The thought spins. I don't even know how to keep all of this straight. I feel completely overwhelmed. Donney throws his arm around me, telling me that he'll be okay with whatever I choose. I can't help but think of Bethany's story from earlier. I picture the pill bottle being shoved from my bloody hands to her pale hands. I can't picture what I did for them, and frankly, I don't want to.

"I don't think I can say yet," I say, standing up. "I am going on a supply run tomorrow with Noah and Eliza. I have to give these people a chance. If they don't hurt anyone, what is the real harm in keeping the people you love safe?"

"Talia, I don't think you want to do that," Lily warns. She stands with me, her hands pressing me to think about this more.

"Lily." I grab her hands. "Give me time. Let me figure out if I can stop this before anyone has to fight." *I'm so damn tired of fighting.*

She nods and drops her hands. "Do us all a favour—don't tell anybody about what I've told you. Pretend you know nothing," she pushes.

"So, basically relive the last few months of my life. Yikes, hate to, but can do."

Midnight comes quick when you aren't looking at a clock. I refused to sleep in my old bed. No offence meant to Lily or Cat; I just wasn't willing to sleep in a room without Donney. It's how we spent the last couple months, him sleeping on a stupidly big chair to protect me from people trying to kill me. I guess it's my turn, minus the chair, of course.

We stay in the room Donney woke up in. The one where Lily, Donney, and I had our conversation earlier. The only room I've seen with four beds. Donney sleeps on the bottom bunk, Clary sleeps on the top. I have the bed closest to the door, and Greg has the bed in the middle. He's kicked the blankets to the floor.

I try not to think, and I try to close my eyes, but the idea of having another dream is frankly terrifying. But eventually, I doze off. The only reason I know this is because the next time I open my eyes, the sun starts to break through the window.

I try to hide my face underneath my pillow but it's too hot, so I roll off the side of the bed and the floor graces me with its immediate presence. I roll my eyes and force myself up off the ground and onto my feet. I look at the bottom bunk to see that Donney's swelling has gone down a lot, like, it's not even swollen anymore. Just a shiny array of blues and deep purples.

That'll make Bethany proud. Knowing her, she'll see it as a reminder that no one can take her down. That just makes me fume. Donney's hair is an absolute mess. With it being so short, you'd think knots are impossible, but I'm convinced that he would struggle to run his hands through it and not get them caught. The mental image makes me smile.

Donney's eyes open up and immediately sees me staring at him. *Awesome.*

"What happened last night? And please tell me I'm going to regret it." He smirks at me, and I reach up to smack him in the arm. "Too early for violence." He wags a finger at me.

"Do you not remember what happened last night?"

Donney sits up and dangles his feet off the side of the bed. He looks up as if he's trying to physically look into his brain to see the memories. "Right, danger. Awesome." He jumps down right in front of me, so we are less than two inches away. He's almost a whole head taller than me, so he backs up to look me in the eye. "How are you handling the whole thing?"

"Me? I'm fine. After all, I'm the one with superpowers."

"I see it's already going to your pretty little head." He laughs as he flicks my braid over my shoulder and reaches around to grab the nape of my neck. He pulls me closer until I'm engulfed in a hug. "I know you're worried," he whispers into my ear, "but don't be, okay? Everything will be alright. This might be a hell of a ride, but we'll walk off it in the end."

I don't worry about replying. I just hug him back. He hasn't bothered to change clothes, no matter how many times the boys offer. He said his clothes are his clothes.

"We should go for a walk," he says as he slowly lets me go. "It'll help us to clear our minds until everyone else wakes up." I nod, and he leads me out of the room. "Actually, first …" He turns back to the hallway and runs to the bathroom. I roll my eyes.

I sneak quickly and quietly into my room and change my clothes. I meet Donney in the hallway, and he shakes his head as if hallucinating before shrugging and leading me up the stairs with him, which I happily oblige.

We walk outside under all the trees. It's colder than I thought it was going to be. "I'm glad to see you've changed your shirt," he says, pulling on the collar of the teal polo I slipped into on our way out.

"Yeah, well, I don't need to be silver inside and out." I try to laugh but I'm sure Donney realizes that it's fake.

"Hey, we don't have to stay here if you don't want to." He stops and turns to look at me.

"But Lily said—"

"Forget what Lily said. We don't have to go with her either. We could register as a family and just get replaced into a squad. No one would have to know. Sure, we'd have to come up with a good story, but we could hike to the east coast or the west! An ocean is an ocean. I'm not picky." He smiles, and I let the idea dance in my mind for a bit, no questions asked, no amnesia girl, no monster, just me. I wouldn't even have to be alone. Donney, Clary and Gregory would be with me. I could just be me.

"I can't." I surprise even myself with those words. "Let me try to finish this here. At least let me go on this supply run today." We keep walking. "This is a really advanced game of chess, and it's not my turn. You'll have to trust me when I say that we're winning."

"Do I have a choice?" he asks, throwing up his arms.

"No." I smile. "But if this goes south, take the kids and do exactly what you said. Register as a family and get replaced. Keep those kids safe."

"Fine, be that way. But don't for a second think that I'm leaving you, ever. Wherever you go, I go. Don't forget that."

My blood warms. "Okay, I won't."

CHAPTER
56

When we get back, we smile as if nothing happened. Jenna and Eliza are laughing in the kitchen and Nick is playing music in the living room and twirling on the carpeted floor.

"Talia!" Nick yells over to me. His hair is down in perfect ringlets. "Come on! This one is your favourite."

"Nick," I yell back, "I told you I don't remember how to dance!"

"Dancing isn't something you think about, it's something you do. Just because your brain doesn't remember doesn't mean your body doesn't!" He runs over and grabs me by the hand. He pulls me to the living room and starts moving to the music. I follow his steps, trying to mimic his moves to the best of my ability and ...

I'm dancing?

"Holy cow, Tal, you *can* dance!" Donney laughs from the side of the room. I run over and grab his hand, trying to persuade him to dance too. "I, on the other hand, cannot." He just sort of ... wiggles. Nick and I both die laughing. "That's it. I'm done." He backs out of the room.

"Nooo! You're the best wiggler I've ever seen!" I say, trying to drag him back to the middle of the room.

"And that's the *last* time you'll ever get to see that!" he yells back as he storms downstairs. I, however, stick with dancing with Nick. It just feels nice.

We move together fluidly. He sways left, I sway right. He kicks left, I kick right. Eliza and Jenna move to the couches, watching us dance. We both have the biggest smiles on our faces. Nick stops for a second to turn up the music, sure to wake anyone still sleeping before rejoining me in the middle of the room.

"I missed this!" Eliza yells over the music. Jenna nods in reply.

We dance to the entire song and then the next, and then the next, and a few more after that, until I think I'm going to cough up a lung. Nick seems to be having the same reaction and runs over to turn down the music.

"It hasn't been the same without you, Tal," Nick says, violently whipping his head from side to side, trying to get the sweat off.

"Is this where we get to vote who was better?" Jenna says from the couch. "'Cause even without knowing what she's doing, Talia is the best."

Nick pouts before laughing and swinging his arm around me. "One of these days … I'll catch up to you," he says breathlessly.

"Now!" Eliza claps her hands and rubs them together. "Breakfast?" Everyone agrees like they haven't eaten in a million years.

Donney, Greg, and Clary join us once breakfast is ready. Clary's hair is tied back in a braid of her own. I'll never know how she is so good at that. Gregory, however, looks like he messed his hair up specifically for this event.

I take a seat at the table right next to Nick and Cat. Jenna places plates down in front of each of us. Eliza is still laughing about how even with no memory I can still dance circles around Nick. He, however, says that I got pity votes for that exact reason. We're all laughing as Bethany and James enter the room. I give them each a smile. Bethany is quick to give one back, happy to see us all happy.

She takes the spot next to Clary. "I like your braid," she says.

"I can do one for you if you want!" Clary offers. Bethany smiles.

"Sure! Thanks. After breakfast?" Clary looks to Donney, who smiles and nods.

"Okay!" she agrees. James seems to be giving a half-smile like he wants to be happy, but something is bothering him. Is it what I said yesterday?

"James! Come sit. Jenna made bacon and eggs." He smiles at me and comes to sit down at the table. He sits down on the other end from me, clearly not willing to chat. Jenna offers him a plate, which he takes with a simple nod in thanks.

"Alright! Hands on the table," Jenna says.

Donney, the kids, and I look confused. Everyone else takes their hands and lays them flat on the table. We copy them. "Wait, what are we doing?" I ask.

"Everyone wants all the bacon, so everyone starts with one piece, but that is more of a suggestion. Hence the hands rule—we're all starting fair and square in a bacon-grabbing ready position. Now, hands!" Jenna says with a huge smile. We all place our hands down and Jenna slowly places the bowl down in front of us. Before she moves her hand, she says, "Oh, and no forks this time!" Eldon and Noah laugh.

"I still have the scar from that," Eliza says.

"Well, yeah, *genius*. That's why they call it a *scar*," Noah quips back. We all laugh.

"1 … 2 … 3 … go!" Jenna shouts and removes her hand. Everyone quickly reaches in and grabs as much bacon as they can get. I get a healthy two and a half pieces, Donney has four, Eldon seems to have about six, Gregory has none. It completely breaks my heart, but I'm *not* giving him any of mine. Thankfully, I don't have to. Eldon sighs before giving him two pieces of his stack.

It warms my heart; I know I couldn't do that. Very selfless.

The eggs are placed down next. Much less fighting there—everyone passes them around all civilized-like.

For the rest of breakfast, we all giggle about things that don't matter, and it feels nice to be carefree. When we finish, we all help clean up the plates and reload them in the cabinets before going our separate ways. Eldon and Nick are going to work on the garden, Jenna and Eliza are going to cut the grass, Cat and Lily, just kind of … disappear.

"Why don't you go try to help them with the garden. You're a pretty good gardener," I say to Donney and Gregory. Greg nods and Donney seems relieved with doing something other than a board game. Clary says she's going to find another hair elastic for Bethany and runs off.

Bethany hands Noah the remote and hands mostly empty backpacks to each of us, containing a couple of granola bars, to be refilled later with the supplies we "acquire." She gives us a quick nod and sets us on our way.

We gather the Silver Men. Watching Noah work the remote makes me want to throw up, just knowing what these things can do and how messy it got last time we lost control of them. I knock on the wooden door on our way out of the cellar for good luck.

"Ready?" Eliza asks, bumping into me and shaking me out of my shock.

"Do I have a choice?" I ask, starting to follow behind Silver Man One.

"It helps if you pretend you do," she replies through pressed lips.

"Let's just go," I say, though my stomach seems ready to heave any minute. I'm not willing to waste that bacon, though …

I adjust my baseball cap to hide my eyes from the sun. I watch as the Silver Man glides his feet in a perfect fluid motion. It's trippy watching them move. They're like complete liquid metal that just happens to be taking the shape of a human, only to go solid when touched. *Trust me, I know.*

We march for hours in the stupid sun. I use the back of my arm to wipe the sweat off my brow, and I see that my stupid wound is still open.

Dammit. Remember to have Donney fix this before it gets infected. A self-note that I know I will forget by the time we get back.

"We're here," Noah says as we approach a big house with white pillars holding up a gorgeous awning.

"How do we know if anyone is here?" I ask, looking for any reason to turn back.

"We have access to a few government systems, one of them being housing placements and medical staff locations in case of an emergency. This one just happens to have a fancy doctor, which means that they get more supplies than they'll ever need," Eliza states plainly. "If it helps to know, they have more than enough to share. We don't take anything from anyone who can't spare it."

Oddly enough, that does help.

We approach the front door. The three of us take the lead, and the Silver Men stand behind us. Noah knocks on the door. For a minute, no one answers, but I am freaking out. My heart won't calm down. I feel like I could cry at any second and I'm about to throw up. Another minute passes ...

"I don't think anyone is home," I say.

"They're home." He knocks again, louder this time. "If you know what's good for you, you'll open up!"

"Hey!" I hit him in the chest, and he scowls at me. "There's no need for threats."

"What do you think we're doing here? Collecting food for a charity?" He bangs on the door again and an older man opens it. He has dark, olive skin and stunningly black hair that is swept back.

"Can I help–" He looks up to see the Silver Men and tries to close the door, but Noah shoves his hand on it, stopping him.

"We just need food, please, if you have any to spare ..." I try to ask politely but that just gains me three weird looks.

"I don't have any food to spare. I'm sorry." He tries to shut the door again, but this time Noah forces himself inside.

"Dr. Putzig? Yeah, we know who you are. Show us to your kitchen. We'll be in and out in a matter of fifteen minutes, hardly a disturbance to your day." The doctor steps aside, letting us walk in. The Silver Men follow us inside.

"No! Those must stay outside," he demands.

"Sorry, buddy, you aren't the one calling the shots here," Noah says as he marches the Silver Men in behind us. The doctor points in the direction of the kitchen. Noah, and Eliza pillage through it like it's nothing they haven't done a million times.

I look around the house briefly. It's gigantic. There's a wonderful chandelier hanging in the middle of the foyer.

"You have a lovely base," I say in pure awe. The doctor nods to me before following Noah and Eliza to the kitchen. I spend a little more time looking around before I spot a little blonde girl sitting at the top of the staircase watching everything attentively, without a shred of fear in her eyes. I wave to her and she waves back.

"What's your name?" I call up.

"Amanda," she says softly.

I smile at her. "Hi, Amanda. Do you have any friends you can go play with for a little bit?" She just shakes her head. "Okay. I understand that. I don't have many friends either." She smiles sweetly. Her blond hair shifts with her gaze. I follow it to see the doctor standing in the doorway.

"Amanda, go back to your room."

"But, Papa, we're making friends."

He smiles at her and then softly at me. "Please, mon amour." She nods and bounces back up the stairs. He looks over to me as soon as she leaves.

"I'm sorry, I didn't mean any harm. I wasn't trying to—"

He holds up a hand to stop me. "I can tell you mean well. You seem different from your friends."

I laugh. "Thanks." His gaze falls to my wounded arm.

"I can fix that for you if you'd like. A few stitches should solve it."

"Oh, that's okay sir, I appreciate the offer, but I don't want to be any more of a bother than we already are."

"Nonsense. People like you are why I became a doctor all those years ago." He holds out an arm for me to follow him into another room. I hesitate before obliging.

The next room is bigger than the last. Several couches line the walls, and elegant paintings cover the wall. One looks familiar immediately.

"Did you do these?" I point to a painting depicting Amanda. He laughs.

"No, my wife, Amanda's mother, did. A very talented woman. She'll be doing afternoon yoga with the rest of our squad in the yard right about now."

So bougie.

He gestures for me to take a seat on the couch as he grabs a medical bag much like Doc's. He grabs a tube first, a cream paste, and rubs it on my wound. It doesn't sting; rather, it cools and then numbs my arm.

"A numbing agent so the needles won't hurt too much." I nod as he ties the black string around the needle before poking it into my arm. I feel nothing. It's a miracle. I laugh and smile. He smiles back at me. He ties the first knot and moves onto the next stitch.

A few more and he's done. It looks even better than before.

"Thank you. You are a very kind man." He gives me a sad smile before welcoming me to rejoin my friends, who have filled all three of our backpacks.

"Talia, perfect. You're back," Eliza says, tossing me my backpack, which I quickly swing around my shoulder.

"Great, can we leave now?" I press.

"One last thing. We need antibiotics: penicillin, amoxicillin, and doxycycline." Noah claps his hands. "Chop, chop."

"I'm sorry, but that I just cannot do," the man says. "We too only get a certain amount each year. It's the middle of the year, and if I give you what I have now and any of my family gets sick, we'll need it. If someone you know is sick, I'll give you what they need to get better, but I cannot give you everything I have."

"Talia," Noah calls without removing his eyes from the doctor. "Where did he sew up your arm?" Confused, I point to the room we came from. I hadn't even noticed that he noticed my arm was fixed.

"Liz, go get the medkit." Eliza marches past him into the other room. With the Silver Men standing beside me, I feel uneasy about the whole situation. When she comes out with the leather bag, she smiles at Noah.

"It's all in here! We really scored!" The doctor grabs her as she tries to leave.

"I can't let you take those! I have my own family to think of. Please." He looks at me with pleading eyes. I want to tell him that I don't have a choice here. I want to fight with him, but it's a losing battle.

"I'm sorry, Dr. Putzig." I nod to him, but he starts crying, crazy and frantic, and he dives towards Eliza's hand.

"That's it!" Noah says, and he lifts the remote to his head and presses the red button.

"No!" I yell as the Silver Man steps forward and places a gentle hand on the good doctor's back. He recoils as the blue shocks jump over his body. He shakes and pales quickly until he falls lifeless to the ground.

"Papa!" I look up to see Amanda sitting on the stairs. She runs down to see her father.

"Run!" Eliza yells, and we all make our speed out the door, putting as much distance between us and the base as we can.

We run until we can't. We reach the tip of a small city street with some houses torn apart by looters and others for firewood. I stop by a house that must've been red at one point, now bleached pink by the sun. I lean on their mailbox and empty my stomach onto the gravel driveway.

"You murdered him! He wasn't hurting anyone! He had a family, you *monster*," I spit at Noah.

He just seems to shrug it off. "If we need these meds, we'll have them now. If we left them with him and we needed them, we'd be dead. I'm not willing to lose anyone else," he says heartlessly. "Don't worry, Talia. They had two doctors living there. They'll still get plenty of support. His daughter will be fine."

"She just watched her *father* get *murdered*. Who would be fine in that scenario?" Eliza and Noah just shake their heads.

"Their family is none of our concern. Only ours," Eliza says as they start walking back to our base. The walk home will be stone silent.

CHAPTER
57

When we arrive home, I'm mostly out of it. A mixture of fear, grief, and anger seems to be stirring in every corner of my mind. I know they'll all have the same reaction as Eliza and Noah, so I don't say anything.

Bethany seems excited at the loot. She digs through the med bag to find all the medications. "Geez, we're safe for a while!" she exclaims. I just push myself back down to my room. I grab a change of clothes and a towel and go to take a shower.

I let the water fall on my face. *Drown me,* I beg it. I scrub the grime away, but I can't scrub away the image of the doctor taking his last breath or the face of his daughter when she realized what happened. No. Those will haunt me for the rest of my life.

They're not getting away with this. I thought it was just taking what people can spare, intimidating, no murder. Looks like I had all of this wrong. They have to be stopped.

Bethany has to be stopped.

I waste the rest of my night in the silence of my room, save for a few conversations with Lily. I watch the hands on the clock on the wall tick with each passing second until I can rightfully make my next move.

The clock strikes 2:00 a.m. and Lily meets me at our bedroom door.

"Are you sure about this? There's no coming back. Not again."

I look at one of the pictures on the wall, the one of me, James, and Bethany smiling like we have nothing to lose. "I'm sure." I swing my backpack over my shoulder. In it is nothing more than a few shirts, shorts, and underwear.

She goes to grab a couple of other things, and I make my way to Donney and the kids' bedroom. I creak the door open quietly, softly waking each of them.

"Talia, what the hell is going on?" Donney asks, slipping on the shirt I throw at him.

"We're leaving. We're going to stay with the Children," I say, tossing him a backpack filled with clothes.

"What happened to waiting for your move?" he asks, shaking Clary alert.

"They made their move, now I'm burning the board."

CHAPTER
58

The four of us take our time to climb the stairs and tiptoe to the front entrance. We reach the front door, jump outside, and run to the spot where we are meeting Lily.

"Where did she go?" I ask. "She should be here!" At the same time, Lily pops out from behind a tree.

"Sorry I'm late. I was just getting us a ride." Lily looks ... badass. She's wearing a black leather jacket that fits her perfectly. Half her hair is pulled back into a ponytail. She's wearing army-green combat boots that just scream "I'm ready to kick ass." Shy little Lily, a super badass.

I really like this one.

"No worries, lead the way," Donney says, grabbing Clary by the hand. Lily takes us through more forest until we see a desolate road and an army jeep parked right in the middle of it.

"Get in," she commands. By her will, we all step in. "Seatbelts!" she sings as she bends over and plays with some wires until something sparks and the jeep turns on.

"Just how far is this place?" Donney chimes from the back seat.

"Far enough that I wouldn't get back before light, but not far enough that we won't get there with hours to spare with this bad boy!" she exclaims as she rubs the steering wheel.

"Hey! Princess." Who, me? *Not a princess.* "Open that drawer in front of you." I bend down and open the compartment, and in there are a couple of papers and a CD case. "Awesome! Whadda they got?"

"Uhm …" I open the case and read her some band names: "The Cargoes Brothers, Mary-Anne's Greatest Hits, Rubber Ducky Gonna—" I skip the last part, considering the audience. "Jake's Lost List."

"That one!" she yells. I pop it into the CD player and the music starts blaring. Somehow, Lily knows all the words. She sings, "*I think I'm gonna diiieee, I don't care whhhyyy, So I write this song with all my heart, my love I give to yooouuu.*" Cheesiness at its best.

♟

Two hours of speeding and loud singing and we finally got here.

Where is here, exactly? Good question.

Here is a dark building that looks like it could fall any minute. No doors, barely any roof, and most of the walls missing.

"There's no way that this is it," I say, checking the whole thing out again. Nope, it doesn't look any better the second time.

"This is it!" Lily says, throwing her hands up as if it's some big presentation.

"Maybe we'll just live off of bark and wild berries for the rest of our lives. I like my chances with that better than entering that *hovel*," Donney says, running from one side to the other. The building is comically small.

"You guys have no sense of adventure!" Lily whines. "C'mon." Donney and I look at each other and push forward, the kids within reach behind us. "So, this is where you'll be staying …" Lily shows us the kitchen that is missing a wall.

"I really, and I mean *really*, hope you're kidding," Clary says from behind me. Lily throws her arms down in disappointment.

"Of course, I'm only joking. You all have rooms. Keep coming." She opens a hatch on the wall of a staircase that leads down. We don't go down the stairs; instead, we climb into the hole. One at a time. Donney goes first, followed by the kids, and then me, and Lily follows behind me. There's a small, dark room on the other side that is nothing special. "I know, I know, now check this out."

Lily pushes a hidden button, and the back wall completely opens up. Bright, blinding lights shine through. My eyes adjust quickly, and I'm able to see the metal staircase that leads downwards. Lily rushes down.

"C'mon, guys! I've only gotta couple hours, and I'm not ready to waste it!" She waves for us to follow. I follow her down immediately, and I honestly love what I am seeing. It's a very open space with a few lights here and there, but I can see a bunch of others that aren't turned on … because it's nighttime?

A big, burly man with a well-trimmed long beard and a red flannel gets almost tackled by Lily. "Little? What're you doing here?"

"I brought you a princess!" she says, gesturing to me, and then she kisses him hard, like, awkwardly hard.

"Uhm, not a princess," I chime in, but she doesn't seem to be wanting to listen. I can't believe I once thought this girl was timid and shy, 'cause right now? Badass to the max.

Finally, they pull apart long enough for him to speak. "Hey! It's Amnesia! No way, heard great things."

"Really? Like what?" I ask.

He pauses for a second as if trying to think of something. "Okay, I haven't heard much, but here. We'll make you into a legend. Hold me to that, I dare ya." He smiles at me and looks around to Donney and the kids. "Family?" he asks me, pointing to them.

"Yes," I say without hesitation. They are my family.

"Okay, no problem. There are a few kids for the young ones to hang out with. It'll keep them out of danger and amused. The boy can, uh, I don't know, what canya do?" He speaks directly to Donney.

"Kick your ass." Okay then, too early for Donney.

"Got it. Pouty face needs his beauty rest. We'll put you with the cooks for now, maybe trainer later ..."

Donney rolls his eyes. "Where can the kids sleep?" Lily looks to Big Burly Man, who nods, and she takes the kids by the hands. Donney steps forward, ready to fight her.

"Relax, Pouty, they'll be in room two-thirteen. There's no one else in there tonight, so even with your nervousness, they'll be safe." Donney turns to look at me.

"Don't worry, Donney, I trust her," I whisper for his ears only.

"Doesn't mean I have to," he snarls.

"It's fine, Donney. I'm just tired, okay?" Clary says with her big doe eyes.

Donney leans down and places a kiss on her forehead. "Okay, go get some rest. I'll see you as soon as you wake up."

Lily leads them down the hallway and Big Burly Man turns back to me. "Alrighty kiddo, this is where things get real."

CHAPTER
59

Big Burly Man shows us around the main area. He lifts his hands like Poseidon lifting a big wave. "This is the Silver Palace. Safe haven for Silver Children and their families. For a while, we had nothing to worry about, but as I'm sure you know, we do now." He shows us a room filled with mats and metal rods on the walls. "This is where we will teach you to fight, how to properly use what has been given to you."

"Oh, I'm Jerry by the way, but everyone calls me Timber. Little—or Lily—is my girl. Poor girl is undercover, and I never get to see her."

"Little is a very fitting nickname," Donney says, nodding.

"Yeah, everyone around here has a nickname, like you, Pouty."

Donney is shocked, to say the least. "Wait ..." Donney says in a rush.

"Anyway, where were we? Ah, yes, combat room."

"Wait!" Donney continues. "That will not, I repeat, *not*, be my nickname."

"Then you had better change your attitude before the morning. First impressions here stick."

"Wait now," I chime in. "Does that mean my nickname will be Amnesia? 'Cause ironically, I'd rather forget about that."

Timber laughs. "Alright, then, tomorrow." He pauses as he walks us to the next room. "This is the kitchen, where you'll be working ..." I can see Timber struggle to avoid calling Donney Pouty. Donney notices too because his fist clenches, ready for a fight. I grab his arm, trying to get him to calm down. He looks at me, takes a breath, and unclenches.

It takes about thirty minutes before the tour is over. This place is oddly large. There was a game room, a movie room, a large food court, an underground garden centre, and a ton of hallways with nothing but living quarters. I like it, it's homey, which I suppose says something about the homes I've had. Finally, we meet up with Lily back where we left off.

"What took you guys so long?" Lily asks, obviously tired of waiting patiently for us to bring her boyfriend back. She immediately hooks onto his arm.

"Sorry, Little, I was just giving a wholesome tour." Lily pouts and pulls on his arm. She looks at her black watch that takes up an unnecessary amount of space on her wrist. "Well, we've got time. How's about you give me a tour?" She raises her eyebrows at him.

"Of wha–of course, my love." They run off, and Donney and I share a look of astonishment before bursting out laughing.

"Are they ...? Did they just ...?" Donney says through laughter. "Holy crap." He pouts. "They didn't even tell us where we'll be sleeping."

"There, there, Pouty." Donney scowls at me. "I saw some couches in the movie room. Let's go."

I find myself unable to sleep again. Maybe it's the whole "first night in a new house" thing. Maybe it's the little springs in the couch pushing into my spine, or maybe it's the fact that I've just found out I'm a part of a much bigger government plan than ever imagined. The possibilities are, unfortunately, endless.

I wonder about the people we've left behind. What happened to Doc and Bea, or the other little children I grew to know for a short while? Hell, I find myself wondering what happened to Montey. Is he happier now that I'm gone? Does he feel safe? Or does he think he's made a callous mistake? Part of me wonders, and the other part of me says *who cares?* I wonder how Donney feels knowing that there's no guarantee that they're safe. We *did* lead the Silver Man away, so they probably aren't dead.

I hear Donney stirring on the couch in front of me. The couches are layered out row after row, facing a large blank wall. I want to ask him his thoughts on everything, but I don't want to wake him from his potentially first good sleep in a while. Of course, I'm sure he'll never stop being paranoid about my trusting side and how it seems to encompass my personality. I consider sitting up, just to alleviate some of the pressure from my back, but I know if I stir too much, I won't be able to fall back asleep. So, I lay here and stare at the ceiling.

There is nothing special about it. It's a white ceiling in a white-walled room, drastically plain, but the couches look like they've been taken from the side of the road after a family decided they were too trashy to keep. Explains the springs, I guess. A completely mismatched set of a dozen or so sofas are taking up all the space the room has to offer. So much so that to walk around the room you'd have to jump over a few of them.

"Screw this!" Donney shoots up from the couch and startles a gasp from me.

"What?" I follow him into an upright position, and he turns around to face me.

"I'm tired," he says.

I raise an eyebrow at him. "Isn't that what sleep's for?"

He flips me off and stands up.

"Where are you going?"

"I want to go play with some weapons. Stay here." He jumps over his couch and is now standing right in front of me, prepared to jump over my couch when I grab his leg. He puts his foot down and sags his shoulders. "What?" His voice is breathy and tired.

I stare at him for an extra second, studying his shaggy brown hair and the bags under his eyes. "I'm coming with you."

He rolls his eyes. "No, I don't need a babysitter, and I don't need a punching bag."

"Sucks," I say as I jump over the back of my couch. "'Cause I'm coming."

Donney stares at the white ceiling and finally meets my gaze. "Do you ever take no for an answer?"

I shrug, and he nods and jumps over my sofa. He leads us out of the room.

I'm thankful for the detailed tour. We can get back to the weapons/workout/ whatever room with no trouble, despite Donney trying to convince me to make a wrong turn.

I take in the glowing silver of the room. The walls are lined with spotless mirrors, and the floor is taken up by a mat that squishes under my toes. There are a bunch of stands holding different types of weapons—silver swords, long staffs, nunchucks, and so many more, all made completely from a shining metal I assume to be silver or some form of conductive. I am attracted to the small daggers that are lined up on the backside of the door. I grab two and twiddle them through my fingers so flawlessly that even I'm amazed.

I look towards the mirror and over to Donney on the other side of the room. He picks up a long staff and tosses it from hand to hand, measuring the weight of it. He looks at me and smiles like a kid in a candy shop. He quickly diverts his focus back to the staff as he swings it so fast, I can hear it tearing through the air. "Oh, hardcore dibs," Donney says as he checks it out up and down as if it were an attractive woman. "Here!" He tosses me a long staff and holds his up as a guard.

I let it fall to the ground. I had no choice, seeing as how I was still holding the daggers. I toss up my hands at Donney. He mimics the same gesture back. I set the daggers back on the stand where I found them and pick up the staff, and I find myself tossing it from hand to hand. It feels good in my grip. Donney puts himself back into a fighting stance and I follow.

We circle each other around the room until I jump a step forward and swing the staff at him. He blocks it easily, and I find myself more disappointed than I should be. He takes a low swing at my feet, and I jump over it so smoothly it's almost natural. Donney tries to swing again, but during his windup, I see my opening and I take a quick whack at his arms, forcing him to drop the staff. I immediately point the butt end of my staff to his neck, forcing a surrender. He complies and throws his arms up.

"Not bad, not bad." I remove the staff from his throat and allow him to pick up his staff. "But just so we're clear, I totally let you win," he says with a smirk. I scoff at him just as two guys stroll into the room, only far enough to see Donney and not me.

The men are both tall. One is a good six inches taller than the other. The taller one is skinny, with blond hair and scruff on his chin. The shorter one is also blond, but his hair is curly and tied back into a ponytail. The taller one lifts his chin at Donney.

"What we got here, Chimney?" he says to the shorter one next to him. *Chimney, another stupid nickname.* "Looks like our newbie likes to wake up at the crack of dawn."

Chimney playfully smacks him in the ribcage and chuckles. "*That's* a new one." He straightens as if he's just had the best idea in the world. "That'll be his new name! Dawn!"

Donney's eyes widen, and a smile pushes up on his face, but he pushes it down. "A little too plain, I think." He adds, "How's about Dawn-*E*?" The two blondes look at each other as if they just invented chocolate and giggle profusely as they back out of the room.

"Sure!" adds the taller one. "Catchya, later, Dawn-E!"

We pause until they're out of earshot and burst out in a hysterical laughter. "Donney?" Tears and laughter squeeze my stomach. "Did they just name you ..." I pause to breathe. "After you?"

"Shh ...," Donney says through laughter of his own, "that's the best nickname I've ever had!"

"I don't know, I thought Pouty was pretty good." Donney stops laughing, stands up straight, and turns his face towards me, his piercing blue eyes stabbing into mine. "That's it." He rushes me and tackles me to the ground. I swing my arms and legs, trying to get him off me, but he pins me down. His hair flops down, creating a perfect tunnel to his high cheekbones.

I can't help but giggle. "What? This was your devious plan? Put me on the mat that's more comfortable than the sofa I slept on last night? *Cunning*, you really got me." Donney rolls his eyes and stands up, offering me a hand to grab. I attach myself to him, and the second I'm on my feet, he pushes me back down onto the mat. "Oof."

"Oops, sorry about that. Here, let me help you up." He extends his hand again, but I know better than to take it this time. I swat him away.

"Screw off, Pouty."

Donney quickly grabs me and pulls my back into him, covering my mouth. He whispers into my ear, "Do you want people to hear you?" I bite his hand in retort. "Ow!" He throws me away. "Brat!"

I wipe my mouth with the back of my hand. Honestly, yeah, Pouty suits him much better than anything else they could have come up with. Instead of saying all this aloud, I elect to kick the long staff toward him and kick mine up to myself. I push myself into formation. "Round two?"

CHAPTER
60

Donney and I spend the better part of the before-sun morning fighting. Occasionally people stick their heads in, but they quickly duck back out. Not that it fazes either of us. We're used to the gawking eyes from every time I left my room back with Donney's squad or when they used to stare at him for just helping me out. Rather than talking, Donney and I spend the majority of the time at each other's throats, quite literally. After a while, we switch to freehand. I now have a few bruises from that, and of course, so does he. Then we switch to swords and finally, after a nice couple of scrapes, we agree to go out and act normal for the new people we have to meet ... again.

We saunter into the cafeteria. He stands quietly at my side, towering over me, and we scan the room. His jaw is hard, preparing for a fight. I rest my hand on his arm and squeeze, a gesture to make him slow down and recognize that he's safe. To my luck, I see his tight jaw slacken and turn into a forced smile. From him, a forced smile is still a smile.

Chimney stands up from the back of the room. "Hey! Look, it's Dawn-E!"

Timber stands up in the back of the room, and Donney's shoulder's square, daring him to make a correction. Timber gives Donney a quick smirk before bellowing, "Welcome home, Dawn-E!"

"And who's this?" A brave ginger boy around Donney's age, looking like a tall leprechaun, comes towards me, reaching for a hair I can see dangling in front of my eyes.

"Watch it." Donney stands in front of me like a threatening protector. I turn to him and smirk.

"It's okay, Donney, I got this." I step in front of him to embrace the crowd. "My name is Talia Witson of Squad Eighty-Three." I hope they know what that

225

means. Although, some part of me wants to take the words back. I'd hate for them to see me as a threat, but I don't want to be taken advantage of, either. Most importantly, I want to show Donney that I will not let anyone walk over me. "And I … I am a Silver Child." I do my best to stand tall and retain my composure, keeping my voice loud and cold. Everyone around me falls into whispers. Until someone breaks the silence.

"I don't think so," some teenage girl booms out in the far back of the room. My heartrate quickens. *Great, I made the wrong choice again.* "Everyone gets a nickname." Suddenly the entire hall is studying me, trying to figure something out.

"What happened to your arm?" a voice chirps from somewhere in the crowd.

I stand tall and remain almost regal. "I was stabbed," I respond. More whispers.

"What happened to your face?" another voice says, referring to the scar Mary's ring left.

"I was punched,"— I turn my head to over the leprechaun— "for a murder." His eyes are delightfully filled with fright as he stumbles backwards, trying to get away. *Yes, fear me.* The room falls silent. The voice next is unexpected.

"Siren." A child, no older than six, stands on a table.

I furrow my brow and look up at him. "What could you possibly mean?"

"Well, in my books, a siren was a pretty girl who would sing for the sailors and lure them to their death."

I look up to Donney. "I love it," I say proudly.

Timber stands tall and bellows, "Welcome home, Siren!"

"Welcome home, Siren!" the room echoes. I really feel it, too. For once, I really feel at home.

ABOUT THE AUTHOR

Tally is a student at Carleton University studying Forensic Psychology and American Sign Language. Originally from South Glengarry, currently in Ottawa, Ontario. She was introduced to writing by her sister at the young age of twelve and pushed to pursue by her best friend. She was once told that she would make the greatest supervillain of all time. So, read her books so it doesn't come to that.